The Christmas Slayings

One Week. Six Murders.

Inspired by a True Story.

Phyllis K. Walters

Copyright Page

Written by Phyllis K. Walters

Edited by Paula F. Howard

Cover Design by Bob Hurley at TheWritersMall.com

PRINTED IN THE UNITED STATES OF AMERICA
KDP Publishing
First Edition: December, 2019

More copies may be ordered online at Amazon.com
or through
https://www.TheWritersMall.com

Table of Contents

Table of Contents continued...

Table of Contents continued...

DEDICATION

This book is dedicated to my husband, Dan,

who vowed that our life together would not be boring.

So true.

SPECIAL THANKS

I would like to thank Heather Matthews for sharing her journey with me. I pray she will one day be free from her prison, and will continue to rescue young women, leading them out of their darkness while fulfilling her own God-given destiny.

I also extend special thanks to Paula Howard who tirelessly remained committed to editing, advising, and encouraging me throughout the planning and writing of this novel.

CAST OF CHARACTERS

(Alphabetical by First Name)

Amanda Howard	Half-Sister of Angel
Angel Morgan	Defendant
April Chandler	Gang Member
Beverley Stanley	Song's College Roommate
Bill Gorman	Bailiff
Bucky Walker	U of Toledo Baseball Coach
Ellen Prince	Fellow Inmate at JDC*
Judge Charles Lincoln	Friend / Judge
Judge Douglas (D.P.)Tucker	Song Lee's Trial Judge
Judge Kate Brown	Angel Morgan's Trial Judge
Jennifer Kean	Angel's Counselor in JDC
Kristy Delaney	Kitchen Worker at JDC
Daniel Singer	Defense Attorney/Angel
Dr.Rosie Klein	Forensic Psychologist
George Emmanuel	Tavern Owner
Greg Kessler	Half-Brother of Angel
James Abraham	Gang Member
Joel Baker	Son of Missionaries
Laura Robinson	Prosecutor at Song's Trial
Linda Willis	Friend of Dr. Rosie Klein
Matthew Murphy	Lucas County Prosecutor

Marcus Solomon	Gang Leader
Mikey Kessler	Half-Brother of Angel
Mindi Asher	Angel's Roommate at JDC
Paulette Hunter	Administrator at JDC
Penny Tucker	Wife of Judge Tucker
Ron Thompson	Sergeant, Ohio State Highway Patrol
Ruthie Wayne	Dr. Klein's Office Manager
Sally Jacobs	Court Reporter
Sam Strong	Gang Member
Song Lee	Gang Member
Verna Mitchell	Lucas County Jail Corrections Officer
Wes Hall	Investigative Reporter

Victims' Family Members

Doctor William Lee	Song Lee's Father
Naomi Lee	Song Lee's Mother
Joyce Young	Mother of Bobby Young
Margie Bennett	Wife of Brian Bennett
Sheila Brooks	Mother of Richard Brooks

* JDC = Juvenile Detention Center

SOMETIME IN 1981

The Beginning

"Mommy--?" Angel's sweet voice was soft in the dark of the bedroom. "Mommy?" she whispered again.

The blow to her jaw made her see stars before her eyes could focus on the dark figure of her mother rising from bed, an unrecognizable male figure lying prone beside her.

The cast on her mother's forearm had clipped Angel's small chin, barely missing her throat, jarring her head. She fell backwards, landing on the floor, bottom first, hitting her head against the wall.

Somehow, she picked herself up and scampered out of the room before her mother's boyfriend could render harsher discipline. She was learning from experience not to interrupt her mother when she was "entertaining". Her lessons were anything but easy.

In years that followed, Angel would describe how it was her own fault for being stupid and disrespectful. Stupid not to have known where the cough medicine was in the first place, and disrespectful to have intruded on her mother.

Her mother's forearm was in a cast having been broken in a wrestling match with a man twice her size. Twisted by her boyfriend when he found she had shortchanged him from a drug purchase. At the emergency room her mother had told the triage nurse she had fallen out of bed. Angel was threatened never to tell the true story of her mother's broken arm.

Lies and more lies.

MARCH 4, 1994

CHAPTER 1

ANGEL'S STORY

Angel sat in the corner of a holding cell waiting to be formally charged with four counts of aggravated murder. In the same cell, twelve ladies of the night clustered together in groups of three with far less to worry about come morning.

They have more value than I do, Angel thought. *Their pimps will bond them out.*

Her own charges were being delayed pending testimony against former friends, Marcus and James, shooters in six murders. She was being charged along with them for four. But part of the deal for her giving testimony as State's witness against them was to save her soul and hopefully appeal to a compassionate judge.

Why did she ever believe someone could love her? She'd been told all her life that she was fat, ugly, and stupid. Her very own mother said it. Her mother's husbands said it. Even kids at school said it, adding 'white trash' to the labels. Consequently, Angel believed it.

Used and abused, her mother had always entered self-destructive relationships with angry, hostile men comprised of gamblers, alcoholics, and junkies, believing that life was better than being alone. Angel had always thought she would someday escape her mother's fate and never settle for relationships with men who would abuse her and molest her own daughters.

"Why in the world did I walk out of the Juvenile Detention Center (JDC), only to enter into the worst relationships I could ever imagine?" Angel asked herself. "At least the JDC was my stable home for five years. I was away from the ranting and ravings of my intoxicated mother, and the sexual and physical abuse from her husbands and boyfriends. No matter how sterile and drab, at least I was safe."

Angel's two younger brothers, Greg and Mikey, were the product of one of those husbands, Antonio Rossi, by name. The boys were treated royally while she felt like Cinderella with no "ball" or Prince Charming in sight. She mopped and swept floors littered with animal feces and kitty litter. She did dishes and scrubbed toilets often clogged with objects disposed of by her brothers.

Her older half-sister, Amanda, had escaped this trap by moving to her grandparents' home once she turned twelve. In their Midwest state, a child could choose who to live with at that age. Assuming, of course, someone loved you enough to fight for you. Obviously, that was not the case with Angel, besides, Amanda's grandparents were not related to Angel anyway.

Amanda's hand-me-down clothes were useless since they were stained with the evidence of her monthly periods. Before Amanda left, the two sisters had shared the same bed. Afterwards, Angel gained privacy which eventually led to physical violation at the hands of her mother's then-current husband.

At first, she prayed, but finally, took matter into her own hands and ran away. No one looked for her. But that changed when she stole a car. Finally taken to a Juvenile Detention Center (JDC), Angel remembers telling her story to one of the counselors:

"Someone more stupid than me, left his keys in an unlocked car at a convenience store. At fifteen, I thought I could drive the car to a warmer climate where homelessness would be more bearable. But I was wrong."

Instead, she ended up with a five-year stint at the State's JDC for grand larceny. But she figured it could have been worse: "If I had been a real adult, I could have been sentenced up to ten years in prison and a $10,000 fine. Lucky me!" It was rare optimism for Angel.

Upon release from juvenile detention on her 21st birthday, Angel hit the streets again with no guidance and no place to stay. She misled the JDC authorities by letting them think she had a room at a local YWCA where she would receive meals in exchange for housekeeping duties.

On her first evening in fresh air, without knowing it, she met her future in the form of a young African-American girl and her boyfriend seated at a picnic bench outside a 7-11 store near the Greyhound facility.

In her pocket was $98, from her account in the juvenile facility, which she had earned herself over time. No relatives had helped or even visited. Now, she fully intended to buy a one-way bus ticket to Florida where she could crash on the beach and sleep with sounds of gentle waves to drown out the loud, threatening voices and images in her head.

"Hey, where ya' going?" the young man called out as Angel approached to pass them.

"Going in here to buy a bus ticket."

"Where you headin'?" the girl asked.

"Somewhere warm," Angel answered.

"My name's Sam, and this is my girlfriend, April," the dark-skinned young man said. "What's your hurry? Get some food and sit here with us."

"Yeah, join us," April said before Angel had time to think or respond.

"Okay," she simply said. "I guess the ticket can wait."

She went into the 7-11 store and bought a diet-coke and packaged turkey sandwich, then joined Sam and April at the picnic table. The sun was just going down when she realized she didn't have a warm jacket, but neither did they.

The longer the trio talked, the more comfortable Angel became. It felt good to talk and not be told what to do.

"Why don't you bunk with us at a house a few blocks away?" April asked.

Angel thought for a moment, and then accepted, no questions asked. After all, no one else was expecting her, and the bus trip could wait until morning.

She later realized how naïve it was to think they could be her friends without strings attached.

MARCH 4, 1994

CHAPTER 2

DR. ROSIE KLEIN

I loved the life I lived until three years ago when my husband, Oliver, unexpectedly died from cardiac arrest coming off the 18th hole of our favorite golf course. At least he enjoyed a winning game with his Saturday buddies. They were traumatized, but nothing could have saved him.

Together, we had raised our two sons and his three older children, golfed together, traveled together and enjoyed spending time with friends. It had been a wonderful life.

Now, I'm totally absorbed in my career as a forensic psychologist. But, little did I know that my husband had a secret life with a few business ventures that left me deeply in debt. When I discovered everything after his funeral, it resulted in forfeiting practically everything I owned.

Now, on this cold winter morning, I was brewing my favorite Boston Stoker coffee in my downtown office, looking forward to a cup. Jocko and I had arrived earlier and stepped into the warm room which felt like heaven coming in from the frigid outside. Jocko is a large, mild mannered, half lab-half poodle. His big brown eyes mirror my own when I lean down to feed him and assure him how much I care.

I usually keep Jocko on a leash whenever we're outdoors, which is totally unnecessary, really, since he never ventures from my side, except at the dog park. But city laws can be so unforgiving. Labeled as my "service dog", his purpose is supposedly for my protection. Truth be told, Jocko fills the enormous void inside me from the loss of my husband and the 'empty nest' crater from all the children being grown and gone. After such a life filled with family events and a deep relationship with my husband, it's hard to fill my life again. I miss everyone and everything of my old life, at every turn.

On Fridays, I enjoy a downtown office on the 13th floor of the tallest building in our city, the LaSalle Building. I actually sublease it from a psychiatrist by the name of Dr. Robert Siefer. The 13th floor is an oddity since we know most buildings never have such a numbered floor. So, this intrigued me, and I took the office feeling the 13th floor would be lucky for my business, or, at the very least, a great opening conversation topic.

My main office is in the suburb of Summerhill. My dedicated office manager, Ruth, stays there and will call me when I'm at the LaSalle office to notify me of any client referrals that have come in.

She'll often greet me jovially with the comment: "You've been walking the streets again, Rosie." Her comment references the fact that I like walking to and from lunch on Fridays near the Lucas County Courthouse. The proximity allows me to enjoy frequent lunch dates with professional colleagues. If I skip lunch, I shop at two major department stores which have, so far, survived the flight of most merchants to the malls. My visibility primarily helps create referrals from attorneys, promote myself, and have fun doing it. The remainder of each week, I work either at Summerhill, or in my office at home.

In years past, living near Summerhill High School, and my suburban office, afforded me the privilege of immersing myself in the lifestyle of our two sons, Christopher and Stephen. I was a "soccer mom", "hockey honey (mom of a hockey player)", and transporter of the boys and their friends to practices, away games, and summer sports camps. It was a time in my life that I absolutely loved.

The boys also benefited from our family membership at Walnut Creek Country Club and my business membership at the Town Club, a private restaurant on the 26th floor of the LaSalle Tower. It has a breathtaking, panoramic view of the city, when not enshrouded in clouds or surrounded by thick, white, glistening, snowflakes.

Our boys took all their dates to dinner at either one or the other of the private clubs prior to homecoming dances and proms. But, that season of our lives has since passed into sweet memories and life-long friendships. Now I look forward to Stephan's college breaks and spending time with my three-year-old grandson, Joshua, when Christopher and his wife have a date night.

Today is March 4, 1994. No sooner do I arrive at my LaSalle office, toss my scarf and hat onto the coatrack in the corner, unhook Jocko's leash, and grab a mug of strong black coffee, then Ruth calls. I have just gotten comfortably seated in my scotch plaid wingback chair.

"I know your morning is just getting started, but one of your friendly attorneys is on the phone. I'll transfer the call to you."

It was a phone call from a familiar voice, Danny Singer, a prominent, well-respected, local defense attorney.

"Good morning Mr. Singer."

"Good morning to you, Dr. Rosie. I have been appointed to defend one of the female defendants in a case that is being called the 'Christmas Slayings'. My call will be brief. I need you to evaluate her."

He proceeded to describe the case of Angel Morgan. The defendant being one of four alleged perpetrators of the crimes for which she was being charged. "Alleged" because she, and they, are "innocent until proven guilty", the well-known American motto.

"Okay. I have some time to listen now."

The legal community, including lawyers, prosecutors, and judges from surrounding counties, had all grown to respect Dr. Klein's experience and expertise in the field of forensic psychology. Following the death of her husband, they showed her support by referring private therapy clients to her as well as appointing her to evaluate defendants facing trials for serious crimes such as rapes and murders.

Dan Singer was not a public defender, but a defense attorney with considerable experience. He was, however, expected to "give back to the Court" by accepting a "pro se" capital murder case usually once every other year. No local attorney was pleased with this unwritten rule, but all of them lived with it.

"Pro se" means they are not paid for their services. This case could cost them two hundred and fifty dollars or more per billable hour, the customary charge for direct and indirect time spent on the representation of a murder suspect.

As Attorney Singer lays out the circumstances of the case. I sip my coffee, shoes off, legs resting on the overstuffed, matching ottoman in front of me. Listening intently, I scrawl a few notes and mentally determine the case to be "viable". That means, a psychological evaluation of the defendant would be appropriate given the initial details provided by Attorney Singer.

Indicating my agreement to see the defendant, Singer identified her as twenty-one-year old Angel Morgan, being held for the past 15 months without bond in the Lucas County Jail. That length of time had been necessary so she could testify against her co-defendants in a plea deal struck to benefit her.

I couldn't know in this moment that it didn't benefit her at all.

First, however, I needed to be appointed by the Court at the request of the defense attorney. Then, as per my normal procedure, I would review the entire discovery packet of materials relevant to the crimes.

Yes, as in "multiple" crimes. Six murders to be exact. All committed within the week prior to Christmas of 1992. Four murders were perpetrated against random strangers and two against friends of the pack of four defendants.

After our call, I was refilling my ceramic mug with Boston Stoker and snagging a chocolate bagel slathered with cream cheese, when I unexpectedly receive another call. This one is from a professional colleague by the name of Matthew Murphy.

"It's The Irish Assistance County Prosecutor" Ruthie announces to me over the phone, before transferring him to my line. Matthew was on the path to becoming The County Prosecutor as had his father in years past. Matt took mostly high-profile cases. He was currently experiencing the success of having secured guilty verdicts for the two men in these heinous murders, now being called the "Christmas Slayings".

One of the two, named Marcus Solomon, had received the death penalty while the other, known as James Abraham, was sentenced to life in prison without parole. The third defendant was the young woman, called "Angel" whom I was about to evaluate. The fourth defendant was named Song Lee who was still waiting to be sentenced.

"Good morning Rosie. Matt Murphy here."

"Hi Matt. How are you? Your call must mean it doesn't really matter who appoints me, right? I hope my findings and conclusions are useful to everyone involved, namely Judge Brown, but of course, you and Dan."

"Yes. We all trust your reasoning. We have found you to be very thorough. If there is anything my office can do or provide for you, just let us know."

"Thanks Matt. I will keep that in mind."

"Have a great day, Rosie. Be careful. The sidewalks are slick. I heard a rumor that Spring is just around the corner."

"I'm looking forward to the daffodils and tulips. Talk to you again soon."

The Daily Blade investigative reporter, Wes Hall, would no doubt be calling as well. I thought. I'm sure he spent every moment in the court room during the trial of these men, just like he has done in many other cases with which I have been involved.

"What could this young woman have been thinking?" I say out loud to Jocko lying near my feet. Jocko simply looks at me inquisitively.

"I'm probably giving her too much credit," I say to Jocko.

Obviously, she wasn't thinking at all. Who does, getting involved in murder? Oh, I shouldn't be so cynical. There, but for the grace of God go I, realizing my own choices since Oliver died haven't always reflected good judgment. We don't have a clue, yet, about this gal's story. We simply know she was befriended by a group of kids while living on the street.

Based upon news accounts, Angel had been released from the Juvenile Detention Center (JDC) earlier in the week of the murders. She had no plan to live at the YWCA and was not going to work there for room and board as she let JDC believe.

Why did the JDC authorities allow a juvenile offender to be released with no designated place to reside? Here, again, is an example of another juvenile who has fallen through the cracks. How are they expected to productively enter into society as young adults when the system miserably lets them down?

I continue reading the online news reports, finding absolutely no trace of her whereabouts until her arrest which coincides with the apprehension of the three other gang members, Marcus Solomon, James Abraham, and Song Lee.

The actual discovery packet should arrive at the LaSalle office within days and will consist of arrest reports, witness statements, written confessions and the history of the defendant. Accustomed to reviewing these reports, I will also request additional material to include school records and medical records.

A call comes in from Ruth still at our Summerhill office.

"There's a storm coming, so your 1:30 couples' therapy appointment has cancelled. Do you know the expressways are becoming hazardous and the city streets slushy? With the wind chill and the temperatures dropping, the sidewalks will soon freeze over. I suggest you be careful out there, Rosie. And to think: The groundhog saw his shadow last month and scampered back underground for another six weeks. I guess he knew what was coming."

With that in mind, I determine to quickly hike the two blocks to the Lucas County Jail during my lunch hour and conduct a brief informal interview with Angel.

I know I lack the official Court order allowing me private access to this client, but since I'm practically a fixture there, most certainly I can obtain entrance with just my driver's license."

Wearing water-resistant boots, my plan is to hustle back to the LaSalle office building after interviewing Angel, retrieve Jocko, take the elevator to the parking garage and leave the city before the 4:00 pm traffic kicks in. I am really grateful my daily commute is a simple, twenty-minute drive. I can listen to my southern gospel music with Jocko on the seat beside me.

"So, Ruth," I tell her, "Here's what you should do:

"Go home at 2 pm and transfer the phone lines so you can answer calls from home. What I really need for you to do is confirm Monday's appointments."

"Sure, Boss. You are the best!"

I never take Ruth's commitment for granted. It would be terrible to lose her.

MARCH 4, 1994

CHAPTER 3

EARLY RECOLLECTIONS

Sitting in her small, confined cell, head cupped in hands, Angel could not believe she had been so stupid. No longer blaming her mother for her own bad decisions and impulsive actions, Angel was thinking back to memories of the woman she loved yet feared.

One memory she just barely recalled was being removed from the care of her mother at about the age of three. Neighbors had reported to police that Angel was wandering between houses and down the sidewalk wearing only a dirty diaper and filthy tee shirt. Her mother said she thought Angel was napping so had walked to a mini mart for a pack of cigarettes. After that, Angel was placed in a nurturing foster home that included warm baths, hot meals, and being read to at bedtime. That's the part she remembered: Feeling loved for a very brief time.

Then, her mother came up with a safety plan with the help of a Children's Services caseworker and Angel and her mother were soon reunited. She remembered that part because she felt sorry to be going home. The reunion was partially due to the agency's policy not to split up siblings. Angel's older sister, Amanda, was still in her mother's legal custody at that time.

Amanda often visited her paternal grandparents and didn't know about Angel's removal and subsequent reunion with their mother, nor was she subject to other neglect matters. Unfortunately, Angel's mother moved their little family unit to a different neighborhood soon after the incident, so no authorities checked on them or were ever called again.

Soon after that, Angel's mom married for the image of stability, thinking it might look good and help keep her children. But, as usual, her choice was a poor one. Her new husband, Antonio Rossi, was ten years younger, and had an eye for little blonde girls.

A child's attitudes and beliefs are formed by the age of seven, according to experts. Angel's tender memories depicted a lonely little girl isolated from friends, neighbors and extended family. Her brothers were born in the years following reconciliation with her mother. They were a year apart and both in diapers for what seemed to be an eternity to Angel. That's because she always had to change them. Her mother never seemed to be around.

The brothers' presence had both good and bad aspects in Angel's life. The good included a lesser sense of isolation and loneliness. It also meant having some affection and physical touch with another human being not of a violent nature. The bad involved her total responsibility for their care at a tender age herself, particularly when Amanda was at her grandparents' home on most weekends.

One Wednesday night at church, something prompted Angel to go forward when Pastor Butch asked, "If anyone wants to dedicate their life to Jesus, please come forward now." Angel had been told over and over that Jesus loved little children. Her heart was filled with this warmth she had not felt before and her eyes welled up with tears as she looked at the large oak cross extending from the ceiling. She wondered if God could rescue her from this hell she was living and had experienced all nine years of her life.

She took one step out into the aisle and joined several other children walking toward the altar hand-in-hand.

Following her declaration of faith, the congregation gathered around the children and presented each with their own personal children's Bible. This simple ceremony was going to be the hope she needed to face her bleak future. She whispered a prayer on the dark bus ride home and held the hands of her little brothers sitting on each side of her. She silently vowed never to take her anger out on them, and at that moment, meant it with all her heart.

As the church bus turned onto the block where they lived, she saw flashing blue lights and hoped the police were not at her house with her mother. But of course, they were.

Having a search warrant, the police were exercising it without restraint. Dresser drawers were turned over with all contents strewn all over the floor of both small bedrooms. Every cushion was removed from chairs and sofas. Even the refrigerator and oven doors stood open.

When she and her brothers arrived, she saw her stepfather seated at the dining room table in handcuffs. A short, fat patrolman was reading him his rights. Soon after he was escorted to a police car while her mother sat motionless on the floor in the living room.

Someone at school had overheard one of her brothers talking about powdered milk. This talk turned into a rumor that some white substance resided in Angel's kitchen cupboard. Their mother was furious, not with the school personnel or the police, but with Angel's little brothers, Greg and Mikey.

During the middle of that night, they moved to a motel just on the other side of the Indiana state line. Angel still remembered their hurry and the flashing, red neon lights in front of the motel with the words "vacancy" and "pet friendly" flashing on and off. They had no pets but, Angel assumed if pets were allowed, children were too.

So, that's how Angel learned to deal with conflict and

hardship. Simply run. She wondered how long it would take for her mother to replace her stepfather. She also began to believe that Jesus stayed with the church and was no longer available to her.

MARCH 4, 1994

CHAPTER **4**

INITIAL INTERVIEW

"Hi Mel. I'm here to see Angel Morgan. I don't have formal paperwork yet."

I presented my driver's license and was approved as a professional visitor here to see the defendant accused of murdering six people.

Placing my briefcase, coat and hat on the conveyer to be scanned, I was buzzed through and quickly retrieved my belongings.

"Thank you. Have a great afternoon," I nodded toward Officer Jordan, tall and nice-looking, then walked down the hall.

Because of my positive professional track record at the County Jail, I was permitted to come through security without the required court documentation, just as I had hoped. Yes, it really helps having a good reputation, especially in a town like this one.

Another set of doors buzzed, letting me know they were unlocked. Pushing through with my shoulder, I held my coat in one arm and briefcase in the other.

Two Sheriff's deputies, Ambrose and Testerman, were standing at computers in the booking area.

"Hello Officers. I am here to see Angel Morgan."

"Okay, Doc. I guess somebody has to do it," Ambrose said; Testerman gave a short laugh.

Angel was sent for as I made small talk about the weather with the officers. Within ten minutes, the defendant appeared walking slowly down the hall beside Officer Verna Mitchell.

Angel appeared clean in her drab green jail garb. First thing I noticed were her fingernails. They were chewed down to the quick. She had nothing holding back her long stringy hair from her somewhat pretty face.

"Hi Angel. My name is Dr. Rosie Klein. Your lawyer, Daniel Singer, requested we meet and discuss the details of your case. This will help him determine the best way to represent you at sentencing."

"That's a good idea," she said. Her eyes were a little puffy and I wondered if she had been crying.

As customary Angel gave permission for me to see her, and we entered an unlocked, glassed-in interview room. We sat across from one another with a rectangular metal table between us.

"I need your signature so I can share information not only with your attorney, but also with the Prosecutor and the Judge," I explained, producing a standard consent form.

"The information will be in the form of a written report," I told her. "Unfortunately, I can't offer you a confidential relationship."

"I understand," she said and signed the bottom of the paper in large, round, cursive without hesitation.

"Are you willingly prepared to plead guilty to the murder, robbery, and obstruction charges?" I asked.

"They told me if I agreed to the charges, the death penalty option would be taken off the table," she said. "I am not ready to die Dr. Klein."

"I know my testimony helped get the death penalty for Marcus, and life without parole for James. So, I'm praying my sentences might include the possibility of parole."

I produced a preprinted intake form and began asking Angel basic but pertinent information.

"Your last known residence was the County Juvenile Detention Center?"

"Hum huh. I was there five years for grand theft auto."

Angel and I agreed to discuss the details of that arrest and incarceration later.

"Parents?"

She answered plainly: Her family of origin included no known grandparents. Her mother was an orphan and she had no knowledge of her birthfather. Their heritage was unknown. She hadn't heard from her mother during her entire five-year incarceration.

"I figure she's in prison or murdered by one of her violent partners. I can't be positive."

"What is your mother's full name?"

"After she and Antonio divorced, she married one more time to Roger. Her face twisted with distaste.

"He was the last person we lived with. To answer your question, I don't know what name she went by after that. I don't even know where my name, 'Morgan', came from. My brothers might know what her last name is now…If you can find them." She was biting on a fingernail.

"I would appreciate knowing if my mother is alive," she said without emotion. "Even where my sister, Amanda, and brothers, Mike and Greg are living. Amanda would be about twenty-six years old now, and the boys would be eighteen and nineteen. The boys were much smarter than me, you know."

I knew from reports that Angel's formal public education ended during the ninth grade when she ran away. At that point, she was fifteen. She had repeated the fourth grade when they moved again to avoid authorities which, unfortunately, also removed her from the church she had grown to love, and its kind volunteers on Wednesday night.

Angel described her GED classes at the Juvenile Detention facility: "I missed passing the test because of math and reading," she said, "So, I couldn't get my high school equivalency certificate. I kinda feel really bad about that."

My notes reflected her thoughts:

- She was fluent in her description of her childhood history.
- She regretted not having a driver's license or a diploma.
- She did not mention regrets over what got her into this situation.
- She made face contact about half of the time. The rest of the time she looked down but spoke in a normal tone.
- She demonstrated little emotion in voice or posture and showed no mannerisms indicative of anxiety other than her chewed up nails.

I believed she had given me enough to start and began packing up my papers. As I looked at her face, she seemed pleased to have been given some attention.

"Angel, the weather is really stormy. I'm sorry, but I need to leave." Touching Angel's arm, I gave a little squeeze to reassure her. "But, I promise to return soon. Are you willing to take some written tests?"

"Sure. It's so boring in here," Angel said.

I escorted Angel out into the hall where Verna Mitchell was waiting to lead her back to her cell. As I left the facility, precipitation and wind were picking up and stung my cheeks. None the less, I managed to safely return to the office without incident. The dark clouds were dreary, but, at least, the snow was already beginning to lessen.

Ruth, being in the Summerhill office on Fridays when I was downtown, had a routine of recording a voice message listing any messages that had come in for me. I noticed the coffee pot was still on, so I poured a to-go cup for my drive home.

Instead of heading directly to the parking garage, we took the elevator to the lower level. There was a pet friendly, grassy, fenced area behind the building Jocko usually liked. However, he was not happy with the frost beginning to form on the turf. Even so, he wagged his tail with appreciation, after he relieved himself.

The drive home took forty-five minutes. I decided against playing any music, preferring to toss around the particulars of my interview with Angel. I had a lot to think about.

FRIDAY EVENING - MARCH 4, 1994

CHAPTER 5

A NEW DIRECTION

Home is where the heart is and I was grateful my condo included a two-car attached garage leading into the mud room. Once safely inside, I removed my dirty boots, Jocko's leash, and a very wet hat and coat. The warmth of the house enveloped me.

Heading for the fireplace with its gas fire insert, I flipped the button. There may not be the aroma of burning wood, but I loved seeing the flames come to life. My apple-scented candles on the coffee table easily made up for the smoky aroma of firewood that was missing. I never tired of the sight of the flickering blue and red flames. Pouring myself a glass of dark red wine, I thought: For medicinal purposes, and laughed out loud to Jocko. He cocked an ear at me.

Tonight, would be a good night to disengage from my professional life by watching the programs I'd taped earlier this week. However, Friday night, at ten, was usually the live telecast of my favorite show, "NYPD Blue". Most of the shows were dramas, but I preferred ones with female leads, always easily identifying with their roles and emotions. I could do that, I sometimes thought while watching.

As I sipped the full-bodied wine and gazed at the flames, my cell phone rang. I was pleasantly surprised to hear the voice of my friend and colleague, Judge Charles Lincoln. He had always treated me respectfully in his Courtroom and at public appearances. I didn't realize how highly he regarded me until he mentioned the idea of introducing me to two of his personal friends.

"Hello Rosie. How do you like this weather? Are you hunkering down for the week-end?"

"Hi Judge. Jocko and I are doing just that. I think this storm will pass and the roads will be clear by tomorrow evening, don't you?" The Judge and most others who worked downtown knew Jocko and were openly fond of him.

"Well, Rosie, one of the friends I've told you about is going to a University of Toledo basketball game with me tomorrow night. Are you going?"

"No. I'm sharing my season tickets with a friend and this game is not one of mine."

Truthfully, her friend bought the entire season from Rosie but offered to take Rosie to half the games. Rosie's financial status had changed dramatically, for the worse, upon the loss of her husband.

"Is that so?" the Judge said with an upbeat note in his voice. "I was wondering if you would be interested in meeting my high school buddy, a recent widower who has overcome his own battle with cancer? Perhaps you could meet us at Alfie's before the game. If you hit it off, maybe the three of us could get a bite to eat afterwards."

The Judge also went on to say: "My friend is a widower with two adult children and two grandchildren." It was interesting that he was painting such a complete picture of this man in a short time.

"Bucky, had cancer surgery after the death of his wife, and is ten months post-surgery. I think you and Bucky would have a lot in common especially since you are both widowed, are survivors, and interested in sports. He's an avid softball player and follower of the Cincinnati Reds. He's told me he's contemplating picking up golf, too. I just think the two of you would hit off."

I pondered the offer, considering any other options for Saturday evening, and decided to go. It could be a pleasant time. "That sounds like a good idea. What time do you have in mind?"

"Six pm works for us. How about you?"

"That's just fine. Assuming the roads are clear, I'll be seated on a bar stool listening to the Marvin Jones jazz combo."

Hanging up, I somehow felt less isolated and more content to eat a light meal by myself. Tuning in to the local news, there was no mention of the new case I was working on which gave me some relief. There had been reporters lurking around the steps of the County Jail when I left after interviewing Angel for the first time. Probably the winter storm and a desire to get safely to their newsrooms had been on their minds.

I figure the case will be highlighted in the future as Angel comes closer to trial. For now, I'm grateful no one has approached me for a quote. I've got a lot more to find out before I can make a statement, if at all.

Judge Lincoln called his friend, Albert Walker, or "Bucky" to his friends, and confirmed the plans for the next evening.

"Hey, Bucky. My lady doctor friend says she'll meet us at Alfie's before the game tomorrow night. I guess she hangs out there. Kind of a classy place."

"Oh. Okay Judge we can do with a bit of class. Sounds like a plan. Pick you up at five-thirty."

"See you then, Bucky. Nice suggestion!"

The Judge was embroiled in his own nasty

divorce that was dragging on and on for no recognizable reason. Although he felt sorry for Bucky's circumstances, he believed being a widower is in many ways an easier road to travel than being divorced with all the regrets, guilt and anger. To the Judge, being divorced meant sharing the kids on holidays "till death do us part".

Being divorced meant seeing one another at social events given that the couple travels in the same circles, as he and his estranged wife did now. And being divorced carries a bit of a stigma with little or no sympathy from friends who elect not to take sides.

Life sure can be complicated sometimes.

SATURDAY EVENING - MARCH 5, 1994

CHAPTER **6**

DR. ROSIE'S NEW FRIENDSHIP

I met the Judge and Mr. Albert "Bucky" Walker at Alfie's Supper Club as planned. The two men strolled up to the piano bar where I was seated in a black, leather, swivel chair. Judge Charlie, as I liked to call him when not in his courtroom, made the informal introductions.

"Hi Rosie. I would like to introduce Bucky Walker, my long-time friend."

Bucky extended his hand and I shook it and smiled. Nice firm handshake. I like that.

I noticed Bucky's flashing smile and rather slight frame for an almost six foot, 55 -year old- man. Then, remembered the fact he had survived cancer surgery just ten months ago. Being thin and trim was becoming to him with his prematurely white hair and athletic gait. I was not disappointed.

"So glad to meet you, Rosie. I've heard many, many good things about you."

"Thank you," I said looking him in the eyes with a smile still on my face.

At that point, three well-dressed, middle aged women recognized Judge Lincoln and beckoned Charlie to their high-top table. Their motives may have been professional but more likely, since he was getting divorced, of a personal nature.

Judge Lincoln had just won re-election for the third time.

Bucky and I struck up a conversation regarding how we both knew the Judge. The swivel chair beside me became available. Bucky seated himself and began sipping a coke.

"Charlie and I palled around in high school. We played varsity baseball and club ball in the summer."

Bucky shared other stories about his teen age years with Charlie. The time passed quickly, and it was time for the game.

"I'd like to meet you after the game," Bucky said, "It seems I monopolized the conversation and I'd like to hear more about your life."

"Well, you did sort of monopolize the conversation, but I didn't mind. You guys seemed to have so much fun, I really enjoyed hearing about your shenanigans. I do, however, agree to meet you after the game and continue our conversation."

Bucky disengaged Charlie from the women, and they left for the basketball game. I turned my attention back to the jazz combo wondering how long the game would last. I moved to a high-top table which offered a bit more privacy and less noise. For the next few hours, I jotted notes and thought about the process I would use to evaluate Angel. I also contemplated having a late night supper on the dining room side of Alfie's.

Two hours later, just as I finished my planning on Angel's case, the two buddies returned.

"Have you eaten?" Bucky asked.

"No, I've been munching on nuts. Who won the game?"

"Toledo! It was a great game. We'll tell you more, but first, why don't we take you to eat. You must be really hungry. Nuts aren't really a meal. My favorite restaurant,

Marion's, is right across the street," Bucky said. "You in the mood for the greatest pizza you'll ever find?"

Well, the black top parking lot is covered with a layer of white, crunchy snow. But instead of feeling insulted, I chuckled to myself. Bucky's honesty is an admirable trait and one too frequently lacking in other men I've dated.

"C'mon Rosie, it'll be fun and others from the game will be there. It's sort of like a gathering place."

"Well, these boots were made for walking," I said, briefly thinking goodbye to dinner on the dining room side of Alfie's.

Conversation at Marion's focused on the huge win of University of Toledo (UT) over Ohio University (OU). That led to the topic of baseball. Judge Lincoln played college ball at OU, and Bucky currently coaches baseball at UT. He described his team's recent ten-day pre-season tournament in Florida while we waited for our order.

"The team and some fans stayed at The Waterfront Inn in The Villages, Florida," Bucky said. " All rooms look out on Lake Sumter. It's a man-made lake and only a short walk to a number of restaurants nearby. They also have an outdoor square where live music is played nightly. Really nice."

"That's a strange name for a town. What exactly is 'The Villages'? Rosie asked.

"It's a huge retirement community of over seventy-five thousand people, if you can believe it. They expect the population to continue increasing over the coming years. Most residents use golf carts as their main mode of transportation. You can't begin to imagine this place unless you experience it first-hand."

Our order came and we started eating while Bucky continued describing his event.

"High school and college teams from all over the State of Florida enjoy playing tournaments there. The Tournament actually draws teams from states up North looking to get out of the cold weather while developing team unity. Our team played twelve games. We won a three-day tournament and came in second in a four-day tournament. Our preferred bat is the Louisville Slugger, wooden, but the retired guys who play softball in The Villages use aluminum. Makes it easier for them to hit further."

The evening continued filled with pizza and talk. I found Bucky very pleasant company. Then, we all walked back to our vehicles parked between Alfie's and Marion's. Bucky closed my car door and lowered himself to look through the window after I rolled it down.

"Be careful driving. I'd like to call you tomorrow, Rosie, if you wouldn't mind. I guess we still didn't talk about you. But you're a good listener and we got through a lot about sports tonight."

"I'd like that," I said handing him my business card. It had been hidden in the palm of my hand because I had been hoping he would ask.

"You're quite the sportsman," I said giving him my best smile. "And I found it all interesting. I'll look forward to your call."

What I didn't mention was the fact that I was not supposed to drive after 11:00 p.m on any night, but decided to leave that story for a future occasion. I also wasn't sure Judge Lincoln was aware of certain restrictions imposed upon me after an unfortunate incident I had on Valentine's Day. At this moment, I wasn't complying with them, but I guess Bucky was interesting enough to me to break them.

What I couldn't know was about the conversation Judge Charlie and Bucky were having at that moment on the way to their cars.

"Hey, Judge, what do you think if you and Darlene would meet Rosie and me for dinner on Friday at Mancy's?"

"So, Bucky, I take it you like her," the Judge said. "You're stepping up, Bucky, from that other woman you've been seeing. Don't get me wrong, I realize you've been vulnerable since your own battle with cancer. But, have I told you how much I admire your determination to overcome obstacles that life has pitched at you since your wife's passing?"

Bucky was quiet. He didn't respond to the Judge's opinion of his most recent lady friend. He still had some feelings for her but since they were just barely over a parting of the ways, he didn't feel like commenting one way or the other. He did say 'thanks' in response to the comment on determination to move beyond his esophageal cancer. Bucky had recently been advised that the worst was behind him and he was clear, seeming to have won the battle.

"About Friday," the Judge said as he climbed into his car. "Let's do it. I'l talk with you about it before Friday."

On Sunday, I awakened to much more pleasant weather. The wind had subsided, and the sun shone brightly through my bedroom window. After walking Jocko around the condo complex and savoring two cups of hot, black coffee, I read Angel's written confession.

It provided me with more knowledge of Angel's literacy, intelligence, communication skills, and thought process at the time of the murders. School records would be very useful since they pertained to absenteeism, attitude and performance on standardized tests.

I put in a quick call to Ruth.

"Hey, I hate to bother you on the weekend, but would you find out if Angel's siblings are alive and willing to be interviewed?"

"I was told by Danny Singer's office that the discovery packet would be hand-delivered to our Summerhill office no later than 1:00 pm tomorrow, that's Monday. If the siblings have been located, there should be records containing complete names, contact information, and any prior statements, wouldn't there be?" Ruth asked. "Of course, if not, I don't mind getting them for you."

"Thanks Ruth. You were lucky enough to find out about the early release, even with that storm on Friday. We can wait until tomorrow to look through the material."

"Thanks, Boss. What is that word you use about me...'tenacious'? Just doin' my job. "

MARCH 8, 1994

CHAPTER 7

ANGEL'S NEW FRIENDS

Angel appeared more disheveled on Tuesday when Dr. Rosie met with her in the same conference room in the County Jail.

Conversations were, supposedly, not monitored when an attorney, doctor, or pastor was meeting with a defendant or inmate.

Their conversation began with Dr. Klein asking, "Angel, can you please describe exactly what happened upon your release from the Juvenile Detention Center (JDC) fifteen months ago?"

"It was a Wednesday, late afternoon," Angel stated. "I was about to enter a Greyhound station beside a 7-11 store to buy a one-way bus ticket to Florida. A couple of teenagers called to me. The guy said, 'I'm Sam, and this is my friend, April. What's your name?'

"I thought they seemed really friendly," Angel continued, "Kinda like interested in knowing me. They were sitting at a picnic table on the side of the building. It was cold out, and April was sitting close to Sam. They were both black and looked kinda young. She was small and he had kinda like a lot of muscles. They were wearing wool scarves and knit caps. I noticed they wore white gym shoes with no socks and kept their hands stuffed in their pockets. Sam's jacket looked like part of a camouflage uniform like they wear in the Marines. I didn't think it looked heavy enough to protect him from the cold Ohio weather."

Dr. Klein made some notes, then looked up at Angel with a smile of encouragement. So, Angel continued her story:

"I answered him, 'Hi, my name is Angel.'"

" What's your hurry?" Sam asked.

"Oh, I'm going in to buy a bus ticket to Florida."

After hearing Angel's plan, April said, "Why don't you spend the night at our house?"

Angel thought for a moment, realizing no one was waiting for her in Florida, then answered: "Okay."

Sam asked her for a favor. "Do you think you could buy us a six pack of Bud Light and a package of Crispy Crèmes for morning?"

Hesitating only briefly, Angel entered the store and did what was asked with the money she had saved for her bus ticket, not yet purchased. Then, after eating a sandwich she bought for herself, the three of them walked down the narrow, littered alley for about six blocks. There were no signs of other people and back windows of some houses were boarded up. Other houses displayed Christmas decorations in the windows and on shrubs outside. Occasionally, they heard dogs barking as if communicating from one property to another.

Opening the gate of a chain link fence, Sam and Angel entered a back yard with a cracked, uneven, sidewalk leading to the back of a dilapidated, two-story house. Again, Angel hesitated wondering: I might be making a mistake here.

But, because Sam and April were acting so kindly, and laughter had permeated their short time together, Angel entered the yard, too. She hadn't laughed in a long time, and seemed to see the possibility of a future.

Noticing a gray frame garage positioned with its overhead door facing the alley, she saw both small windows on each side of it covered with cardboard. As they approached the abandoned, old house, Sam directed her to a cellar window obscured from view by two dented garbage cans. April crawled through, jumped down, and extended a hand up to her.

Angel bent down and tried entering but could barely get her large frame through the opening. Sam assisted by nudging her from behind. He handed the beer and donuts down to the girls, jumped down to join them, and picked up a flashlight placed on a ledge beside the window. It was dusk and the flashlight provided one of two means of light. The other was a candle with the scent of cinnamon helping offset rancid odors retained from the damp, dark cellar.

All Angel could see on the cement floor were mattresses strewn about and black garbage bags obviously used to cover the people who slept there. She noticed one sheer curtain seemingly torn from a curtain rod, probably from upstairs. It could serve as a protection from the cold, or creeping critters such as spiders. There was no power. No running water or electricity, therefore, no heat. She only saw a drain where she assumed they peed. In one corner was a pot with toilet paper beside it. She later found it was used to carry human waste to garbage cans in the backyard.

"Hey, Angel," said Sam. "Come with us so we can introduce you to some friends in the garage."

April led them up rickety stairs to the back kitchen door which was bolt-locked from the inside. By unlocking it, they could now enter the house without climbing through the basement window.

Out at the garage, they knocked on the side door and waited until it was opened by someone. Angel couldn't see who until he opened the door wider. A young black man seemed startled to see a white girl with Sam and April. They entered the garage and Sam introduced her to Marcus. Inside was another black man he introduced as James. An older, teen-aged Asian girl was also there.

"This is Song," Sam said. "Hey, you guys, this is our new friend, Angel. We met her at the 7-11," he announced.

The men were seated on folding chairs at a card table. There were five-dollar bills in front of each of them. It appeared they were gambling on a card game and drinking Jack Daniels from small juice-sized glasses. Song stood nearby silently watching.

April took Angel's hand and walked her over beside Song who smiled, still remaining silent. Sam pulled up a chair and sat down at the table.

Song was wearing a dark blue and gold University of Toledo sweatshirt. Her straight, black shiny hair was pulled back into a ponytail. Marcus and James wore identical black, hooded, oversized sweatshirts, blue denim jeans, and Nike flip flops with grey socks.

That's a little strange, Angel thought, *but maybe they play in a band.*

A late model, dark green, four door, Honda Accord was parked inside the garage, facing out. A couple of large pizza boxes were strewn on the floor beside the card table. One had the remnants of a veggie pizza while the other was a meat lover's delight and smelled like it.

April and Sam helped themselves to the rest of the cold, greasy pizza.

"Hey, Angel. Want some pizza?" April asked.

"No thanks. Not really hungry."

Angel began wondering how to handle this increasingly uncomfortable situation.

Then, strangely, without so much as a good-bye, the two men stood up and simply left in the Honda.

"I think they're going to find a high-stakes poker game," Song said, "They've been practicing." She remained in the garage with April, Sam and Angel after pulling the door down when the car left. Angel noticed a space heater near the entrance which was providing warmth from the brutally cold air. A heavy orange extension cord appeared to be connected to an outlet on the back porch of the house next door.

Sam went back to the abandoned house to retrieve the beer Angel had purchased. Song and April began chatting while Angel listened. The girls didn't ask, so Angel didn't offer any information about her past.

"I am a Sophomore at the University of Toledo on a band scholarship," Song said. "I play the trumpet, keyboard, and love to sing."

"That's how Sam and I met Song, Angel. We had summer jobs on Hilton Head Island. Sam sang and played guitar for kids. I can sing, but my job was scooping ice cream in a store nearby. Tell Angel what your job was, Song."

"I went through high school on Baden Island. It was a music boarding school. For the summer, I sold ferry tickets to tourists who visited Baden. One day I heard Sam singing to the kids under the trees. And that was the beginning of our friendships."

"Wow, Song," said Angel, "So, you and April have known each other awhile."

"I really want to become a music teacher and get gigs in rock groups and jazz bands now and then. I'm in a jazz quartet, and we're already hired by the University to play at faculty dinners and music student recruitment luncheons."

Angel was not at all acquainted with music opportunities or jazz for that matter.

"What's a gig?" she asked.

"It means you're hired to play," April answered.

Song explained further.

"My parents believe I'm teaching private music students when I don't fly home on school breaks. It costs a lot to fly to Korea at the end of the school year, then back in the fall. They don't like it, but they excuse my absences like at Christmas this year. My parents and younger sisters miss me, and I miss them, but the truth of the matter is that I fell for James," Song said. "James was a local guy I met at an outdoor Jazz concert in a park near campus. He's not a college student, but he's charming and handsome, don't you think?"

April and Angel exchanged glances, but neither responded to Song's inquiry.

"I never had a boyfriend before because it wasn't acceptable in my culture back home," Song went on to say. "Marriages are still arranged, and courtships are watched very carefully."

Later, Angel found out that James only became local after he ran away from his host family to avoid returning to Africa.

Song's story unfolded further: "One night we were drinking Tequila, straight up with a twist of lime. James offered me some weed. He told me I could experience life more vividly and my musical performance more passionately. I must confess it has become impossible to focus on school. All I think about is being with James, getting high, and listening to him perform."

Song didn't mention she hadn't attended classes or band practice in six weeks. James gave her some pills to help stay awake in class, but she didn't even attempt to leave her dorm room. Her roommate, Beverly, who was also in the band, started worrying about her. But Song assured Beverly she didn't have mono, wasn't pregnant, and just needed to spend more time resting.

At this point, Dr. Rosie asked Angel, "Did Song seem to share that information with pride, or did she demonstrate serious regret?"

"I didn't think Song looked like she was high or drunk on anything. Song's eyes were clear, and she didn't ramble like other kids I've known on drugs. She definitely didn't tell me her story with any pride. She seemed very proud of the fact that James loved her."

"Why don't you continue your story, Angel," Dr. Klein said

"Song told me that at first they took up housekeeping in the house next door with James' friend, Marcus. It was in much better condition and even had running water. The owners were simply away for the Winter. Then, they noticed the empty garage and abandoned house next door."

"She even explained that from the beginning of their relationship, she and James lived on the money Song's parents sent her to spend on incidentals while in college. Luckily for her, she kept a post office box, so her parents didn't know she wasn't going to classes."

Although Song had no knowledge of the condition of the house Angel was staying in with April and Sam, she nonetheless offered Angel a sofa in their house, if she wanted.

"I hate being the only girl and am beginning to think there's trouble brewing. I have no idea what it might be about, but I think it could be theft. They said they've been out of drugs for three days." She also added, "I'm not hooked. I just use them to get closer to James."

"So, what are your plans?" she asked Angel.

"I plan to go to Florida and eventually find a job,"

Angel explained.

Intrigued by Angel's courageous, free spirited plan, April asked to hear more and asked,

"Meanwhile, in Florida, where will you stay?"

"I may be homeless but being homeless on a warm beach is much better than being stuck in the nasty North weather," Angel answered.

"Summer on Hilton Head Island was really sweet," Song said, "But it's much further north than Florida beaches. It wouldn't be very comfortable in winter."

I can trust Song, Angel thought, *But not any of the others.*

That night Angel slept on one of the mattresses on the floor in the cellar.

"Dr. Rosie, I was thinking then that if I decided to stay around, I would take Song up on her offer to stay in the warm house. But, the next morning, April and Sam asked me to walk to McDonald's with them, and loan them each the price of a breakfast combo. I had no problem with that offer and decided to delay my bus trip another day. We spent the rest of the morning sitting in the garage with the small space heater to keep us warm. April started telling me her story."

April explained to Angel how she and Sam had spent the summer in Hilton Head two years earlier.

"Then, we suggested that Song come back to Toledo with us and go to college."

"We got back to Toledo and went to see our old friend, George at his Evergreen Bar," Sam added. "He was so happy to see us, all grown up. We first met when April and I lived at the children's home when we were little.

"So anyhow, we started cleaning George's bar after it closed at 2:30 am. He had a small apartment above the bar and allowed us to sleep there. We got to eat the left-over Greek food, not sold during the evening."

"You can see why they seemed to really like George," Angel said to Dr. Klein. "They described him as a short, jovial Greek man with a heart of gold."

"Then, April told me, she and Sam started getting high and not showing up for work at the bar. Liquor began missing and the collection jug that sat on the bar was often empty. It held donations from customers to be used for the orphans. They both denied stealing anything and sincerely believed they were being set-up by customers."

"But George must have had his suspicions," Dr. Rosie added. "He probably felt he had no other choice than to fire them." Then she asked, "How did April and Sam meet James and Marcus?"

"Sam told me that the three of them, Song, April and him, met James at an outdoor concert the fall of '92. Sam said that Song really liked the guy. It was just before Thanksgiving. Then, James introduced them to his friend Marcus. At that time Marcus and James lived in an apartment together and did lawn work and maintenance for the man next door. The job ended when the guy left for Florida for the winter."

Dr. Klein had jotted several pages of notes, took a moment, then looked up at angel.

"Back to your story, Angel. You were at the point where it was the next day."

"Well, around noon, Song and James came over, and Song welcomed me with a hug. I even noticed that James seemed nicer and more open when Marcus wasn't there."

Dr. Rosie made a mental note: *By then, Angel had been so touch-deprived that this gesture probably sealed the idea of a real friendship in her mind.* Rosie hated to interrupt the flow of conversation, but needed time to go to her office and return phone calls. She suggested they take a short break and promised she would return after lunch.

As they rose to stand, Verna, a corrections officer, noticed them and opened the door. Angel was escorted back to her cell.

As she walked back to the parking garage, Dr. Rosie thought: *Sam seems so much different than the other two men. I just can't quite put my finger on why and how he and April got involved with the others. It surely was a bad decision.*

MARCH 8, 1994

CHAPTER **8**

BEGINNING OF THE CRIME SPREE

After lunch, Dr. Klein returned to jail to see Angel. She had returned a few calls from private clients and eaten a small Greek salad she had packed for lunch. Arriving just after 1 pm, she waited while Angel was brought into the interview room and smiled at her as she entered.

At this point in the interview process, Rosie sensed a good rapport had been established. Now, she began pressing Angel for details of the crimes. First, however, she produced an energy bar for Angel, and a bottle of water for each of them. Then, she asked Angel to describe what happened the night the first victim was shot on the sidewalk outside a telephone booth.

"Take your time, Angel, just tell me what you remember."

"It was Thursday around 7 pm. We were sitting around in the garage. Marcus arrived, clapped his hands, and suggested we all go for a 'joy ride'," Angel said.

"The six of us got into the Honda and thought we were just gonna drive around for fun. None of us knew James and Marcus thought shooting someone at random was 'fun'. James was driving and Marcus was in the passenger seat. I was huddled in the back with my three friends."

"You mean April, Sam and Song?" Rosie asked.

"Yes," Angel said.

She had thought of tape recording this discussion but didn't want to scare Angel into silence. So, she had decided not to. Still, she needed all details to be crystal clear.

"Then, Marcus rolled down his window." Angel stopped talking at the memory. Then, with downcast eyes, she told of remembering the bitter, cold air coming in which caused her lips and cheeks to burn. She watched Marcus put his drink down between his legs and withdraw a gun from beneath the seat. The next thing she knew, he pointed the gun out the window and pulled the trigger.

"He shot a young black kid just comin' out of a phone booth!" There was moisture at the corner of Angel's left eye. "Marcus jumped out'a the car and yanked off the bleeding guy's Fila shoes and letter jacket. He checked his pockets for cash and might've got a few dollars. I couldn't believe what was happening!" Her face twisted in a sad expression. Rosie paused a moment.

"Was anything in particular said before the incident? Why this guy?" she asked quietly.

"No warning whatsoever," Angel replied. "This guy was in the wrong place at the wrong time and was definitely wearing the wrong clothes."

"What do you mean?"

"Well, when Marcus got back into the car, he mumbled that 'he got what he deserved'. I think because he attended a rival high school."

"He must have been quite young. Was he dead on the scene?" Dr. Rosie asked.

"I dunno. I heard later he'd died." Angel mumbled. Her eyes were still looking downward.

"What happened next, Angel?"

She seemed to be getting restless, putting her hands together and cracking her knuckles.

"Then we sped off and went on the highway," she recalled, her eyes looking into the distance.

According to police reports, they had sped off and merged on to the Interstate toward Michigan which was north of where they were staying. In Michigan, they exited at the five-mile marker and reentered the highway going back south to Toledo.

"When we got back there, I was just so glad the men let me and April go back to the cellar in the house. Sam stayed in the garage and the guys sped off. Me and April hightailed it through the back door and downstairs as fast as we could go. There was no reason to use the broken window. We were so scared, we didn't care about anything right then."

"What did the men and the other girl, Song, do the rest of the night?"

"I dunno. I just remember it was almost impossible to sleep. Between the hard floor and the memory of the shooting, I couldn't. I don't think April slept either."

"How were you and April feeling at that point?"

"We were scared to death. I worried about Song, too. We sat on the mattresses in the cold, dark cellar. I wanted to know how April and Sam got themselves into this mess. April told me she had grown up in an orphanage with Sam. He was four years older. He joined the Marines when he turned eighteen. She told me, he invited her to meet him in South Carolina when she graduated from high school. They spent the summer at a resort, working part-time and enjoying the beach. Before that, they were not boyfriend and girlfriend. She was still a young teen-ager when Sam joined the Marines. That summer, I guess, they fell in love.

"Then, April and Sam met Song who was at a famous

music boarding school on another Island," she continued. "The three of them basically hung out, working part-time till the end of August when it was time to return to Toledo. They convinced Song to go with them and said there was a good music school at the University of Toledo. I guess she was pretty good, because she got a music scholarship there."

By now, Angel was talking freely. She said that April told her Song did well her first year at college. April, herself, did okay working as a temp employee at an employment agency. Sam, however, could only find occasional gigs and had no steady employment, musical or otherwise. They stayed friends with Song, but she was mostly involved in campus life.

"Then, God sent them an angel by the name of 'George'," Angel recalled. "April said they remembered him as a kind, generous man from their days in the children's orphanage. Now, he owned a bar and offered them jobs cleaning floors and bathrooms after the bar closed at 2:30 am. He also gave them a little apartment above the bar. They slept days and ate left over food George prepared for his customers. But, when George started noticing liquor missing, they eventually lost their jobs and their apartment, too.

"But then, they knew Song. Her dorm room was paid for once a year, by her parents. So, when school was over in June, Sam and April secretly bunked with her in her dorm room. It was easy because her roommate left for the summer. Song's parents sent her money from Korea for food which she always shared with them. Then, when school started in the Fall, they had to leave the dorm. That's when they found this empty house and basically broke in through the cellar window.

"About six weeks later, Song asked them to join her at a jazz concert in a community park near campus," Angel said. "I remember it well because April described it as 'the beginning of the end.'

"James was playing in the band and Song fell hard for him. On one of the band breaks, James came over and introduced himself. Sam was sitting on the ground against a large, oak tree with his guitar in his lap. James asked him if he played Jazz. Sam said 'no' that he played Country and Pop. James said he played in some gigs that are Pops and maybe he could set him up. Then, James turned his attention to Song, and after the concert, the two of them disappeared into the park."

Angel continued talking and said that James and Song moved into the house next door at Thanksgiving when the elderly owners went to Florida for the winter.

"She told her college roommate that she was house and pet sitting. That was also the first time they started seeing Marcus around."

At this point in the interview, Angel was showing emotional distress. Her head hung forward and her voice wavered. But Dr. Klein still needed more information.

"Did you begin to contemplate simply running away?"

"No. I really couldn't think of a plan that would not get me killed. They would know to check the bus station or even the train station. I used thirty dollars between the purchase of beer, donuts and three McDonalds breakfasts. I wasn't even sure I had enough money for a ticket now."

"Listen, Angel, that's enough for today. You did a great job. I'll be back at the end of the week. I know that talking about what you've been through is very difficult, but it's what will help you, I believe. "

Rosie left the jail and it's depressing grey walls behind as she went out the door. She was relieved to smell the crisp, fresh air and see a vivid blue sky. What a terrible way to live life, in a cell without an outside view and an inside stimulation of hope. Hope that comes from faith in a better future. Rosie said a silent prayer for this young woman and a prayer of gratitude for her own blessed life.

Although she had been appointed by the Defense, Rosie decided to stop and see Matt Murphy at the Assistant County Prosecutor's office for a brief chat. It seemed appropriate since he had broken the ice on this case by calling her the day she was appointed by Dan Singer.

Rosie recalled the times she had worked with Matt, on previous cases. He was destined to become the County Prosecutor in time. His father had been in that position for twenty years. The current Prosecutor would retire in half a dozen years and Matt would run unopposed for the office, she imagined.

Matt and Rosie felt mutual respect and had a personal connection through their children. While growing up in different suburbs, their children played against one another on school sports teams. She knew Matt had confidence in her professionalism, and that she was not simply a paid Expert Witness. She always told things as she saw them, given the facts provided to her. She never relied only on the defendant's version of events, but always elicited information from other sources, some human and some recorded in writing.

On the stand, when Attorney Singer would ask her if she had ever testified in behalf of the State, the jury would perceive her as neutral, once she answered, 'yes'. All Matt could do was hope she rendered an opinion favorable to his case.

It was obvious this defendant, Angel, was competent to stand trial. After all, she had testified for the State against both James and Marcus. Marcus was sentenced to death by lethal injection for six murders. James received a life sentence without parole. Of course, there would be multiple appeals. But Matt was certain their cases were iron clad, and the verdicts would be sustained by the Court of Appeals. Rosie couldn't imagine a reason not to stop in to see him.

Matt greeted Rosie in the reception area and escorted her back to his office. It was a corner office on the third floor with windows facing the river. The side windows looked down upon the Court house steps where the press often perched.

As she passed the small offices of his junior prosecutors, Joan Nickels and Freddie Thomas, she was acknowledged with a wave and a nod. Joan appeared to be on the phone while Freddie was on his computer with headphones. For all she knew, Joan and Freddie could be calling upon her services soon. They were not assigned to Angel's case but had helped Angel prepare her testimony against Marcus and James.

Matt asked her a couple of personal questions. For starters, he wondered why he hadn't seen her at the last basketball game. The usual Saturday night tradition held that if the team had a home game, most season ticket holders were in attendance. The student section was far removed from them. As was the noisy pep band.

Rosie didn't want to explain that the wives decided where dinner would be after the game and usually it meant gathering at a local pub, Treasure Island, for fried chicken. Even when she did attend games now, she was out of the loop without her husband. Seldom was she invited any more.

Unbeknownst to most of her friends and colleagues, Rosie had an emotional connection to the University having been a basketball halftime dancer while working on her undergraduate degree. Her participation had opened many doors for her. Professors liked her because they could talk about the game on Monday morning. This led to acceptance into graduate school programs that not only paid for her tuition but also paid a weekly stipend. She made more in grad school than she had made as a physical education teacher.

The second personal item on Matt's agenda was in reference to who she was dating. He had a local attorney in mind. She indicated Judge Lincoln had beat him to it and she was perfectly satisfied with her lifestyle for the time being. He responded by saying he would keep the offer open.

Rosie closed the conversation by asking Matt if there were materials he would like to emphasize when she reviewed them. He indicated that everything was relevant.

She didn't want anyone withholding important information to ensure they won the case. Both the Defense and the Prosecutor should have duplicate copies of all discovery materials. It was unethical to withhold witness information.

As Rosie left the building, she felt satisfied with her interview and the day's outcome. Now, she was heading home with anticipation of a possible phone call or message from her new friend, Bucky.

TUESDAY AFTERNOON – MARCH 8, 1994

CHAPTER 9

A NEW RELATIONSHIP

Sure enough, Bucky had communicated while I was absent from my Summerhill office. He'd sent a lovely plant with multicolored cut flowers inserted in the center. The card simply read:"Spring is around the corner and until then you put Spring into my step. (signed) Bucky."

I thought it was appropriate to call him to express my surprise and gratitude. He answered on the second ring and voiced appreciation on hearing from me so quickly. I was glad.

"The flowers are lovely, and the thought even lovelier. How could you know it was just what the doctor ordered?"

"A little birdie may have told me," he said. "No, actually, the Holy Spirit laid it on my heart."

I was speechless. For him to be unafraid to voice a spiritual thought to me was very special. It was a flag to take this man seriously. He was different. He might be a 'keeper'.

"Have you seen the defendant again?" Bucky asked, breaking the silence.

"Yes," I replied, and it made for an emotionally charged day on both our parts."

"I was planning to call you after baseball practice," he said, "But, I'm glad you called sooner."

"Oh. Is this a bad time? I'm sorry if I interrupted."

"No, no. Not at all. I just need to be at the fieldhouse at 4 pm. I was wondering if you're available for dinner on Friday night and do you eat red meat, like in steak?"

"I happen to have a wide-open calendar this weekend," I said, so glad he had asked. "That sounds great, and I simply love steak."

"Do you mind if the Judge and his new main squeeze join us? He would really like to be out with friends on Friday night."

"I would be delighted. May I ask, is the new main squeeze someone I know?"

"I'm uncertain as to who this lady might be," Bucky replied, "But I heard a rumor she was the Judge's court reporter. Oh, by the way, I need your address. I'll pick you up at six pm on Friday, if that is okay."

"It is, and I'm looking forward to seeing you," I replied.

I headed home to take Jocko for a walk after he'd been cooped up all day. He would not get to run at the dog park until Saturday. But, I would bring him to the Summerhill office on Wednesday, as was his usual mid-week itinerary. The Summerhill office is on the first floor and Jocko enjoys looking out the double doors in the lobby, sort of acting as a greeter to my clients.

This particular Wednesday morning, I would be facilitating my bi-weekly women's support group. Ruth would traditionally make coffee along with delectable, chocolate croissants for all participants. Comfort food always helped dynamics in the group, which were unpredictable and fiery, but developing in an interesting way:

The divorced women in the group were no angels. Several were still currently involved with married men. At first, wives in the group who had been betrayed at some time in their lives were enraged at these women giving lame excuses for fooling around with married men. The 'harlots' told the wives their husbands had roamed because "they simply weren't having their needs met at home". That didn't necessarily mean in a sexual manner since men also needed approval and attention.

As weeks went by, these group members seemed to bond and were beginning to look at the men in their lives as now the source of their problems, instead of the men's wives. Group members who were wives were now saying how their husbands were groveling and begging for forgiveness as they, themselves, became stronger and were facing their husbands with their suspicions. The group members who were mistresses, in turn, were stunned the men were beginning to backtrack in not wanting divorces in order to be with them. This resulted in making the mistresses begin to want to be more honest women.

Everyone in the group always hugged good- bye, vowing to do their written homework which involved journaling feelings and planning how to implement healthier life choices. I couldn't help but think of Angel and Song. Perhaps, in our next meeting Angel would share the hardships she and Song had faced together.

I spent Wednesday night and Thursday, listening to sappy love songs on my CD player while reviewing the discovery materials. I found it helpful to use a yellow highlighter to magnify significant facts I might want to review later. Then, I jotted down notes on a legal pad as a reminder of questions I wanted answered by Angel. But decided to put off collateral interviews until the beginning of next week until I would finish interviewing Angel.

My intent was to be available to Angel and be sure to follow through with whatever I've told this fragile young woman she could expect of me. I didn't want to disappoint her and lose the trust we were building. I wanted her to know that she could depend on Dr. Rosie Klein to be reliable and trustworthy. I don't believe Angel has ever had a relationship with anyone who really had integrity and no ulterior motives. Sadly, I realized even I had an ulterior motive, trying to get Angel to reveal herself, but unlike others in her life, this one really was meant to help her.

FRIDAY EARLY MORNING-MARCH 11, 1994

CHAPTER **10**

THE CRIME SPREE CONTINUES

Early Friday morning, Dr. Klein arrived at the jail just after breakfast. Angel seemed glad to see her. After settling into chairs in the interview room, Dr. Rosie placed a protein bar on the table in front of Angel and a bottle of water for each.

"How are you Angel?" she asked quietly, as Angel looked at her passively. "I've been thinking a lot about you and your story. But more importantly, I've been thinking about you and how you're coping with everything."

"Thank you, Dr. Klein. It makes me feel better just knowing you seem to care. "

"So, can we proceed with your story, Angel? What happened next?"

Angel began describing the next joy ride.

"They made me get into the car, but I didn't want to," she said. "I got in the back, again, with Sam, April and Song. I was sitting behind Marcus who was driving. April and Sam sat next to me in the middle, and Song sat behind her boyfriend, James, in the passenger seat.

"Were you interested in a relationship with Marcus? You sat behind him when he was on the passenger side," Dr. Rosie recalled.

"No way! I didn't think of him like that at all," she answered emphatically. "I didn't even think it ever looked that way."

"That's okay, Angel," Dr. Rosie said in a calm manner. "I was just asking. Please go on."

"It was about a quarter to six on Friday, and still dark out because of it being winter. We cruised slow through downtown streets. People were leaving their offices and hustling to get home from work. James had the music blaring. I think it was Aretha Franklin singing, yeah, 'Killing Me Softly with His Song'. But, there was nothing soft about the level of the music and I started to feel so nervous," Angel started looking agitated, and Dr. Rosie touched her hand on the table.

"Then I saw a businessman dressed in a long, black overcoat, leather gloves, and holding a briefcase. He was standing close to the curb at a bus stop downtown. Sure enough! What I was afraid of happened! James rolled down the window and pointed the gun out the window. He shot the guy from no further than five feet away! I was so scared! The man dropped to the sidewalk and I saw a couple of older kids, maybe college age, bend over and put their backpacks over their heads. For protection, I guess.

"Then I couldn't believe it, but James jumped out and grabbed the briefcase! He barely got back in the car when Marcus drove off so fast. We were all scared in the back seat. I think he was getting away before the college kids could identify the license plate. But I don't think it would have mattered since the car wasn't registered to any of us, and most likely wasn't turned in as stolen even. Then we hit the highway and drove over the State line again before turning back after about five miles."

"Why do you think they thought it was such a good idea to go north to Michigan and then turn around?"

"I think they saw that type of getaway in a movie or something."

"When we got back to the house, James opened the garage door and Marcus backed in. They dumped the stuff from the briefcase onto the card table. They were really happy to find a business credit card and a check book in there. I guess that's what they were hoping to find. Right after that, they left the garage on foot to use the credit card at a convenience store. It was a store where they don't ask for ID if you don't buy more than $100 worth of stuff. The rest of us were left behind, and we just kinda looked at each other. I could see that Song didn't seem happy with her boyfriend. We just sat there without talking at all till they came back."

"That must have been terrible for you all, Angel," Dr. Rosie said quietly. "What were you guys thinking?"

"I know what I was thinking," Angel said. "We were involved in two murders. We couldn't really run, and we couldn't go to the police. We needed to find a television to watch the news and see what information they had out there," She added, "James and Marcus returned so quickly we never were even able to come up with a plan."

Noticing Angel anxiously digging her fingers into the palm of one hand, Rosie asked: "Do you need a break?"

"No. Sometimes it helps me to tell my story to somebody who seems to care," Angel answered. "The next morning, me and April and Sam were woken up with a banging sound on the side of the house. It was James and Marcus who was calling us to meet them at the car in ten minutes. This was strange because they usually played cards, drank, and used drugs all night. It didn't feel right. Usually, they didn't wake up until about two in the afternoon and then they were usually starving.

"By now, I couldn't think at all. We just did what

we were told. It was a sunny day, but really cold. Song was already in the back seat of the car holding a large cup of black coffee. We drove out to a quarry where the teens from town go to swim in the summer when no one's around. There're never any lifeguards, but there are rafts and cliffs to dive from into the deep water. I would have liked to do that in the hot summer, but now it was cold and empty.

"Marcus told us to get out of the car. We did as he said but wondered what in the world he was up to. He said they had watched the morning news and saw information about the business guy's murder. It didn't say where the info came from, but it was probably the witnesses at the bus stop. But Marcus and James decided it must have come from our group."

"Why would they think that? You guys were the only friends they had," Dr. Rosie said opening her eyes wide in surprise.

"They were getting paranoid and still definitely high, not thinking straight," Angel said. "They told everybody but Song to kneel on the ground. We were in the parking lot facing the quarry. I got down on my knees and began praying softly to Jesus. Suddenly, I heard 'pop, pop' and saw Sam and April fall forward on their faces with bullet holes in the back of their heads. I don't know why they didn't shoot me, too. I just couldn't believe it. I couldn't hardly breath. Then, they ordered Song and me back into the car and just left. The bodies were still lying there on the cold ground." Tears were streaming down Angel's face now.

"Maybe God is real," she said softly. Then, with a weak, choked up, voice, she struggled to tell the rest.

"The four of us drove back to the garage and parked the car. The guys told me to bring my stuff into the house next door. They said I would be staying with them now.

"Song said absolutely nothing the rest of the day. It was Saturday and they watched sports while me and Song sat quietly at the kitchen table. There were herbal tea bags in the cupboard. We sipped our tea and warmed our hands on the sides of the steamy cups. I felt numb all over and so sad.

"It was obvious to me that Song was giving a fake smile when her boyfriend looked her way. Dr. Klein, at that point, I knew we weren't going anywhere any time soon. The guys played cards and drank as if nothing happened.

"Nobody talked about April and Sam anymore. It was like they were never there. I thought since they were orphans, with no parents or relatives to tell, who would look for them? I didn't know what was going to happen to me or Song."

"Angel, you are very brave to retell such a frightening story," Dr. Rosie said. She knew Angel had gone through enough memories for today. A person could only do so much.

"Try to get some rest now and be sure to eat something for lunch and dinner. You need to regain your energy and strength after telling me your story"

After hugging Angel, and promising to see her again soon, Dr. Klein left, nodding to Verna Mitchell as if to induce her to be gentle with the defendant.

Rosie walked to the parking garage and drove to her suburban office. She needed a hug, herself, from Ruth. Ruth was such a faithful friend, working such long hours while having an ill husband at home. Just before starting the car, however, she picked up her phone to make a call.

"Hi there, Ruth. Would you mind putting in a to-go order at Bob Evans for us and I'll pick it up on the way? Order something for your husband, Ralph, as well."

Rosie's appetite at this point was really shot. Her usual salad with dried cranberries and walnuts had lost its appeal. She decided a bowl of tomato bisque soup might hit the spot.

Back at the office, she settled into an afternoon of providing marriage counseling. Several of the women in the Wednesday support group were being seen with their estranged husbands. For once, she looked forward to hearing about the conflict between bright, articulate, middle class couples in contrast to the life and death story she had just heard. Time to eat the salad and "change her hat", so to speak.

Before the end of the day, Ruth provided her with the schedule of collateral interviews for the following week.

"Hey, Rosie. Next week, your first collateral interview will be with the arresting officer, Sergeant Ron Thompson of the Ohio State Highway Patrol. He was assisted by three other Sheriff's Deputies, but the Sergeant's version of the events should be enough

"You're right. The other officers' written reports likely concur with Thompson's account. I think I will review them prior to meeting with Sergeant Thompson."

"Your second interview will be Angel's older sister, Amanda. She told me she might be bringing two preschool kids with her. I assured her there are plenty of toys and coloring materials in our waiting room."

The waiting room was just outside Ruth's office door which made for easy supervision. There was a small portable TV that could be turned to cartoon stations, if needed.

"Thanks Ruth. It is unlikely she can offer much of Angel's childhood beyond the age of nine. Their lifestyles differed dramatically after Amanda left their mother's house to live with her grandparents. Schools were not the same. Church was not the same. But I am sure, whatever she recalls will be useful."

Angel didn't have much else going for her.

FRIDAY EARLY EVENING-MARCH 11, 1994

CHAPTER 11

DOUBLE DATE

I toyed with the dilemma of whether to wear boots or shoes to dinner with Bucky. He's such a gentleman, if the parking lot is not shoveled clean, I'm certain he'll leave me at the door to the restaurant and not make me walk in from the lot.

I decide to wear black flats. As an olive skinned, brunette, my best color is red, or so I've been told. So, I choose a red turtleneck sweater, matching it with a hand knit red shawl, silver dangling filigree earrings, and black slacks.

Bucky arrives right on time. Jocko appears excited to see him. He tells me, 'I look great' and offers his arm to escort me to the car. The Judge and his friend, Darlene, are already in the back seat.

This dinner date is serving several purposes. It's a pleasant reprieve from the stress of engaging in such highly personal interviews with Angel. It's also allowing me to step back into a mid-American, mid-life, typical Friday night lifestyle I haven't enjoyed since my husband died. And it's offering me an opportunity to make new friends.

Sharing laughter is just what the doctor ordered. I can't help but think how important laughter was in the beginning of Angel's new friendships, which in her case, masked the overall red flags of bad intentions, and turned out disastrous for her. But that wasn't laughter's fault.

One always needs to be aware of their

surroundings and the actions of others, I thought. Being aware of this, I wonder just how significant laughter will be in my own new journey.

During dinner, I find that Darlene lives in the same suburb as I do, and that we shop at the same privately-owned grocery store. Most likely, we've passed each other in the aisles and never knew it. We might even have sipped complimentary, flavored coffee while waiting for our individual numbers to be called at the Deli, completely unaware of each other.

"But, I can't imagine buying baking supplies next to you," Darlene says, "Because I buy all my baked goods in the bakery."

"Me, too!" I answer her back. Again, laughter.

After a delightful dinner at Mancy's, Darlene invites us all back to her place for drinks and dessert. Later, the Judge remains at Darlene's where he left his car before the double date. Bucky escorts me back to my front door and steps into the foyer. He notices there is no sound from Jocko at first, but very quickly, Jocko is there, greeting him happily.

"Jocko only barks when I'm accompanied by a strange visitor," I tell him. "Now that he has your scent, and likes you, he won't bark when you approach our door by yourself."

"I take that to be good news," Bucky says. "Do I assume, when I read into your remarks, that you'll be seeing me again?"

"Of course," I smile at him.

Bucky glances toward the coffee table and notices the flower arrangement he sent to my office earlier in the week is front and center. I nod toward the arrangement.

"I brought them home on Wednesday because I was reviewing records at home for a few days," I explain.

"They're simply beautiful and I didn't want to leave them alone at the office. Such pretty flowers should be looked at often. It breaks up the monotony of a day. Again, I want to thank you for sending them."

Feeling myself blushing, I hoped Bucky wouldn't notice under the dim light.

"Yes, I'd like to see you again."

"Good," he said happily. "I'll call you in the middle of next week." He had said at dinner that as a baseball coach for the University of Toledo, he'd be out of town recruiting from Sunday until next Wednesday.

The University would be on break for the week of St. Patrick's Day. In prior years, students always celebrated with lots of green beer and vandalism on campus. This year, the University decided to use the week for Spring break. They couldn't afford to keep replacing burned mattresses in the dorms.

After Bucky left, I put on my knee-high boots and took Jocko for a walk around the condominium grounds. Although the pool wasn't filled, the surrounding lights remain on all winter and the American flag waves in the night unless there was rain or snow.

On this night the moon is full. The stars seem to be sparkling a little brighter than they have been of late. I can't help but smile in the darkness as Jocko and I walk along.

MONDAY MORNING-MARCH 14, 1994

CHAPTER 12

COLLATERAL INTERVIEWS

On Monday morning, Sergeant Ron Thompson arrived precisely on time. Not in uniform, since it was his day off, he greeted Dr. Klein who thanked him for taking time to drive to her Summerhill office and clarify details of the arrest.

Declining a cup of coffee, he accepted a bagel with crème cheese and a small glass of orange juice. Although they had never met, he had heard her testify in another case in which he had been involved. Her testimony had been relevant to the jury, he told her.

"May I call you 'Ron'?

"Certainly," he replied.

"Please, call me 'Rosie'. Now, Ron, I'd like you to tell me exactly how Angel and her co-defendants were identified and apprehended two Christmases ago."

"It was Christmas Eve, 1992," he said. "On the police radio, the Captain had just notified all officers of shots fired in a West Toledo residential area called in by two separate neighbors. They'd watched a car leaving the scene and gave the license plate. I saw a late model Ford merging on to I-75 North from the ramp at Superior Street and noticed its plate matched, so I began following the vehicle. I saw two women in the back seat, straining their necks to view the patrol car. It was dark and I couldn't make out faces, just long hair.

"According to Sgt. Thompson, once the driver noticed

the patrol car, the vehicle began to pick up speed. It wasn't long before it greatly exceeded the speed limit. At that point, Sgt. Thompson had probable cause to pull it over. Turning on his lights, he called for back-up and began pursuing the vehicle ahead.

"Three Sheriff's cars soon joined the chase, all tailing the Ford as it sped toward the State line. Sgt. Thompson's Highway Patrol car led the others with blue and red lights flashing.

"Pull over immediately!" he called out on his loudspeaker. He repeated it several more times before the Honda began slowing and pulled over to the shoulder of the highway without further incident.

"Police cars surrounded the Ford," he said. "I used the loudspeaker again and ordered the driver to open his window, put both hands out and drop the car keys. He complied, and I ordered him to open the door from the outside and step out with his hands in the air. He did so immediately. Then, I told him to keep his hands up and walk backwards until I told him to stop. Again, he did as commanded. Lastly, he was told to drop to his knees at which point one of the officers stepped forward and handcuffed him. The others kept their eyes on the remaining passengers in the Ford."

Rosie was quiet as she listened. Sgt. Thompson seemed to remember the incident in every detail and Rosie wondered if that was a natural ability.

Was he really remembering this case or just one of his many routine stops? Or had his recent testimony at the trials of the men stirred his memory?

Sgt. Thompson continued his story and stated that the other three suspects were each instructed to do the same thing and all had complied without incident.

"Not a single one of them asked any questions or said

a word," he continued. "The two passengers in the back seat turned out to be a young Caucasian woman and a young Asian woman.

There was no eye contact between the women and the men, but the women looked at one another, and cried a bit."

Rosie decided he knew the exact case and was reporting the right one.

"Once they were all cuffed, they were placed in separate patrol cars and read their rights," he continued. "The County Sheriffs' deputies were on the scene and transported all of them to the Lucas County jail. That's where they would be interviewed and probably booked on suspicion of robbery and murder. I had received a report on my police radio that Mr. Brooks had been shot and did not survive. DOA on arrival at the hospital."

"Okay, Sergeant, I really appreciate hearing about the case from you," Rosie said. "At this time, I have no further questions, but I might in the future. Would it be alright if I got back to you if I do?"

"Absolutely," he answered while standing and offering his hand. Dr. Klein stood and shook it.

"Thanks Ron, for taking your personal time and for your cooperation. Let me see you out."

"I'm glad to help in any way I can. This little gang created fear and havoc in our city and getting them off the streets without more deaths was a huge benefit to all citizens."

"In a way, it was a Christmas gift to know the rest of our community was safe," Rosie said as he left. She topped off her black coffee and continued reading the discovery materials. It appeared the Public Defender assigned to Song's case, Chickalette, had encouraged her to plead guilty. Therefore, a trial had been avoided. She was facing a life sentence without parole for her role in the crimes. He had advised her there was a slim chance a jury would hand down a lesser sentence. But, she would need to appear extremely remorseful, accept responsibility for her actions, and possibly speak to the Judge and families of the victims in the courtroom. She'd refused thinking she would have a better chance at clemency from a single judge.

When both shooters went on trial, they were convicted of all charges. At that time, the victims' families did not come forward with statements. Their emotions were still too raw, and the handwriting was on the wall as to the verdicts. The records showed Marcus received the death penalty and James received life without parole, just as Angel had said. Angel's testimony most likely influenced the judges to hand down unanimous verdicts of guilt on all charges and the recommended sentences.

Angel was led to believe her own sentence might be lessened by her willingness to cooperate with the State by testifying against the shooters. Unlike Song, Angel had a past record because she had stolen a car as a juvenile. Now it was coming back to haunt her.

Dr. Rosie and Angel would be at the upcoming sentencing hearing for Song. They wouldn't miss it. It could indicate what might happen to Angel.

Rosie barely had time to scratch down a few notes before Ruth announced the next witness. It was Amanda, Angel's big sister. Ruth led her back to the office and offered her a soft drink or water. Amanda politely declined both.

Dr. Klein pointed to an overstuffed love seat positioned across from her chair. She noticed Amanda was wearing a heavy, wool, black cardigan and a long red scarf with fringe on the ends. No jacket. No hat. No gloves. She was twenty-something and looked responsible, a grown woman with children of her own.

"So, Amanda, where do you and your children live now?

"I live in a small rural town about 30 miles south of Toledo," she responded. "It's kind of like a small farm community. I work part time in a hardware store, there. The kids are with my grandparents today, the folks who raised me from the age of twelve."

"I hope you didn't mind coming in to talk today. It seems like a bit of a drive for you," Rosie offered.

"I don't mind," she said. "Really, I prefer coming to Summerhill. It's easier to get to than downtown, and parking's free," Amanda said. "Although, I really don't see how I can be much help. I haven't had much contact with Angel once she was sent to Juvie," she looked down at her hands folded in her lap."I remember only a handful of times that my grandparents and I actually saw Angel once I went to live with them. My mother was extremely resentful of me and couldn't say anything nice about my grandparents, so I didn't much like visiting with her.

One Christmas, we even placed presents on the doorstep. We knew everyone was home, but my mom or her boyfriend, wouldn't allow Angel or the boys to answer the door. So, we left. That was the last time I tried."

Amanda described the house appearing vacant soon after that winter.

"If they were gone, we had no clue where they all went. Once, the police came to my grandparent's house asking if they knew my mother's whereabouts. But they didn't know. She could have been living in Indiana or Michigan or anywhere." Amanda wasn't smiling.

"Once I moved away, my mother jumped around with the three kids not to get arrested. She could have been charged with anything from child neglect to dealing drugs. I say, 'good riddance'."

Rosie looked at this young woman who had decided at age twelve to liberate herself from her mother, a bad influence. She had been lucky to have had loving grandparents who wanted her. Angel had not been so lucky.

"I told the boys to expect phone calls from you, Dr. Klein. They said they would be glad to talk to you." She referred to Angel's little brothers, themselves, not so little anymore.

Amanda provided telephone numbers for them. She said her grandparents had been notified once the boys were removed and put into foster care. She also said the kids resented their mother for her treatment of Angel, and her failure to protect all of them from some horrible men.

"Amanda, would you like to see your sister, now?" Dr. Klein asked.

"Yes, I would," Amanda answered, "But I don't know if she's forgiven me for abandoning her, and then for not visiting her in Juvenile Detention."

"I will ask her when I see her again," Dr. Klein offered. "If she says 'yes', which I'm sure she will, I'll contact you to make arrangements."

The interview did not last much longer. Rosie gave Amanda her business card and asked her to call if she came up with any more childhood memories she would like to share.

"Sometimes, it takes a while for memories to come back," she explained.

Especially if they've been pushed down so deep, they seem buried forever.

MID-MORNING, MONDAY- MARCH 14, 1994

CHAPTER 13

THE STORY OF JAMES

Dr. Klein asked Ruth to hold all calls. She wanted to begin reviewing the cases of James and Marcus. Refilling her favorite coffee cup, she gave a brief scratch to the top of Jocko's head and sat down in her plaid chair. She planned to read for an hour before taking Jocko out for a brief walk. The snow had subsided, and the groundhog had not seen his shadow. This meant Spring was certainly on the way. Comfortable now, she opened a thick folder and began reading:

> James Abraham came from Zambia. He and his mother lived in the adjacent village across the river from a property known as the Baker farm, home of American Baptist missionaries, Robert and Rachel Baker. James had three siblings younger than himself and three older. This placed him smack in the middle with few expectations by the elders for academic or sports performance.
>
> His younger sister, Caroline, had her first baby at age thirteen. James hated the older cousin who lured Caroline into a relationship only to take off for Lusaka, the Capital, once she became pregnant. Caroline at first believed he had gone to find work so he could provide for her and their son's financial support. James knew that wasn't so, and his heart

ached for his little sister. He thought: "if I could find him, I would kill him."

Being the older brother, James took pride in helping Caroline care for the toddler she named after him. He would put little Jimmy on his shoulders and carry him across the small bridge that led to farmland on the other side of the narrow river. Part of the year, the river was nearly dry which made it an easy walk, usually barefooted, over stones forming a bridge across the water.

The Baker farmhouse on the other side of the river sat on two-thousand acres of fertile land on which the Bakers raised cattle. They also had a well and provided clean water to the village people.

James' mother, Rebecca, and some other women from the village worked in the missionary garden. They were paid a wage and allowed not only jugs of clean water but freshly picked vegetables and fruits to take home. In return, they were expected to attend a weekly Bible study, led by Rachel in the farmhouse.

Most people in his village were ignorant. They were illiterate in reading and writing the Tonga language, as well as English. They were at the mercy of the storekeepers when purchasing merchandise in town. Mrs. Baker would help them barter for supplies. She was very assertive on the villagers' behalf and on that of her family.

She provided those she could with egg cartons so when they ordered eggs, they'd have a safe method of transporting them back to the village. Mrs. Baker thought about raising chickens, but feared they could not protect them, or their eggs, from predators at night. So instead, she raised fruits and vegetables that would survive in the arid climate.

Mrs. Baker also served as their great white lady doctor when first aid, infection, or fever required attention.

Looking up from her reading, Rosie remembered a psychologist she had once heard speak at church, going over to volunteer at the Baker farm.

At the request of two old great-grandparents, Rachel Baker and the psychologist went into the village to diagnose a six-year old girl. The grandparents believed she was possessed by demons. As it turned out, she suffered from Epileptic seizures that could easily be prevented by taking the proper medication. There was a medical clinic in Choma, but to be treated there required a medical referral. This made no sense since there were no private doctors within four hours of this little community.

As the psychologist sat in the thatched roof hut with the grandparents, Rachel Baker translated their version of the child's condition. The psychologist invited the girl to sit on her lap by patting her knees. Rachel translated the doctor's non-verbal request. The child appeared dazed, was drooling and somewhat weak and immobile. She nodded her little head affirmatively, and Rachel placed her on the psychologist's lap.

Given the history provided by the grandparents, it took no time at all for the psychologist to determine a valid diagnosis. She and Rachel returned to the farm where the psychologist wrote a letter to the director of the Choma clinic. She later heard the girl was receiving Dilantin, an anti-seizure medication, and no further seizure activity was taking place

Spring brought torrential rains. In Summer, it was exceedingly hot. In the Fall, there was a drought from four months of no rain. Sometimes, the Farm had electricity and sometimes it went out without notice. The village, of course, never had electricity.

A Baker son named Joel would accompany his mother, Rachel, to the village just across the river where James and his family lived. James enjoyed kicking a soccer ball around and eventually, he and Joel Baker become good friends. Joel paid attention to him by taking him fishing, tubing on the river, and walking into town together. The small town was called Choma in English. It consisted of a café and a few stores on both sides of a dusty, dirt road. Most days carts pulled by oxen could be seen hauling supplies to the farmers. If you wanted eggs, you took your own cartons and money into a store and requested they be filled. If you wanted flour, you went to a separate store. There was a small clothing store owned by a Hindu Indian family. Women purchased fabric to make wrap around garments, head coverings and cloth for infant swaddle carriers.

Joel bought James penny candy in the General Store. James gave some of it along with the cellophane wrappers to his little sisters and nephew to decorate the area behind their cots. For the walk back to the village, Joel purchased James a bottle of Orange Fanta. The bottles could be redeemed for a few cents that Joel allowed James to keep.

James' two older brothers attended a boarding school in Livingston. It was two hours away and he rarely saw them. That Spring of his fifteenth year, the Bakers announced they were going on a furlough to their home in the United States. Of course, they were taking their daughters, Mary and Caroline, (the same name as James' younger sister) as well as their son, Joel. This meant they would return to the United States for about sixteen months in order to provide their son with an American higher education.

The Bakers owned property on acreage near a small Midwest Ohio town, Moss Creek. Their son, Joel, would attend his senior year of high school in their local Christian school. Upon completion he would be admitted to a Christian College where he would major in Bible Studies. After he became settled into a dormitory on campus, the rest of the family would return to Zambia.

James was invited to go with the Baker family. His parents agreed and he flew to America on a three-legged journey. The first seventeen-hour leg was from Lusaka to Miami Florida. After going through customs, they flew on to New York City, then the final leg to Toledo, Ohio. The tall buildings, busy streets, and foreign language overwhelmed him. Mary had tutored him in English, but the American kids spoke too quickly. What helped him adjust was the fact that they lived near a small town with only three traffic lights. Life went at a much slower pace.

James was placed in an eighth grade Special Needs class, based upon his age and his achievement levels. As a seventh grader, the Bakers' daughter, Caroline, was in the same building as James. She was in the school band but they only crossed paths at lunch and recess. Mary began her freshman year in high school and earned a spot on the volleyball team. Life with his American family was sweet. He showed respect and in turn received hugs and encouragement from everyone. Since his grades improved dramatically, he joined the track team and enjoyed doing something he had experience in: Track. He used to run like the wind through the fields in Zambia.

When the Baker family began to pack up to return to Africa, James suddenly became uncertain of his future back home. He missed his parents and siblings but was thinking about wanting more in life. With limited intellectual capabilities, he could not qualify to attend boarding school as his older siblings were doing.

James had managed to earn an allowance during the school year based upon completion of chores. Since the Baker residence sat on an acre of property, some wooded and some not, both boys worked hard. During the summer and fall, they mowed grass, planted flowers, weeded and raked colorful leaves. In winter, they shoveled snow from the long, winding driveway leading from the county road to the front porch and attached garage. Neighbors even paid James to do yard work and shovel snow. It had been his first experience with that cold, white substance and he enjoyed it immensely.

James gave ten percent of his earnings to Moss Creek Christian Church. They called this donation his 'tithes' which was a way of showing thanks for his blessings. James did not view this giving as a sacrifice but as a privilege. He was extremely grateful for the life he was leading in the United State of America. He saved several hundred dollars under his mattress and was now contriving a way to stay in America.

When Joel became settled in his dorm at the

Christian university, James missed him terribly.
He already knew he would soon miss all the
Baker family. Mary and Caroline had become like
sisters, sharing everything during that memorable
year. He loved and admired Mr. and Mrs. Baker.
They were the Spiritual father and mother who
bestowed so much love and encouragement on
him.

He knew that staying behind would cause pain
and appear as though he was ungrateful for their
unwavering commitment to him and to his village.
But, as planned, the evening before the family left
for the airport, James disappeared out his bedroom
window. He left a 'thank you' note and said he
wanted to try to live on his own in the United
States. Taking a duffle bag of belongings, his high
school ID, his savings, and a second pair of shoes
in case he had to walk long distances, James left
the family. But he had no clue as to where he was
going, or how he would get there.

The family was devastated to say the least.
They had no choice but to leave. What on earth
would they tell his family? The girls cried and the
adults hung their heads in disbelief and shame.
None of the Bakers saw this coming or they would
have tried to change James' plan.

Without knowing it, James had led a sheltered
life under the supervision of the Bakers. Their
Christian lifestyle centered around church
and volunteer activities in their small, quaint
community.

Rosie looked up and out the window. Then, returned
to the file and wondered: How did James ever connect with
an inner-city kid like Marcus? Then, she continued reading:

James took a bus into the city and slept on

a bench beneath a church overhang. The next day he wandered into a shopping arcade with a food court. Some black teenagers noticed him and asked him where he was from. Although he appeared similar in skin color, his distinct accent alerted them to his foreign roots. They found him interesting and although he seemed a little odd, it did not stop them from befriending him. In appearance, James thought he looked just like them, and figured it meant they thought like he did, even though the Bakers' little Christian school had only white students.

They invited James to their house, about a mile from downtown That night he was introduced to pot in a pipe and "happy pills". He felt he needed something to restore joy because he was already sad about all the pain he'd caused his family and his spiritual parents.

But one thing led to another. After that night, his decision to keep these new friends turned him toward a life of crime. Small crimes at first, to support his new habits and help his desire to fit in with his new friends. The one thing his choice didn't offer was a way of turning back. Not realizing it, his path in life was now made.

MONDAY- MARCH 14, 1994

CHAPTER 14

THE STORY OF MARCUS

Rosie broke for lunch and went to meet her friends, Penny Tucker and Linda Willis at Giovanni's. She figured if she had a Greek salad and a small veggie pizza, it would serve as lunch and dinner.

Both her friends worked in the inner city of the large, Toledo school system. Penny was a school psychologist and Linda, a school nurse. Rosie had first met them when she served as a school counselor at Jefferson High School. Ordinarily, Rosie didn't discuss work-related topics with friends. But, this time, she decided to tell them about the case of the Christmas slayings. She thought they might know one of the local gang members, Marcus Solomon, and perhaps fill in vital information about his past.

When Linda and Penny were asked about Marcus, Linda said his name was very familiar to her although she didn't know him personally. At Jefferson, she had known three high school girls who were each pregnant by Marcus. One by one, they had come to the nurse's office suffering from nausea on different days. In confidence, they each told her about the boy they loved, Marcus Solomon, and the babies they were carrying.

Later that year, as each one gave birth, the three baby boys were all named Marcus. Each new mother thought he would love her more if their son was named after him. Marcus, however, had no interest in the girls, nor his sons.

All were fourteen and learning hard lessons. He liked them young.

Penny, on the other hand, recalled Marcus from many interactions in the past.

"A special education teacher, Lou Jacobs, and I led a group twice a week for 'drop-ins'," Penny explained. "That's when we invited kids with serious attendance issues to come to our group. The rule was: If you were on the absent list the day prior to group, you could not attend. We made the group very interesting, so it was popular. Our rule increased attendance dramatically," Penny said. "Group was held on Tuesdays and Fridays." So, according to Penny, the kids would come to both days of group, and attend school both days preceding the group.

"Only Wednesday could be a skip day, and if they took one, they needed an excuse in Home Room first thing Thursday morning."

According to Penny, the kids were crazy about Mr. Jacobs. He had played professional football for a season before serious injuries barred him from playing. They also knew him from passing in the hallway between classes and end of day. He always greeted them with a huge smile and high five. They were not offended when he told them sternly: "Remove your hats, guys." Some knew him from his classroom where they began making academic progress for the first time. And some affectionately referred to him as "Bear" because he appeared so burly. Penny also thought he gave many of them a positive male image for the first time in their young lives. They were drawn to his magnetic personality.

During Marcus' junior year, it looked like he might decide to play football. Coaches had identified his athletic ability in gym class. But he lacked eligibility unless he joined the counseling group and improved his grades.

"Without more self-discipline, there was no way he could adapt to the rigorous physical and mental training required of a high school football player," Penny said. "Mr. Jacobs and the kids in the group encouraged Marcus to go for it. At the end of the school year, they vowed to get together again in the fall, but Marcus never returned to school.

It turned out that Marcus had dropped out of school. All anyone heard was that his mother was dead, and his father, recently released from prison, supposedly shot and killed Marcus' mother and her lover who also happened to be their next-door neighbor. Marcus apparently left the neighborhood. Penny and Linda heard nothing more about him until they found out he had been arrested for multiple murders.

"I remember asking Marcus way back in ninth grade what he wanted to do when he grew up," Penny recalled. "He told me: 'I plan to go to prison.' He sounded so firm and matter of fact that I asked him: 'Why, Marcus?' He replied without hesitation: 'My granddaddy lived out his life in prison. My father is in prison now. And as the man of the family, I plan to go to prison too.'" Penny looked at the others for a moment.

"I wonder," she continued, "if Marcus had met Mr. Jacobs in the ninth grade instead of his junior year, would he have revised his future goals?"

They all looked sad thinking about the future of this young man. Then the three women decided to make lunch together a monthly date, and parted with hugs.

Dr. Rosie began to wonder what James and Marcus could have in common, other than the color of their skin. Marcus was streetwise having grown up in the inner city. While James had grown up in an African village, then lived with a missionary family in a small, rural town.

Perhaps, Angel might be able to provide an answer to

that question. Rosie wrote herself a note to ask Angel during their next interview. Then she continued to think and figured the answer might be isolation. Neither one of them had a family. No sense of purpose.

Rosie decided to find a way to connect with the Baker family in Zambia and try tracking down Joel Baker now enrolled in a Christian college. But the question was, "which one?" Her second question would be to ask Joel if he had ever known or met Marcus Solomon.

Reaching her office, she found Ruth busy at her desk.

"Will you contact the high school that Joel, his sisters, and James attended. I need to talk with them," Rosie said. Ruth found the assignment quite easy. She immediately connected with Mrs. Barlow, a guidance counselor at the only Christian High School near the Baker residence. Amazingly, it was the right one.

"I'm inquiring about a family that attended your school last year. Can you assist me?" asked Ruth in her most charming voice. "I work for Dr. Rosie Klein in Toledo, Ohio."

"What can I help you find?" Mrs. Barlow asked.

Mrs. Barlow sound mature and professional, Ruth thought, pleasantly surprised."We'd like to contact a family known as the Bakers who live in South Africa, and their son, Joel, who's attending high school here in the States. We may have donors who would like to provide resources to Joel and the family.

I am not really lying, Ruth thought. After all, Rosie has a big heart and supports several charitable causes. This might be another that I'm researching for her. What better way than helping to feed or clothe needy African children?

Mrs. Barlow was proud to say she had been instrumental in getting Joel into Adrian College with a full academic scholarship.

"Joel stayed with our family over Christmas break and may be coming to our house for the long, week-end, Easter break."

Mrs. Barlow gave Ruth the email address on file for Joel and asked they not disclose it to anyone else without her consent or Joel's should she find him.

As far as the Bakers address in Zambia, Mrs. Barlow said she would look in her personal address book at home. She asked for Ruth's number and promised to call her with the information as soon as possible.

"The Bakers are always in need of things for their ministry and their meager farmhouse, Mrs. Barlow informed Ruth. "I keep their address so our community can support them with financial resources. And by the way, please call me, Nancy."

Ruth thanked Nancy Barlow profusely and couldn't wait to let Rosie know about her fast and successful fact-finding mission. She wished Nancy and her family an early Happy Easter with a "God Bless You" tacked on the end.

Leaving the office to use the rest of her late lunch hour, Ruth hurried to check on her husband. He had Parkinson's disease and often drank broth from a straw. Knowing he enjoyed soup with vegetables and beef, she stopped for some at Panera. This kind of lunch needed Ruth's steady hands to help him. Afterward, returning to the office and finding Rosie pouring over some files, she provided her with the good news about her assignment.

Pleasantly surprised, Rosie was really astonished to hear Ruth had also tracked down Joel Baker and a significant family friend. She immediately sent Joel an e-mail saying she would like to chat about his friend, James. She also let Joel know that she, herself, had attended Adrian her freshman year. This was true. After all these years, she wrote, it would be wonderful if he could show her around campus again.

Then closed the email by saying she looked forward to hearing from him soon.

Would Joel be able to help her connect the dots? How had James met Marcus? Did Joel have any further contact with James after he ran away from the Baker's house? If so, did James ever visit Joel on campus? It was about 35 miles from Toledo to Adrian, Michigan. Did Joel, in fact, have any idea James planned not to return to Africa with his parents and sisters?

She had so many questions, but they would have to wait until she received communication back from Joel. Hopefully, it would be soon.

LATE AFTERNOON, MONDAY- MARCH 14, 1994

CHAPTER 15

THE ORPHANS

After sending her email to Joel, Dr. Klein began reviewing materials on Sam and April which she had obtained through the courts. On the letterhead of the orphanage where they had stayed, the name: "Sister Camille, Director", stood out. Rosie made a mental note to connect with Sister Camille soon.

Sam and April's backgrounds were a necessary part of the investigations since they were brutally murdered. Records showed that a young Sammy was dropped off outside a Toledo fire station as a toddler. An anonymous 911 call advised the fire station that a small, Latino/Black child was standing alone outside the retractable gate. When a paramedic went out to follow-up on the lead, sure enough, there stood a little boy in a snowsuit and rubber boots just staring through the gate. A handwritten note pinned to his front zipper simply said: "Please take care of Sammy, because I cannot!" After checking him over, the Captain told two female paramedics to take him to the Children's Home temporarily.

Life in the orphanage was not bad for little Sammy. He was cute with brown skin, black curly hair and an upturned nose. Quick to learn, he enjoyed kicking a ball around and watching cartoons. He rarely cried, and then, only when someone hurt him. He liked sharing toys and food. He also liked to be held by the staff, kissed frequently, and read to whenever he held a book up to a willing stranger. No one ever came to claim him. Once the Fire Department staff members began providing him with clothes and toys, they ended up doing the same for all the children who lived there.

When Sammy was about four years old, a newborn baby girl was brought to the Children's Home by an EMT who had been directed there by a nearby hospital. Her birth certificate simply said: "Unnamed-Unwanted". So, the Nuns were entrusted to give this baby a name. It was Springtime of that year, so they called her "April".

April's skin tone was a light black. Sammy's was a medium brown. They were the only children "of color" in the entire orphanage holding several dozen children. Some of the young, blonde haired, blue-eyed, white kids were eventually adopted and left the facility. Each time one of them would leave with a new family who had picked them, the rest of the children would wave good-by through the windows and begin missing them right away. Inwardly each one wished it would soon be their turn for a family to want them.

Records showed that elementary school was held at the orphanage, taught by two of the nuns. Sister Hagar provided classes for kindergarten through third grade, while Sister Rahab taught fourth grade through sixth.

Sisters Camille, Hagar, and Rahab lived on the premises and were blessed to have volunteer cooks for breakfast and dinner, and volunteer janitorial help. In return, church members in the community were very appreciative of the nuns running the children's home.

Busing was necessary for all junior high and high school kids. Local kids rode city buses using bus card passes, or walked from nearby neighborhoods. Children from the orphanage rode in a fourteen passenger, blue van easily identified with the name, "Saint Anthony's Villa" printed boldly in white on both sides. They were often taunted by other students because they were getting "special treatment" being brought to school in such a conspicuous vehicle.

Some new friendships were made, but it wasn't as if orphanage kids could invite friends home with them, so friendships were confined to the school yard. But as they grew older, April and Sam survived the taunts and cruelties of youth throughout their school years because they rode the van together, understood one another, and always returned to the safety of the orphanage which they called "home".

Rosie noted the name of George Emmanuel several times in Sam and April's files she was reading. He, apparently, was a kind man whose local tavern was near the orphanage. Having had a few rough years of his own during his youth, he became sort of a guardian angel to the kids who lived there. He would personally provide tickets for all the kids to go to the circus when it came to town, and to opening day of the local professional baseball team, The Mud Hens, each year. He kept a jar on the bar for donations to buy Christmas gifts and several large Christmas trees. One year, he even bought them a red, upright piano with Christmas songbooks.

Sister Camille and the other nuns showed their gratitude and appreciation by sending George hand-drawn thank you cards to string above his bar. Once a month, Sister Camille produced a letter of approval for George to take Sam and April on Sunday outings.

When Sam turned eighteen, he could no longer stay at the orphanage. The home was mostly supported by government funds and designated for minors. So, the nuns had no choice but to send Sam packing. They suggested he join the military, which he did, signing up for the Marines. The day the recruiter picked him up to begin his journey to Parris Island, South Carolina, for basic training, April cried. She didn't want to see him go.

Rosie marked the file notes and put out a call to

Sister Camille. Pleasantly surprised to be connected immediately, Rosie explained who she was and inquired as to how April reconnected with Sam after the Marines. Sister Camille told her that when Sam left, the kids all cried like April and promised to write him. For a while, a lot of the children did keep in touch. But April was the only one to treat him like a brother. She never missed a week of sending him a letter with all the news about her high school career. She was a dancer in her high school's production of West Side Story. She sang and danced her way to and from the dining hall each evening.

April also told Sam the rules at the orphanage had changed for the better. The tavern keeper, George, provided bus passes for them so they no longer rode in the van to school, therefore, didn't stand out as different. The nearest bus stop was right in front of the Orphanage. However, she boarded and exited two blocks away regardless of weather. That way, she wasn't recognized as an orphan even though her heart ached because she never forgot she was originally "unnamed and unwanted". The longing never seemed to end.

In Spring of April's senior year, she was going to turn eighteen. She had taken secretarial studies and was going to be very employable when she graduated. A future employer paid for her room and board the last six weeks of school and the nuns bent the rules for her. They turned an unattached garage into a small efficiency apartment and were going to allow April to remain there and pay rent.

Sammy, now known as Sam, was going to complete his four-year enlistment just as April graduated. He had saved some money and intended to attend college in Toledo in the fall. He suggested that April ask her employer if she could defer beginning work until August. He said she should also ask the nuns to hold the apartment for her. He wanted her to join him on Hilton Head Island, South Carolina, for the months of June and July. His basic training was held so close to the Island, yet he had never had the opportunity to spend time there along the beach. So, if she would join him, he would pay for it all, and they could get temporary, seasonal work, if they needed extra money.

April began to envision time on the Island. She imagined blue skies, white sand beaches, palm trees and warm, soft breezes. She agreed to Sam's invitation and began to make arrangements.

As it turned out, her future employer could not hold the job for more than two weeks and the nuns were totally opposed to her joining a man with whom she was not related. She could not convince them that she felt he was her brother after all those years in the orphanage.

Sadly, after a small graduation party, she bid good-bye to them all and flew to Savannah, Georgia. She was met by a much taller, more muscular version of the Sammy she remembered. After all he was now a Marine. He rented a car for a week so he could pick her up and they could stock up on groceries. His plan was to buy bikes for them to use on the Island and purchase a used vehicle at the end of the summer. He wanted to go into law enforcement, and it required an associate degree. He thought perhaps April would go on to school too.

Dr. Klein decided she had read enough material for one afternoon. Although she was curious as to how Marcus and James met, that could wait. She told Ruth she was heading home. Jocko might be treated to a dog park outing. It was almost Spring. Although the primary focus was her evaluation of Angel, she couldn't get poor dead April off her mind. Dead at the hands of two ruthless men.

TUESDAY MORNING, MARCH 15, 1994

CHAPTER 16

MORE COLLATERAL

While Jocko was running around the field with other dogs weighing over forty pounds, Rosie stood leaning against a split-rail fence. She decided to call her friend, Bill Gorman, bailiff of Judge D.P. Tucker. On most Tuesday mornings, Judge Tucker's Court was not in session which meant that Bill was simply answering phones and completing paperwork.

"Hi, Bill?," she questioned when he picked up the phone. "When is your charity golf tournament scheduled?" Each year the proceeds provided financial support to the local Suicide Prevention Organization and Casa Hope, a transitional living home for young men struggling to break the stronghold of addiction.

"Hi Rosie. I was just thinking about you." he said. "I need you to be my playing partner after all. I was remembering how many of your drives our team used last year." The teams consisted of three Jacks and a Jill, which meant three men and a woman. The women's tees are usually forty yards ahead of the men. After each person teed off, each team member hit the second shot from the best drive. Since Rosie was quite a proficient golfer, with the advantage of the women's forward tees, her drives easily went further than most men. They also were straight down the middle. She was always a valuable player for any team.

"I'm happy to assist for such a worthy cause." She said. "Did you know I'm volunteering now at Casa Hope?"

"No, I didn't."

"I'm teaching anger management and other courses taken from books I've written. I also counsel guys to help avoid relapses when they return to their communities. But, Bill, if you have a minute, I have a question about another matter."

"No problem, Rosie. Shoot,"

"I was wondering if any details stand out in your mind about Angel Morgan's testimony in the trials of James Abraham and Marcus Solomon."

"I remember those cases well. One thing that stood out was the range of emotion Angel displayed. At times, her voice quaked, and she spoke very softly, barely audible as tears streamed down her face. At other times, she leaned forward and expressed outrage. This was primarily when asked to discuss the execution style murder of her friends, Sam and April. But you know, I'll think about it and get back to you if I remember anything else.

She thanked him and turned her attention back to Jocko. When finally back home, Rosie expected to enjoy a glass of dark red wine "for medicinal purposes", as she often explained. Her phone rang and she recognized the number of the Toledo Daily Blade. Grabbing a legal pad from her briefcase, she sensed an interview with Wes Hall was about to begin.

"Hi Rosie. It's me, Wes."

"I knew you'd be calling. The news about my involvement in Angel Morgan's case has piqued your interest. Right?"

"I'd like to meet for breakfast. Where can we talk face to face?"

"Well, my schedule the next two days is light until I

return to jail on Friday. Where do you want to meet?"

Wes was waiting at a booth in the corner of a restaurant where their conversation would be more private. The small, quaint restaurant was decorated with four leaf clovers. After a few inquiries into the lives of their children, she began to describe her role in the Angel Morgan trial.

"I'm not at all surprised that Danny Singer has engaged your services. But I have to say, I doubt the case will ever go to trial."

"Really? Why, Wes? Why did Danny Singer bother to have me evaluate his client if that's the case?"

"It makes it look as if he's providing Angel with thorough representation," Wes said. "I brought you a copy of the notes I took during both James' and Marcus' trials. Angel's description of events was so compelling, I'm sure it was an influencing factor in Marcus' death sentence by lethal injection. James' lack of criminal background only got him Life in Prison."

"I think Angel Morgan was offered a plea deal in exchange for her testimony." Rosie said. "She was so afraid of the Death penalty because of her past troubles that she gladly told her story to stay alive. But, even so, her sentencing is still coming and she'll still need help establishing a reason for leniency."

"There probably was a plea agreement, Rosie. Even so, I believe your expert testimony will be very important in her sentence hearing"

"I agree. I plan to obtain as much mitigating information about the life of this defendant as possible. These factors might warrant Judge Brown seeing a different side to Angel's story. By the way, Wes, I'm sorry I can't provide you any details about Angel in return for your information. You know it would violate ethical standards since Danny is my client, not Angel, right?"

"I know, Rosie. Singer would have to sign a release in order to share any verbal or written information about Angel," Wes nodded. "I'm aware." At this point only the Prosecutor, Court, and Defense were to hear or read any information Rosie would submit.

He, then, started to talk about two other members of the gang.

"I spoke to the nuns at the orphanage. They had no idea that Sam and April were murdered. They absolutely could not comprehend how the pair would been part of a plan to take the lives of others. The nuns had kept in touch with Sam during his years of service to the country, and in their eyes, he had become a conscientious, kind, young man. As for April, they thought she was naïve and impressionable, and knew she looked up to Sam."

"You know, Wes, as many cases as I've handled, I'm amazed at how people get into so many different kinds of trouble. It's like Life is just a huge pot of Greek briami."

Later that afternoon, Rosie met with private therapy clients, and afterwards grew pensive.

Oh, the human condition. So many seem in need of short-term counseling, encouragement, and mostly, hope. I'm just grateful I've got my good and faithful Jocko, she thought reaching to pet his shaggy grey head.

If only life could be as simple.

TUESDAY EVENING, MARCH 15, 1994

CHAPTER 17

THE ROMANCE BEGINS

I had errands to run before giving some attention to my lonely dog, Jocko. While sipping a complementary coffee in the popular Dorothy Lane Market, I received a call from Bucky.

"Hi! So glad you called, but may I call you back when there isn't so much background noise?" I asked him while hearing a constant buzz of shoppers around me. "Fine. I'll be waiting for your call. I am at the airport. Just got back from a recruiting trip. It's really noisy here, too. I'm heading to the baggage claim area."

He seemed eager to talk. I certainly was glad he'd call and was eager to talk with him as well. But I took my time and finished shopping, somewhat like a robot since I was still wondering how Sam and April came to know Song. I must remind myself to ask Angel what she knew about their relationship, and how she personally felt about Song. I made myself a note on my phone's "To Do" list. Knowing that Angel and Song were being kept separated in the county jail, it would be easy to talk with each one separately about the other. Both of their hearings were pending.

Just as I reached my patio door, I noted a slight glimpse of moon appearing among scattered dark clouds. My cell phone rang, jarring me back to the present moment. It was Bucky.

"Hi there. I thought, perhaps, I'd missed your call," he sounded like he was smiling.

"Actually, I just got home and was planning to call you back in the next few minutes. How was your trip? Find any special players?"

He'd interviewed a couple of high school seniors and their coaches in the neighboring state of Kentucky. He'd also watched a pre-season community college game in Dayton.

"I'm excited about the possibility of one particular transfer student to fill out my roster in the outfield next year. He really looks promising," Bucky said. "But what I really wanted to ask you is whether you'd want to come to Saturday night's Toledo basketball game? We could have an early dinner beforehand."

I felt butterflies in my stomach. He was asking me on a date, and I wanted to go.

"It's the beginning of the League Tournament; the game starts at eight with a women's game preceding it. I thought if we went to dinner at five, we could be in our seats for the last fifteen minutes or so of the women's game."

What I later found out, which Bucky didn't mention at this time, was the fact that the girls' basketball coach was the woman with whom he was on sabbatical from their relationship. Looking back later, I was glad he didn't. I might have chosen not to go.

"Oh, sounds like fun. I'd love to go." I said happily in the moment."Do you have any favorite restaurants near the fieldhouse?" he asked.

"As a matter of fact, I do," I answered. "My very favorite seafood restaurant takes reservations. It called Redfish Grill. Would it help if I called to make reservations?"

Bucky seemed pleased to hear me take the initiative in

finding a special restaurant.

What I failed to tell him in this moment was that I had recently "retired" from there. I had taken a part-time job for some evening socialization. They called me "The hostess with the mostest". I always wore a little black jacket and pineapple pin. My job was to "razzle dazzle" the guests as my boss, Eileen, would say.

Eileen was from Boston and I really enjoyed her accent. We became close friends by the time I decided to "retire". Being with Eileen and the younger generation had served as a good distraction from the grief of my husband's passing. It offered me some productive use of evening hours. I had also formed relationships with some of the regular customers. As time passed, I had watched some of the young waitresses graduate from college, become nurses, have babies, and get married. When I decided that part of my life needed to end, I gave a month's notice. They gave me a surprise party on my final shift which really threw me for a loop. I assured everyone I would visit often. Being there with Bucky would prove I was feeling like a whole person again.

"That's great," Bucky was saying on the phone. "I'll look forward to seeing you Saturday. I'll pick you up at 4:30 pm, sound about right?"

"Fine," I agreed. "See you then." When we closed off, I realized I really wanted to see him again. I would also pick up the tab for dinner since it was likely they would provide me with a substantial discount. The last time Penny, Linda and I ate there, Keith, our server and my dear friend, generously discounted the bill by twenty-five percent.

"Keith, that is unexpected and unnecessary," I remember telling him.

"Rosie, let me remind you, you will always be part of the Redfish family."

His kind gesture brought tears to my eyes. I had

tipped him as if I had been charged the full amount and slipped an extra ten dollars under the plate. Servers bussed their own tables, and I was certain he would find the money.

My thoughts were a mixture of gratitude and affection. Gratitude to my former boss at Redfish who had taken a chance on a senior citizen when she hired me back then, and affection for my co-workers, such as Keith and Savannah. They had all played a part in helping me get through my life's challenges at just the right time.

FRIDAY MORNING- MARCH 18, 1994

CHAPTER **18**

THE STORY OF SONG

Song Lee was being represented by a Public Defender named John Chicalette, known to his friends and colleagues as "Chick". He had not requested a psychological exam of his client. Apparently, she had no history of emotional problems or mental illness. She was obviously bright and talented and only 18-years old with no prior criminal history.

There was nothing preventing Rosie from connecting with Chick if she didn't disclose details about her interviews with Angel. She would put calling him on her to-do list for Friday when she would be downtown again.

Early Friday, she called Chick and surprisingly caught him free to talk on the phone. She brought him up to date on her role in the pending trial of Angel.

"By the way, congratulations on your expert testimony in the Marlene Ringer case," he said. "My client and I appreciated it. As you know, so did the Jury."

The defendant he represented was found not guilty. The jury determined Marlene had, in fact, feared for her life, therefore, acted in self-defense when she shot her husband dead as he slept. Dr. Klein had educated them on Battered Women's Syndrome. They came to understand how she had been terrorized and abused, defending herself in the only way she could, while he wasn't looking.

"Rosie, how about meeting me at The Oak Club for

lunch today?" Chick asked.

It meant leaving the downtown area, so she surmised he thought it best if they were not seen talking together by judges and attorneys who frequented restaurants within walking distance of the Court House.

"Okay, great idea, Chick. I'll see you there."

Chick was waiting just inside the door when Rosie arrived.

"So, how did you celebrate St. Patrick's Day?" Rosie asked as they waited to be seated.

"You'll probably find this hard to believe, Rosie, but I simply worked through happy hour."

"You're right, Chick, it's hard to believe." But, he seemed proud to tell her that he had driven directly home.

"So, how did you spend St. Patty's day, Rosie?"

"Well, basically, I worked and focused some on the needs of Jocko, my labradoodle. He was feeling a bit neglected." They laughed together at their mutually tame lives.

"Thanks for asking me to lunch. I would have settled for a telephone consult, but I'm wondering how and where Song met Sam and April. I was hoping you could tell me."

"Well, it's my understanding, they met on Hilton Head Island. Apparently, Sam and April were there for the summer. Song was attending Baden Music School, a boarding school on Baden Island less than two miles off the Hilton Head Island shore.

"It's a school renowned for performing arts," he continued. "Children ages 11 to 18 years old come from all over the globe and reside there nine months of the year. Academically, it's an accelerated school program that prepares boys and girls for college scholarships and careers in music."

"Wow. Talented young girl."

"Song told me that students are permitted to remain on campus during the summer only if they live on a different continent and they part-time summer jobs. Song took a job collecting tickets on the ferry boat between Baden and Hilton Head Islands. She was also to check that passengers were secure in their seats which is how she began talking with Sam and April.

"Sounds like she was a go-getter."

"Definitely, and she had personality, too. She told me that Sam and April were working summer jobs near the pier on Hilton Head. Sam played a guitar and sang children's songs under the shade of a large moss tree. Tourists would gather around him with their kids, sit on cedar benches, listen and sing along. April scooped homemade ice cream at a nearby souvenir store.

"One day, Song's curiosity led her to the area where the children were listening to music. April was apparently on break and sitting there listening to Sam. Not knowing April had a relationship with him, Song sat down next to her.

"When they began talking, April explained that she and Sam were childhood friends from Ohio. She didn't mention that they also grew up together in an orphanage. But when Sam took a break, April introduced Song to him. The three decided to meet for an early lunch the next day since their shifts began at noon, and that's how the relationship began," Chick said.

During lunch, Chick told Rosie that on Song's days off, she was permitted to leave the boarding school and simply enjoy the town square on Hilton Head Island. Because tourists swarmed the Islands on weekends, Song's days off were Monday and Tuesday. This coincided with Sam and April's one day off on Monday. They told her that if she had a bike, Song could ride to their apartment and hang out. They, themselves, had rented a car for just a couple weeks, as planned. Thereafter, they all used bikes to go to and from work, and even ride on the beach when they were so inclined. Song kept a bike at her dorm on the Island and brought it on the ferry the following Monday.

The weeks went by as the three became fast friends. Soon their talk turned to plans for Song returning to Ohio with them at the end of summer. They began devising a way for Song to attend the University of Toledo's music program. Because of her musical talent, and the fact she wasn't Caucasian, they thought she was likely to get a full scholarship.

With the help of her guidance counselor, Mrs. Goodwin, who remained on the Island during the summer to recruit students, Song was able to secure a band scholarship. It was a school she had never heard of, in a state she had never visited. But to Song, The University of Toledo was the same as Badan Music School.

Mrs. Goodwin assured Song that the school not only had a great music department but was also nestled in an upper middle-class neighborhood where many professors and their families lived. This would afford Song safety and, even more, a chance to teach music to their children.

Meanwhile, April and Sam had no idea how they were going to make ends meet back in Toledo. The Island atmosphere was very appealing, and thoughts of brisk, cold winters not inviting at all. However, they decided to take a bus back and see if April's old job might still be available, or another one with similar wages. Sam figured he could sit in with local bands who needed a guitar player that could sing.

"It saves a band money not to hire a vocalist," he told April.

"But you know about the best laid plans of mice and men,"

Rosie laughed as Chick finished his story just as

dessert came. "Sounds like both girls relied on Sam's maturity and decision- making. Now, to give credit where credit is due, Sam's intentions were good. He likely believed the three of them would be just fine in his hometown. Don't you think, Chick?"

"My client did in fact, complete her freshman year at Toledo with outstanding grades in both her major and other required liberal arts classes," Chick said. "But now, here's the rest of the story: No one could believe how Song's personality changed once James entered the picture. She not only stopped going to class but dropped out of marching band which was a requirement for all music majors with scholarships. I have notes from my interviews with Song's roommate, Beverly, which I'll provide to you."

"I would love to review them," Rosie said. "Thanks for all the background. It's always a help in any case to know more."

"I know," Chick said. "That's how I feel when an attorney is helpful to me. I'll leave the notes at the front desk in the Public Defender's office."

"That would be fine," Rosie answered. "I'll pick them up after seeing Angel at the County Jail."

Rosie had intended to have Ruth contact Song's college roommate, Beverly, for a personal interview. But possibly Chick's notes would have something more in his interviews that would give a different slant on it all. If not, the college campus wasn't that far from her downtown office. After reading his notes, she would decide.

FRIDAY AFTERNOON-MARCH 18, 1994

CHAPTER 19

THE LAST KILLING SPREE

On Friday after lunch, Rosie again parked in the garage and walked two blocks to the County Jail. Angel was brought into the interview room and both seated themselves in chairs opposite each other with a table in between.

"How was your week, Angel?" Dr. Klein asked. But before she could answer, Officer Verna Mitchell, opened the door.

"Angel, here's your lunch tray." Officer Mitchell said. Then looking at Rosie, she added: "Angel didn't eat breakfast and we don't want her skipping lunch." Angel glanced at the food tray with no expression, then looked at Dr. Rosie. Officer Mitchell quickly backed out of the room and closed the door.

Angel left her lunch tray untouched, yet this very conscientious officer thought it was important to bring it, Dr. Rosie noted and wrote on her pad. *Angel doesn't appear interested in her bologna sandwich, fruit cocktail, and white milk.*

Officer Mitchell opened the door once more and poked her head around the opening. "Hey Angel, your sister, Amanda, just called about visiting you. What do you think?"

Angel looked up smiling. It was the first smile Dr. Rosie had seen since she met Angel.

"Sure, put her on the approved list." Her mood

seemed much lighter than a week ago despite her lack of appetite today.

Dr. Rosie began asking Angel about the next murder. "Song and I were totally scared after they killed our friends for nothing. We couldn't believe it. They hadn't done nothing wrong!"

"How did that make you girls feel?"

"Man, I had horrible nightmares, and when I was awake, I kept seeing the awful pictures in my head. Pictures of them kneeling on the gravel next to me. And then suddenly hearing 'pow-pow' and looking at them flat on their faces. There was blood comin' out of the back of their heads." She closed her eyes and bowed her head.

"I am so sorry," Rosie said, giving her a minute to grieve before asking: "What happened next?"

"That night, the men held a poker and pot party in the garage. We stayed in the house, sort of relieved to have some space alone. On Monday evening, Marcus and James asked Song if she had received any money from home. She told them it was too early in the month. They made us get in the car and the four of us took a ride to her post office box just to make sure. There was nothing but junk mail in the box which made the guys mad."

"So, no money. What did they do next?"

"They pulled in by a mini-market store. They left Song and me in the car with the motor running. I thought about escaping, but we just sat real still in the back seat of the car. We didn't even look at each other. The next thing we knew, we heard three shots. Then, Marcus and James came running out the front door. James had money in his hand and jumped in the driver's seat. Marcus got in the right side and stuck his gun in the console between the front seats.

"Damn! Can you believe we only got $45 for all that?"

James yelled.

"It'll have to do for now," Marcus replied.

Angel looked up at Dr. Rosie, both eyes lightly starting to tear up.

"We didn't know it yet, but they had shot this young woman cashier. Later we heard she was dead when they got her to the hospital. Again, James drove to the state line. Then we turned around and went back to the house. That's how they liked to do it. They said it was their 'decoy getaway plan'. After that, Marcus and James stayed in the garage with the car, gamblin' and smokin' with a couple of Mexican guys,"

Angel still wasn't eating, but Dr. Rosie could understand why. Who could have an appetite when they were remembering such a story?

"We were told to go to the house. We watched the 11 o'clock news and saw the story of the robbery. It made us sick to see Marcus shoot the owner's daughter, Sophia Pappas, point blank in the forehead. The cops saw the whole thing on the store's video camera, and they showed it on the news. That was very wrong to do."

"While a security camera had filmed the whole thing inside the store, nothing was captured from the outside of the store or in the parking lot.

"Song and I decided not to mention what we saw on the news to the guys. That night, we slept huddled together, sort of like for security," Angel said. Her face was showing the stress of telling her story and reliving her memories.

"As far as we knew, they never did see the video until it was shown for the judges during their trials."

Angel believed, without a doubt, that the video was one of the most influential factors in the outcome of Marcus' trial.

Needing a stretch break, Dr. Rosie offered Angel a

bottle of water and an energy bar. They stood, stretched, and sat back down to resume the interview.

"So, when and how did the final murder happen?"

"We stayed low for a couple of days. The car stayed in the garage. The guys walked or used skateboards to go anywhere. They always kept the hoods of their sweatshirts over their heads, and Marcus carried the revolver in his pocket. I don't think James had a weapon of his own, at least not a handgun," Angel picked up half of the sandwich on her tray and took a bite.

"Two days later, Marcus and James drove us to Song's mailbox, again, to see if the check came from her family. I was in the back seat with her. The guys and me stayed in the car by the curb, and they made Song go into the post office.

"Where was this post office box?"

"On campus," Angel answered. "The mailboxes were in the hallway next to the University bookstore. Now, it was the middle of the afternoon. All the students were on Christmas break so nobody else was anywhere around. We could see her through the window.

"Then, this guy came up to Song and began talking to her. It kinda looked like they knew each other. We watched as he handed her something. Then, she opened her box and got the mail and came right back out to the car. But, James asked her first: 'Did the check come?' and 'Who was the man?' Song said 'Yes, the check came and the man was Mr. Brooks who worked in the bookstore.' She said he wondered if she was interested in tutoring students who needed help with English.

I heard James ask Song what she said back to the guy. She said she told him she would think about it in Spring, but she was too busy now with classes and music students of her own. The man gave her his business card and told her to call when she was ready to work. James asked her for the card, and she gave it to him."

Angel went on with her story, telling Dr. Klein that Marcus then drove them to the bank where Song cashed her check. James told her to be sure and bring some of the free popcorn back to the car. They made one more stop at the liquor store, then returned to the garage to get the car out of sight. The girls were allowed to go back to the house where they watched out a window. They saw several men that Song didn't know come to the garage on foot and enter. Presumably, they were all inside smoking dope and gambling for the afternoon. Since Marcus and James used all the money Song's parents sent, the girls wondered what they would do for food.

"Later, Song told me there was a notice and sketch on the board next to the mailboxes. The sketch resembled Marcus with a message from campus security with a warning that he was armed and dangerous! If anyone saw him they should report it immediately. Campus police wanted to know his location."

Tears were now streaming down Angel's face and into her mouth. She took a sip of water andher tissue

"I'm okay," she said while wiping her eyes. "I want to finish telling you my story."

"I know how difficult this must be for you, Angel," Rosie said in a comforting tone.

"Well, early on Christmas Eve, James told Song to call the guy on the card and ask when he could stop by to talk about possible work opportunities. Song was to tell Mr. Brooks that she was off campus staying at a girlfriend's house. Mr. Brooks said he had to first take Chinese home to his disabled mother, then he would be available to come over about nine, if it wasn't too late.

"'Do you drink wine?' Song asked him. So, when he said 'Yes', she told him that she and her girlfriend would have wine and cheese and the three of them could relax and celebrate a little. She gave him the address," Angel said. "I guess that's when Marcus and James began to develop their plan. The guys took us to the grocery store to get some things like the wine, cheese and crackers while they waited in the car.

"On the way to the store, Marcus and James said they were sure the Honda had been identified and it was dangerous to stay around town any longer. That's when we knew the guys were going to rob Mr. Brooks and steal his vehicle for a final get away. But we were too scared to say anything. We just did what they told us. I felt bad about it but couldn't figure what else to do. Song just kept moving like nothing was happening. We did what we were told.

"Later that night, the porch light was on for the very first time when Mr. Brooks arrived. We wanted the house to appear inviting. Song introduced him to me, and I took his coat and hat. We told him he should take off his shoes since they were wet from the snowy sidewalk. We were barefooted and wore tight, black capris, and slinky, black silk blouses. That was Marcus' idea and part of the plan to rob him.

"Once, he was sitting on the couch, we lit a candle on each end table and dimmed the lights. Then, we started asking Mr. Brooks personal questions like if he was married, and where he lived. He told us he was divorced and lived with his eighty-year old mother in an apartment near the University. We invited him upstairs to the bedroom where Song and I would give him a back rub. But when we went up, we also knew it was where James and Marcus were waiting in the closet.

"Suddenly, Marcus leaped at Mr. Brooks, knocking him onto the bed. Song and I backed out of the room, into the hall. The bedroom door remained open. Our eyes were glued on poor Mr. Brooks and Marcus."

"Oh, my goodness, Angel. You had to be terrified and

shocked by the scene."

"James tied him to the headboard with the electric cords he had cut off the lamps with his knife. Then he duct-taped Mr. Brooks mouth and ankles. Marcus reached into his pockets for his wallet, money, and keys. They tossed the keys to Song and shouted for us to grab our stuff and hightail it to Mr. Brooks' car. We did.

"Before running out the front door, we blew out the candles and turned off the porch light, then ran to the car as fast as we could. We jumped into the back seat before we heard a sound we didn't want to hear. The gunshot told us that Mr. Brooks could no longer identify any of us. The thought of his poor mother ran through my mind. I am really, really sorry," she cried.

Rosie cupped Angel's hand in hers and told her that she had done a really great job recalling the final murder. She waited a few moments while Angel cried softly, not really wanting to leave Angel in her present emotional turmoil. Still, she had to leave. Rosie gave her a warm, reassuring hug and handed her over to Officer Mitchell before leaving the building.

She walked quickly to her downtown office with eyes straight ahead, not acknowledging anyone on the sidewalk as they passed her. Thoughts of Angel's story were milling around in her mind.

While Angel knew that her sister would be visiting, Dr. Rosie also knew that Angel's brothers would be coming with Amanda to see her the following week. She had decided not to mention it to Angel this time because, after recounting the last murder, it could be upsetting, especially if they didn't show up.

Relationships were always complicated. Even the good ones.

SATURDAY EVENING- MARCH 19, 1994

CHAPTER 20

ROSIE'S PAST

Bucky arrived on time and Jocko wagged his tail in approval. I grabbed my purse and jacket and he helped me into the car.

Old-Fashioned manners. I like that.

We drove to the Redfish Grill talking small talk the whole way. Entering the restaurant we were greeted exuberantly by Savannah and Katie, the hostesses at the welcoming host station. Bucky looked taken back and surprised to be introduced to at least three other employees prior to our being seating in a reserved booth. It was nicely positioned in a quiet spot in front of a window with a view of the beautifully landscaped patio area. My friends were taking special care of me and I appreciated it very much.

"I guess I failed to mention that I worked here the past four years," I said with a smile. Bucky looked great and I was very happy to be with him. "The medical bills began mounting the year before my husband passed, and then the job served as a distraction in the three years after his death."

"What exactly was your role? What did you do here?"

"I wore a little black jacket with a pineapple pin and schmoozed the guests. I tried to have the servers' backs when they were confronted by dissatisfied customers. I even held the door and welcomed folks with a smile. I learned a lot about people," I revealed to him.

"We have a lot of regulars here. Some couples eat here three times a week. Sometimes they'll just order appetizers and drinks at the bar. Other times, they'll have a great seafood meal in the dining room. Still, another time they will reserve a booth in the bar and just order the bang-bang shrimp and a salad."

Bucky couldn't help but smile at the words.

"Wednesday night is bang-bang shrimp night," I explained. "That's a popular appetizer with a reduced price that night," He had an amused look on his face.

"Can you believe, people wait up to ninety minutes, and spend more on drinks than they will save from the discounted item? That says a lot about people, don't you think?

He simply nodded, at a loss for words, I guessed.

"Although they often complained to me about the wait, it never stopped them from coming back the following week. Many customers treat this restaurant as if it's their own private country club."

"Wow! How's the management?" asked Bucky."They appreciated me. My immediate boss, Eileen, gave me a surprise retirement party my last night working here. I waited until after New Years to leave. She had all the hosts, bartenders, and servers sign a card. My nickname is 'Yaya', which is Greek for grandma, you know."

"I guess you did what you had to do. I respect that."

"It began that way, but I grew to love the Anglers. Since it's a seafood restaurant the employees are known as Anglers. Get it?" I smiled at him.

"They also understood that I didn't work on Sundays. Sabbath is a day of rest, right?" He looked at me in approval.

After being seated and greeted by a few more servers, they left us to look over the menu and during our entire meal, our privacy was honored.

During dinner, he told me of the loss of his wife and how he overcame esophageal cancer himself. I was impressed with all the things he had accomplished despite life's drawbacks. He, in turn, said he was impressed wih me and saw my life as far more colorful.

"You were very strategic in planning a successful fuure after your unexpected setback," he said. "This even includes the slight detour of becoming a hostess in a three-star seafood restaurant. You are a very humble lady, indeed."

When the tab came, Bucky was shocked to see a fifty percent discount and was even more surprised when I told him I would pay because it was my way of sharing our evening. He added a gracious tip to equal twenty-five percent of what the total tab would have been. On the way out, hugs were given all around by those who recognized me, including some old regulars.

We left the restaurant and made it to the game just as Bucky had predicted. Fifteen minutes was all we saw of the girls' team win. The boys' game began at precisely 8:00 pm as Bucky said it would. The national anthem was sung by a trio of music majors. Their music brought Song to mind and I wondered if they were friends of hers. I also wondered if Song had regrets about the decisions she had made.

At half time, Bucky and I went to the concession area. Lo and behold, we ran into Attorney Dan Lieber and his lovely wife, Debbie. I introduced Bucky to them, and Dan informed Bucky how well- respected I was in the legal community.

"I really appreciate your willingness to join the team appointed to represent Angel," he said to me. My face flushed a little as I realized I was pleased for Bucky to hear this praise.

Upon returning to our seats, we were approached by a tall, slender man who identified himself as Bill Gorman. Of course, I knew him well, but he politely said his name in case I hadn't remembered him. Bucky stood to greet Bill as they shook hands.

"Do you play golf, Bucky?" he asked. "I'm looking for players to join in my charity tournament."

"No, actually, I don't," Bucky said. "But I would be more than happy to sponsor the sixteenth hole. Sixteen is in my lucky number and I always have it on the back of my softball jerseys."

"Great! As a hole sponsor, we'll advertise your company and your name will appear on a sign in the ground at the tee and in the program distributed to all players," Bill said happily. "It also means you and a guest of your choice will be invited to the awards dinner," Bill said with a wink of his eye in my direction. The two men agreed to talk during the week, then exchanged business cards.

The team lost the game, therefore, wouldn't be moving on in the League Tournament or be given a spot in the NCAA tournament.

"So, sorry, Bucky," I tried to ease his disappointment.

"Not at all, Rosie. In all honesty, I think this was a very winning night for me. I couldn't be more pleased with your company." His smile enchanted me.

Perhaps, Bucky and I are moving on to an exciting new dimension of our relationship, I thought. It's been a wonderful night for me, too.

MONDAY MORNING - MARCH 21, 1994

CHAPTER 21

THE BROTHERS

Dr. Rosie arranged with her landlord, Doctor Siefer, to use his downtown office on Monday morning. Dr. Siefer spent mornings at the hospital so there was plenty of space available. It was simply a courtesy for her to ask.

The brothers, Greg and Mike were seated in the waiting room when Dr. Rosie entered the office suite with Jocko by her side. They seemed engrossed in Sports Illustrated magazines. She personally had no use for those publications, but Doctor Siefer provided them along with the daily edition of the Toledo Blade and the U.S.A. Today. The young men's attention was quickly diverted to Jocko.

"Hi, I'm Greg and this is my younger brother Mikey," the tall, young man said standing up. His eyes immediately settled on Jocko.

"Jocko would welcome petting," Dr. Klein said, "especially if you scratch behind his ears."

Mikey also stood and nodded. He made eye contact, displaying big brown eyes beneath long, brown lashes and dark, full brows. Greg and Mikey's similar appearances suggested matching DNA.

At that point Dr. Rosie decided not to interview them separately. If she needed them to testify at Angel's sentencing hearing, she might do one-on-one interviews soon. Rosie noted they were both well mannered and well-groomed. Their hair and nails appeared clean. Crew neck sweaters, jeans, and shoe boots, not designer, but neat and appropriate given the weather. She thought to ask if they needed parking passes for the parking garage beneath the building or money for the expense of coming today.

Once they were all introduced, she led them into her office with Jocko tagging along side.

"Where are you living?" she asked. "Did you have to travel far to get here?"

"We're living in an apartment together about fifteen miles from downtown Toledo," Greg explained. "We graduated from a joint Vocational High School in Indiana. I am almost nineteen and Mikey turns eighteen next month. I am the handsome brother and Mikey is the smart one." They all laughed together.

"Mikey graduated early so he could get done with me," Greg said. "We both studied computer science and now we're going to Owens Community College."

"Every other week-end we go home to our adoptive parents," Mikey said. "When we turned sixteen and fifteen, we were blessed to be adopted by our long-term foster parents. Our last name is Kessler now. Mom expects us home to do laundry while she cooks us some meals to take back to our apartment. Those meals include cookies. Greg is known as the cookie monster for good reason." More laughter. "We also attend church as a family and help our Dad fix things."

"We have never been separated," Greg said looking at his brother. "Even when we went into the foster home system, we were kept together. You might say we're quite used to one another's habits by now, both good and bad.

"When we were taken from our mother, she ended up in prison. We aren't sure but we heard she was wanted in two separate states. As minors, we could visit her twice a year. Once was around Christmas and the other was around Mother's Day. Our foster parents drove us from Richmond to Indianapolis to make that happen."

Dr. Rosie thought for a minute. *At least she is not incarcerated at the Ohio Women's Penitentiary where, in fact, Angel will likely be spending a great deal of time.*

"Why is she in prison in Indiana? What did she do to end up there?"

"She didn't really take care of us. We were living in Centerville Indiana with her, her husband, Roger, his parents, and his younger brother, Buster.," Mikey said. "I remember wondering why no one went to work and worrying about why we weren't going to school. I used to see the big yellow bus come to a stop in front of our property. Other kids our size boarded it from across the road and got back off in the late afternoon, but we never did. Angel was forced to go to school, and she didn't want to. We think it was because she was embarrassed. Her shoes were torn, her clothes were too small."

"Fact is, Dr. Klein, we smelled," Greg chimed in with his head down and his hands stretched out on his thighs. "Because we were only allowed to play out back in the yard, if you could call it that, and tha's where the outhouse sat. I guess, we were never given baths back then. The yard had a brown broken privacy fence around it, and was too small to play catch let alone kick a soccer ball. But that's all we had.

"The men sat on the front porch and smoked and drank Coke laced with Jack Daniels," Mikey added. " I used to wonder what exactly Jack Daniels was. Once I sneaked a sip and nearly puked. That answered my question!"

"What memories do you have growing up with your sisters, Amanda and Angel?" Dr. Rosie asked.

"We don't have memories of Amanda, just of Angel,"

Mikey said.

"She was the one who basically took care of us," Greg said. "She fixed supper and got us ready for school in the morning. For breakfast she would toast some bread and slap a piece of Velveeta cheese between the slices. We dipped it in coffee left over from the night before."

Rosie made note that what they were saying was confirming the accuracy of Angel's story. They had nothing but positive things to say about her.

"It's different now," Greg said. "We see Amanda, her husband and kids often and have some good times together. But we haven't seen Angel in years."

"How did you happen to live in Indiana to begin with?" Rosie asked.

"It was normal to have police knocking on our door back then," Greg said. "It didn't matter where we moved to. It was typical for mom and her boyfriends or husbands to be reported to the cops. She took us to Indiana to avoid arrest, we think."

"After Angel ran away, Mom and Roger moved us from a few miles outside of town to the middle of a bigger, nearby city. Mom was afraid Angel would tell the authorities about our living conditions and how we were abused at Roger's parents' place.

"We lived all crammed up in a two-bedroom house with some friends of Roger's. We were sad that mom never tried to find Angel or report her missing. Angel left no note, so we weren't sure she had even run away on her own. For all we knew, she could have been kidnapped by a drug dealer or sex pervert."

"The F.B.I. finally found us," Mikey said. "They stormed into the little Indiana house and searched for drugs and weapons. We were driven to the office of Children's

Protective Services and our mom along with the rest of the men in the house and backyard were taken to jail."

"A Christian pastor, Mark Kessler and his wife, Ann, took us in," Greg said. "We'd met them once at a neighborhood church festival. We used to sneak out of a window unseen by our mother or the men. She would never allow us to go near a church or folks she didn't know. But when we went to live with the Kesslers , they bought us new clothes and gave us the opportunity to go through junior high and high school. It was the first time we experienced a stable lifestyle and we learned about a loving God."

"Would you both like to see Angel and would you be willing to testify at her sentencing hearing?"

"Yes." They said in unison.

"I assure you; I will be back in touch. I can't thank you enough for your honesty. Some of your story has to be painful to tell."

After saying goodbyes, both young men patted Jocko and headed to their car parked at a meter in front of the building.

MONDAY - MARCH 21, 1994

CHAPTER 22

PREPARATION AND PLANNING

Dr. Rosie drove to her Summerhill office with Jocko in the backseat taking his midday nap. She intended to spend Monday afternoon reading and highlighting the discovery materials related to the six vicious murders. She wanted to prepare to evaluate Angel on Tuesday. She also wanted to ask some of the previous questions in slightly different ways to see if Angel would contradict her stories.

Dr. Rosie waved at Ruth who was on the phone trying to convince an insurance company to authorize payment for counseling of a bereaved widow.

Jocko snuggled against Ruth's legs and Rosie let herself in to her office. She poured over the old newspaper articles about the crimes. Not everything she read was necessarily true, she realized, or that the professionals interviewed by reporters had been truthful. Even if what they said was reported accurately, she planned to follow-up with her own brief, direct contacts with them; defense attorneys, assistant prosecutors, victims' survivors, detectives, even Angel herself.

Ruth gently opened the door. "Hi boss lady. Here's some freshly brewed Starbucks coffee. Is there anything I can do for you?"

"Thanks, and as a matter of fact, yes. Would you please contact someone from the defense teams for James, Marcus, and Song? I will speak to them one by one, if possible.

"Sure thing."

Soon Ruth buzzed Rosie. "Pick up line one. James Abraham's lawyer, Jeffrey Masters, is on the line."

"Thanks Ruthie," she said picking up the receiver. "Hi Jeff. It's Rosie Klein."

"Hi Rosie. What's up?" The tone of his voice suggested he was not excited about speaking to her. She assumed he resented the fact that Angel had turned State's witness against his client.

"I just wanted your point of view on what should go down at Angel's sentencing hearing."

"I don't think Angel was truthful about James' and her roles in the murders," he said. "I think she testified against him just to save herself and believe she helped mastermind a couple of the murders as well. I don't believe she was just waiting in the car."

"Really? Why is that?"

"I think she acted as the look-out and drove the getaway car following the convenience store murder."

"I appreciate you sharing your position with me," Rosie said, realizing further conversation would only go downhill from here. "Well, I won't keep you any longer, Jeff. Thanks, again, and have a nice week."

"Good luck, Rosie. Your client is lucky to have someone who cares about her working on her case."

Dr. Rosie dialed Victor Hamilton's number herself. She knew it by heart from all the cases they were both involved with over the years.

"Hi Victor."

"Hi Rosie. What's up?" he chuckled, recognizing her voice.

"I just got off the phone with Jeff Masters and wanted your take on Angel Morgan's testimonies. I obviously wasn't there for Marcus Solomon's trial."

"First of all. I can't believe Dan Singer had you appointed to evaluate her. What a useless assignment! She was anything but a victim so, don't expect to find life circumstances that would cause her not to be involved in that entire scheme." Victor obviously had deep feelings about it.

"She wasn't a hostage. She wasn't terrorized. She was coached by the Assistant Prosecutor all defense lawyers know and love...NOT... Joan Nichols. I strongly believe that Angel Morgan's testimony fried my client."

I made a mental note to follow up on Attorney Hamilton's perspective by calling Joan Nichols in the next few days.

"You do know I've elected to have Marcus tried by a three Judge panel rather than a jury," Victor added. "No need for jurors to view the remains of six corpses."

In the end, that strategy didn't do any good. The death penalty was imposed by a unanimous vote, 3-0. The verdict wasn't a surprise but the imposition of the death penalty was shocking considering two of the three judges, Judge Carl Greenberg and Judge David Lowe, were known as extremely liberal.

The press went crazy. They tripped over themselves dashing out of the courtroom, each hoping to be the first network to release the news."

"I understand your feelings, Vic," Rosie said. "Look forward to seeing you at a basketball game."

Rosie walked out to the waiting area and beckoned to Jocko. She needed air and knew Jocko would gladly strut his stuff outside for a few minutes. Upon reentering she looked over at Ruth.

"Please call Song's attorney, John Chickalette. Last, but not least, right Ruthie?

"Sorry, Boss Lady, Chick is away on vacation according to his receptionist."

"Okay. Song's sentencing hearing is just a week away. It's likely Chick simply needs to isolate himself, and possibly his defense team, in preparation for the upcoming hearing. I already spoke to him at length, but I wanted to tell him I decided to sit in on her sentencing."

At the urging of her attorney, Song had pleaded guilty to one count of aggravated murder and multiple counts of conspiracy and obstruction. Song was charged with fewer counts of murder than the other defendants because she had no prior arrests or convictions. According to the BMV, she didn't even have a moving violation at the time of these offenses."

"Why obstruction?" Ruth asked.

"Well, when you know about a crime and don't report it, they call it obstruction."

"And conspiracy?"

"If you're with those who commit a crime, it's presumed you helped plan and execute the crimes. Angel's conviction as a juvenile could be used against her because she served a sentence for grand larceny until the age of twenty-one. If her sentence was served while she was under eighteen, it would not have been admissible.

"Since I'm not a witness," Rosie continued, "there's no rule against me sitting in on Song's sentencing hearing. If I was to be a witness, the rule prohibiting witnesses from hearing the testimony of one another would prevail. That's known as 'separation of witnesses,' Ruth."

Dr. Rosie, then, tried to touch base with Attorney

Singer but the phone in his private office went unanswered.

She wanted him to respond to a quote she had seen in the newspaper. It said that he had filed a motion with Presiding Judge Kate Brown to allow Angel's trial location to be changed. Attorney Singer's rationale was that there had been so much publicity regarding his client's testimony in the Solomon and Abraham cases, it would taint prospective jurors' beliefs and attitudes.

The quote said that Singer reminded Judge Kate how sensationalized the cases had become. He stated his position that there was enormous community outrage toward the suspected perpetrators, including Angel. Judge Kate had considered his motion but ruled against it. That's why he decided it was in Angel's best interest to avoid the trial phase, plead guilty to all charges, and pray for the sympathy of a judge rather than to rely on a jury for sentencing purposes.

MONDAY AFTERNOON - MARCH 21, 1994

CHAPTER 23

A BIT OF CULTURE

Rosie called Bucky and apologized for not accepting his call earlier. She explained how inadvertently she had neglected to tell Ruth to put his calls through unless a client was being seen. Bucky accepted her apology. and Rosie felt relief, realizing now that Bucky was becoming very important to her.

She also wanted to invite him to a Toledo Philharmonic Orchestra Pops Concert on the following Sunday evening, Palm Sunday. Their relationship had progressed to where contact was initiated by each of them. With season's tickets, she could think of no one she would rather take. This would make their third date in one weekend.

I'd better ask him before he makes others plans for Sunday evening.

One of her friends, Carol Robin, was a featured vocalist and would welcome them backstage after the performance. Carol was going to sing, "I Left My Heart In San Francisco." Behind her would be a screen with the Golden Gate Bridge on it.

I wonder what it would be like to travel there with Bucky. He was in her thoughts a lot of late.

"What will that entail and what should I wear?" Bucky responded. "I must admit, I've never been to the

Toledo Performing Arts Center. But, I'll be glad to accompany my favorite doctor to the moon and back," he quickly added.

"I assure you, whatever you wear will look great on you," Rosie laughed. "I've never seen you looking anything but dapper."

"I'll be sure to send Ruth a box of Esther Price chocolates so she might be more receptive to my calls," he laughed.

"Sorry to spoil your fun, but Ruth is diabetic. Do they make a No Sugar Added kind? Usually, with good chocolates like Esther Price, those will cost a bit more. Oh, and by the way, Ruth prefers the dark caramels."   They both laughed

"I would also like to know if you would consider going to church with me on Sunday. It's Palm Sunday. I believe you'll enjoy the music and the message by my pastor. No pressure. Simply an invitation to get to know more about my lifestyle choices."

"I'd be honored to go with you. Should I bring my Bible?"

Rosie could almost hear Bucky smile when he told her it wouldn't be necessary. What she couldn't know was that her answer pleased him very much. Now he knew she had some background in Christianity. Since they hadn't discussed religion or politics, just as they hadn't discussed marriage or children, their relationship had been very superficial to this point. Her answer had opened a possible future with him.

"On second thought, bring it if you want to. I usually take mine, but copies are provided in the pews with the hymnals. We don't use hymnals in our services. One service has praise singers, a band, and contemporary music with lyrics on gigantic screens. The other service has a choir and more traditional music, but everything is still on the screen. The Pastor's message is the same in both services."

"Which service do you attend?" Rosie asked.

"Usually I go to the early, contemporary service, but if I have no other plans for the day, I tend to go to the later, traditional service. It breaks up the day and gets me out just in time for a nice lunch which I intend to take you to, my dear."

"Oh, really? Is it a mystery lunch? Or will you let me know ahead of time? Should I use the restroom at church before we take off on that quest?"

"You most definitely should use the restroom. That leaves the cat out of the bag, doesn't it? We'll be traveling at least an hour. Actually, not quite."

"Do I need flat shoes?"

"No. We're not hiking till next weekend."

"Next weekend? You're looking ahead to next week-end?"

Hoping he hadn't overstepped his expectations, Bucky was thinking that he might have actually found a partner who would respect him, enjoy his interests, and expand his experiences in a positive, healthy manner.

"Yeah, well, it keeps my calendar happy," he said. They both laughed, then agreed to make plans for next Saturday on Thursday evening. Bucky would remain on Rosie's mind until their next contact.

All in all, the conversation served as a great distraction from the serious nature of Dr. Rosie's professional tasks at hand, namely Angel.

TUESDAY MORNING - MARCH 22, 1994

CHAPTER 24

JDC INTERVIEWS

On Tuesday morning, Rosie called Paulette Hunter, administrator at the Juvenile Detention Center.

First, she asked if Paulette knew Angel personally, then asked about her cellmate.

"I grew quite fond of Angel in the four plus years she was here," Paulette replied. "She often helped younger girls adjust to their new circumstances and always showed respect to the staff. She demanded the other girls respect us as well."

Paulette was shocked to hear Angel was part of the "downtown posse"who had terrorized the city as reported in the papers. She told Rosie it had been obvious to her and everyone else that Angel's self-esteem was poor. She seemed to grow more confident after helping others and receiving appreciation.

"I could tell that Angel was desperate to be loved; she welcomed hugs," Paulette said.

"Can you tell me anything about Angel's cellmate?"

"Her name was Mindi Asher," Paulette said. "She was white and came in about a month before Angel. She was charged with a felony for shop lifting over seven hundred dollars of electronic equipment from a Wal-Mart store and she had a pimp too. He would sell her services, and the items she stole, to purchase drugs. Fortunately, he was arrested and tried as an adult.

"Mindi's charges weren't as serious as Angel's charges because Angel stole a vehicle and crossed the state line. Even so, after Mindi was released, she was on parole and when she came to see her parole officer, she would visit Angel. The last year or so, she's been off parole. I understand she returned to her family in Kentucky somewhere. Her last name is Asher, if that helps locate her."

"Was counseling available to the girls, and did Angel participate?" Rosie asked.

"Yes, and yes," Paulette answered. "Our counselor's name is Jennifer Kean. She takes a very personal interest in the girls and sees them individually as well as in group."

"Do you think she would be willing to speak with me to help evaluate Angel's state of mind when she entered and when she left the juvenile facility?"

"She'll be limited in terms of confidentiality between a counselor and a client, but I am sure she'll be more than willing to help in any way she can. We used to talk over coffee about both Angel and Mindi in terms of their future on the other side of the bars. Quite frankly, we saw a brighter future for Angel than we did for Mindi."

"What made you think that?"

"On the day Mindi was released, she hopped a greyhound bus to go visit her old boyfriend in prison. Angel, on the other hand, was going to live at the local YWCA. She told us they offered her a part-time job cleaning the bathrooms, hallways, and canteen in exchange for room and food vouchers. There's a food court at the shopping arcade next door. At times, Jennifer took the girls there for ice cream, the ones who were unlikely to bolt, that is."

"Wow. Angel posed no risk, then. Is that what you're saying?"

"She seemed to have goals, and mentioned an interest in attending a nearby beauty school," Paulette said.

"Who was responsible for following up on the girls' placement after their release?"

"That would have been Susan Shell. She's no longer employed here but was reassigned to a women's state prison in Marysville. Basically, there was no follow up for the girls who were not on parole. Angel had served her complete sentence and was no longer a juvenile."

"Thank you very much, Paulette. You've been extremely helpful. I would like to follow up with Jennifer, Angel's counselor. Is she available at this same number?"

"Yes, and if you come over, I can walk you to her office. Timing is everything. Next week she goes on maternity leave for four months.

"That would be great, Paulette. By the way, please feel free to call me if you think of anything else to help me develop a profile on this young woman. I take it you have no knowledge how I can reach Mindi.

"I'll check with her parole officer. Once she turned twenty-one, though, I think she was off the grid. But she may have a follow-up address in Kentucky. I'll definitely get back with you one way or the other."

Jennifer Kean answered the tap on the door. Rosie introduced herself and asked Jennifer if she was aware Angel was now in prison.

"Please, come in," she said, warmly welcoming Rosie and offering a seat. "Yes, I'm aware and it greatly troubled me when I first heard," Jennifer said.

"I had hoped that girl would make it. When I heard

she was arrested with the 'downtown posse', it made me sick to my stomach and I wasn't pregnant at that point in time. I tried to see Angel but, the authorities wouldn't allow it."

Rosie explained about her role with Angel and began her inquiry.

"Did you or Susan Shell make the arrangements for Angel to live at the Y, and was there was any follow up once she walked out of the detention center?

"Because Angel was twenty-one, she was simply encouraged to make her own arrangements," Jennifer answered in a defensive tone of voice. "She informed us verbally of her plan to live at the Y. No one had reason to doubt her. It sounded logical. "

"What can you tell me about her state of mind when she left? Was she still in individual and group counseling?"

"She actually developed her exit plan in group," Jennifer's voice softened a bit. "The other girls thought it was so cool. They planned to model their own future after Angel's."

"Did she say anything about her family?"

"Yes and no. She talked about her family in individual counseling, but had no plans to reunite with any of her siblings or her mother. No one had visited her in the entire five years she was here. I thought she received a stiff sentence, I might add. Even though stealing the car was wrong, I can see why she felt she had to. She saw herself as a victim with no other way out but to run away."

The two women looked at each other thinking thoughts of how other victims handled their situations.

"She seemed very interested in beauty school," Jennifer continued. "She was taking GED preparation classes led by volunteers. However, somehow, she was never ready to take the reading and writing portion of the test. I think she could have passed the math if she didn't become too anxious, and if she remembered to wear her glasses. But she never got that far. We did provide her with eye exams and dollar store reading glasses which made a huge difference in her academic performance.

"But, with Angel, it was a slow process improving her reading from about the fourth-grade level to the sixth-grade level. That's the level at which all newspapers are written, I believe. If she was going to make it in beauty school with all the science and reading required, she would need to bring her reading comprehension up to that level. There were times she became very discouraged. That's when the group helped her the most."

"Is there anything else you can tell me about her? Did she take care of her personal hygiene? How was her weight and fitness? Did the facility deal with anything like that?"

"Her hygiene was hit or miss," Jennifer said. "Some days she brushed her hair and had clean fingernails. Other times, she arrived at counseling with nails chewed down to the quick. Eventually, she learned to control her anxiety and stopped biting her nails. The nurse, Janet Sloan, told me her periods were also hit or miss. They were irregular and produced extreme cramping and passing of clots. You might want to check more on her medical history. I'm not privileged to tell you."

"What exactly are you referring to?"

"Maybe you could get a release from Angel or subpoena my counseling records and Janet's medical records. Otherwise, we can't disclose the extent of her childhood trauma. And yes, there was that."

Rosie hesitated and made a note to remind herself to look for sexual abuse problems.

"Thank you so much for your time. One last thing: I take it you did not see signs of a propensity toward violence. She demonstrated no angry outbursts directed toward other girls?"

"That's correct. Her anger was directed inward and manifested itself by depression with suicidal ideation. Although there were no actual attempts to take her own life, she did write about it. I can tell you that much. There were times in group, when she expressed it toward the men who had abused her and the mother who didn't protect her. As time went on, she learned to express anger appropriately and you could see it in her interactions with the other girls. She would bring her journal entries to group and share them openly. She was making good progress."

"I wonder what became of those journals. Would she have taken them with her?"

"Well, nothing was left in the cell. It never is when a resident is released. She either trashed them or had them in her duffel bag. Other girls left with stacks of white envelopes containing letters from family and friends. Angel had nothing like that."

"Thank you for our discussion, Jennifer, it's been extremely helpful. I understand you'll be on maternity leave soon. Do you know what gender your baby is?"

"As a matter of fact, I do. We're having a little girl around the first of May. We are naming her Esther. Are you familiar, Dr. Rosie, with the story of Esther in the Bible?"

"Yes. I can say I am. She was married to the King and through her courageous acts, she saved the Jews from extermination. Isn't that where the phrase "For such a time as this" was coined?"

"Exactly. We're not Jewish. We're Christian. But Esther's story has inspired me over the years to take risks to benefit those who have no voice concerning their future. Our little girl is a gift from God, and we don't take our responsibilities lightly."

Rosie gathered her notes and Jennifer walked her to the door.

"Have a blessed day, Rosie. Thank you for all you're doing in behalf of this troubled, young woman."

Deep in thought, Rosie walked to her car.

For such a time as this.

LATE TUESDAY MORNING - MARCH 22, 1994

CHAPTER 25

BATTERED WOMEN'S SYNDROME

Rosie listened to talk radio on the way downtown to see Angel. It was a local radio station and the discussion featured the pending sentencing trials of both Song and Angel. From what Rosie could hear, absolutely no one held sympathy for the two young women, nor was any insight brought up regarding whether they could just have been in the wrong place at the wrong time, or somehow held captive by the two men who pulled the triggers. They did talk about motivation for the six murders so close to Christmas in 1992.

It had recently occurred to Rosie that Angel might be suffering from Battered Women's Syndrome, (BWS).

Oh my gosh. This helps explain Angel's sense of hopelessness and helplessness when confronted with a dangerous situation.

Rosie began mentally preparing how to share this finding to Judge Brown:

Girls and women who have been physically, mentally, and emotionally abused, do not see that they have any control over the circumstances of their own lives. It does not have to do with how frequently they have been abused. It's like the studies of mice in a cage with an electric grid preventing them from escaping. At some point, the grid can be turned off, but the mice will not attempt to leave the cage.

Rosie felt hopeful that she was on to something that could help Angel:

"Battered Women's Syndrome is usually the result of abuse over time but may occur after an extremely traumatic event. Symptoms can manifest immediately. In some cases symptoms lie dormant in the absence of contact with an abusive person and simply don't appear for years. This is called 'the sleeper effect'. Symptoms may include sleep disorders, nightmares, eating disorders and intrusive recollections. Intrusive recollections are times of visualizing the incidents of abuse. There may be obsessive thoughts that interfere with the ability to pay attention and focus. It is an anxiety disorder so extreme that it can produce panic episodes." She finished her notes just in time to leave.

Rosie arrived at the jail just as Attorney Singer was leaving. They met near the front door.

"Hello, Dr. Klein," Singer said seeing Rosie walking toward him. "I just spoke to Angel about testifying at Song's trial. I think it could be to her benefit in her own sentencing trial. As you know, Angel never pulled a trigger or held a weapon. But according to Angel's story, neither did Song."

"That sounds like it could be a strong testimony for both girls." Rosie replied. "By the way, I was going to ask if you could subpoena Angel's counseling and medical records from the JDC? I spoke to her counselor at juvie and due to confidentiality requirements, she couldn't say much. But, she strongly indicated there was lots of material there to support a background of quite a bit of sexual abuse."

"Absolutely, Rose. It sounds like a great idea. I am always impressed by your thoroughness. I will have my staff get on it, right away. Just give us a couple of days, then stop by for the subpoena. Have a good visit with our girl."

They waved good-bye as Rosie bid him to: "Have a good day!"

Taking her usual seat facing the glass windows across from Angel, Rosie noted that Angel's back was toward the windows. This was less distraction for Angel while sitting in that position. Rosie could also see law enforcement officials moving through the hallway and others standing at computers across the way. After their usual greetings, Rosie began asking Angel about her extensive time in JDC.

"What did you think of your JDC counselor and the group counseling sessions?"

"Those meetings were the best part, I guess you would say, otherwise, the weeks were boring. I hated weekends and holidays, especially my birthday and Christmas. The group sessions seemed almost like family time that I never really had."

"Really? Please tell me more."

"Well, most of the girls were younger and would come and go with short sentences. I didn't want to get too attached and never see someone again, and I missed my little brothers."

"Let me ask you a personal question, Angel: Did you then, or now, have any problems with your periods."

"My periods are what the JDC nurse called 'heavy with clotting and cramps'," Angel said, looking at her as if she was a mind reader. Then Angel broke into tears and put her head into her folded hands, sobbing while her shoulders shook.

Rosie produced a tissue from her purse, handing it to Angel who was gaining back a little self-control. She looked up at Rosie, bit her lip and crossed her arms against her chest.

"Angel, did you always suffer like that from your periods?" Looking up and breathing heavily, she responded quietly.

"Only after the abortion I had when I was thirteen."

Rosie was speechless. Managing to compose herself, she asked, "Who took you for an abortion?"

"My stepfather, Roger Jones. It was his baby. He raped me each time my mother went out to the grocery store with one of my brothers. Sometimes he was drunk and sometimes he was just mean."

"She only took one of your brothers?"

"Yes. Roger knew if he kept one of the boys at home, she would never leave him or tell anybody how cruel he was. She was never allowed to leave with both of the boys."

"Where were you living?" Dr. Rosie asked while taking notes feverishly.

"In Indiana, not far from Ohio. I remember there was just one rest area between our town and the sign on the highway that said,:"Welcome to Ohio"."

"Who did you tell?"

"No one. I tried to tell my mother that other men had molested me, but she didn't believe me, so I didn't see any sense in telling her about Roger. When he found out I was pregnant, he took me to an abortion clinic in Columbus, Ohio. He used an excuse that he was taking me and my brothers fishing. I'm sure my mother had to wonder about his sudden interest in fishing."

"He wasn't happy when we got to the clinic and the woman said he had to sign for me because I was a minor. They also needed to know the town we lived in. He lied and gave the name of some little town, I think it was something like Greenfield, Ohio."

"Him and the boys left me there and really did go fishing. They were told to return in two hours, to pick me up, which they did. I was kind of out of it and slept in the back seat with my youngest brother, Mikey. My other brother, Greg, rode up front with Roger."

"What's the next thing you remember?"

"I remember going to school on Monday like nothing happened. I could hardly walk but nobody noticed, or maybe nobody cared."

"Did your mother and Roger stay together? Was he there when you ran away?"

"Yes, and yes," Angel said. "But I think they might both be in jail now for drug distribution. My mom will get out long before I ever do."

I most definitely will follow- up with her brothers to see if they remember this fishing field trip. Rosie thought, making a mental note.

"Do you mind if I obtain your medical and counseling records from the JDC, Angel?"

"That's okay, Dr. Klein."

Dr. Rosie decided to focus on clinical testing during the rest of the interview. She took out a plain, white, 8x11 sheet of paper and some fruit scented markers from her purse.

"Angel, can you draw a picture of yourself?"

"Okay." Angel picked up a strawberry-scented marker and began to draw.

Dr. Rosie was not surprised that Angel drew a small stick figure facing forward with short hair and ears sticking out. Arms were behind the back with no sign of hands or feet. Legs extended to the bottom edge with nothing else on the page.

"Angel can you put some clothes on the figure and draw some surroundings?"

Angel nodded and put baggy pants and a shirt on the figure, but it still didn't depict the person as being male or female. No jewelry or buttons or belt. She added a line across the bottom to depict a sidewalk.

"Thank you, Angel. Good job."

Dr. Rosie passed Angel another sheet of plain, white paper. "Would you please draw me a house?"

"Sure. That one's easy."

The house was large and rectangular, but looked like an institution. No curtains in the windows. No handle on the door. No flowers or sidewalk leading to it. The roof had no chimney.Everything was drawn in one color-black.

"Nicely done," Dr. Rosie said.

"Last request, Angel: Please draw me a tree. You may draw it with anything you want." She pointed to the colored pencils and markers.

Angel's tree had no blooms on it, just a black trunk with a circular hole in it and bleak branches without green leaves.

A hole drawn like this is thought to be symbolic of past traumatic experiences, Rosie mentally noted. She felt sorrow for this girl whose life was destroyed long before she befriended the downtown group and the murders occurred.

Rosie decided an I.Q, test was unnecessary for purposes of sentencing this defendant. Based on Angel's vocabulary and verbal communication skills, she was obviously not retarded. Rosie then administered simple reading, spelling, and math tests.

After these, she determined that giving a written, standardized personality test to rule out severe mental disorders and establish truthfulness, would not be valid with Angel's limited reading skills.

Angel may not meet the standard for being considered literate. Literacy requires a sixth-grade reading comprehension level. But being more than two years behind her last grade level will qualify her as having a learning disability. Particularly being under stress, it may also have impaired her understanding of her Miranda rights. Not that Judge Kate Brown would use that as criteria to influence sentencing at this point, Rosie thought.

She began to assess Angel's memory by asking Angel to remember three words. Ten minutes later, Angel repeated them flawlessly. Her memory appeared intact. She seemed grounded-in-reality. No impairment there.

"Why did you lie to the detention folks about where you would be staying?"

"I was embarrassed to say I had no other plans and had no one who cared," Angel said.

"I used to daydream about living near or on a warm, sunny, sandy beach. Once, I saw a television program that featured life at Ormond Beach, Florida. I kept that picture in my mind during long, dark, sleepless nights."

When asked about the time she tried to commit suicide, Angel answered quietly.

"I wondered what heaven would be like. But I was afraid if I committed suicide I would go to hell. If I had to be in hell, I might just as well stay where I was in hell on earth."

"Angel, I will try to sit right behind you at Song's hearing. That is, if you are called to testify. How do you feel about that?"

"I wouldn't mind. Even though I've had enough practice being questioned in the first trials. I really don't want to have to do it again. But I guess I should do it to help her. She was very nice to me. You know we were kept apart in separate pods. I haven't seen her in all the months we've been in jail."

Song was not being held as a State Witness against the two men as Angel was. She didn't understand why they were being kept apart except perhaps the Prosecutor was afraid they would not tell the same story. A contradicting testimony might result in the judges throwing out Angel's testimony, which they couldn't afford to have happen since they had made a plea deal with her so she would testify against the two men.

"I absolutely told the truth, the whole truth, and nothing but the truth, so help me God," Angel said. "I remembered everything very clearly. I repeated the same story in both trials. Both of my testimonies were so much alike, they believed I had memorized them. "

Dr. Rosie finally stood to leave and hugged Angel who showed no resistance. She even briefly put her head on Rosie's shoulder.

"You have been terrific today. I have one more thing to ask of you. I'm leaving you with a list of forty incomplete sentences. I would like you to finish each sentence by writing down the first thing that comes to mind. I will go over your answers when I come back. Don't worry about spelling. And Angel, there are no correct answers, no wrong answers and if you must leave some blank, don't worry. These sentences simply reflect your feelings, ok?"

Rosie left the building and breathed the fresh air with more appreciation of her own nuclear family.

No more taking them for granted. I need to call them tonight and bring them up to date on my new main squeeze. Although, she and Bucky hadn't kissed let alone squeeze.

Answering machines at her sons' houses were her only contact. She left brief messages saying she would like a call back at their convenience. No emergency; just Mom wanting to update them. She sent her love to them. Every conversation or note ended in that manner.

At 6:45 pm on Wednesday evening, with Jocko beside her, Rosie unlocked the door to her suburban office.

I wonder where in the world Ruth could be this evening. Ruth always has the coffee, herbal tea, and chocolate croissants ready by now. No call. No note to say she has stepped out.

The first two ladies who were attending tonight's support group pulled up to the curb. They had traveled thirty minutes through the countryside from a nearby, small town to participate today.

On rotating weeks, Dr. Rosie facilitated either this grief support group or a post-abortion support group. Some of the women attendees experienced guilt and grief over the loss of their babies. Most in the group were young and coerced into that choice. Many developed severe depression years after the actual event. And others, were the mothers of the pregnant girls who recognized the pain and suffering of their daughters and the loss of a grandchild for themselves.

Women in both groups were referred by their pastors who had seen them for marriage counseling with husbands or in their own grief counseling.

Ruth pulled in beside them and quickly got out with goodies in her arms. She apologized for being late by saying her husband had fallen in the bathroom this afternoon.. She was just returning from the hospital where he would remain under observation for another day.

"You have nothing to be sorry about, Ruthie. And stopping for the pastries was totally unnecessary. Was your hubby unconscious? Bleeding?" asked Rosie.

"Not unconscious, just moaning. I guess he passed out. He had fallen off the commode onto the cement, tile shower head -first. I had no idea what I would see when I rolled him over. Fortunately, there was just a cut above his eye that created lots of bleeding, but no damage to his eye. Probably a concussion. He has no memory of what happened."

"Do you feel comfortable leaving him? We will be fine here if you need to get back to the hospital."

"He's finally sleeping, peacefully. I'll go back in the morning when there should be more information about his condition. Thanks, Rosie."

The other four women arrived and prepared their beverages, taking pastries before sitting in the chairs making a circle. The group began discussing everyone's journaling since the last gathering that each had completed. Then, they began sharing any updates to their circumstances.

Jocko received his fair share of pampering and Ruth came in to top off their coffee.

Everyone seemed comfortable as the routine of the group session began.

THURSDAY EVENING - MARCH 24, 1994

CHAPTER 26

WEEKEND ESCAPE

Promptly at 7:00 pm on Thursday night, Bucky called. I had just finished watching the six o'clock news and eating my tomato bisque soup and BLT.

"Is this a good time?" he asked.

"Absolutely," I said, feeling relieved to hear a sweet voice after such a harrowing week.

I remembered my most recent boyfriend, Jerome, used to call on Thursday to solidify plans for the weekends. Although we'd never discussed being exclusive, it was assumed the weekends were reserved for one another. Neither was expected to explain how we spent the rest of our week. But little things had begun to go wrong, and that relationship had ended in October. We had mutually agreed it was better to part as friends. So much of our time together had been swimming, golfing, and dancing. And booze. Lots of it. Once I realized he would never get high on life with me, absent alcohol, it didn't seem worthwhile to continue. Jack Daniels was his best friend and I would never replace him.

"Do you think three dates, including church on one weekend, is too much too soon?" I asked.

"Of course, not," he replied.

Then I reminded him of the concert coming up on Sunday evening and asked Bucky to accompany me to a charity dinner and art auction to be held on Saturday evening at my country club, Walnut Creek.

"You're keeping my calendar very happy," he laughed in response.

"The auction proceeds will benefit children who reside at the Lucas County Sheriff's Ranch," I explained. "They attend public school but live in villas on the sprawling grounds of the ranch. Some are there temporarily because their parents have lost their jobs and have no one who can provide for their children. Others are there because they've been removed as a result of abuse or neglect."

"I can see you're a woman who likes to help others, a lot," Bucky said. "I find that a very endearing quality, Rosie. You are certainly my kind of woman."

"I'm just in awe of the house parents who provide structure, discipline and love. They work 24/7 for two weeks on, then their off a week. I don't know if I could do that," I said.

I wondered how Angel's life would have turned out differently if she'd had the opportunity to live with nine girls and caring house parents.

"Rosie, I'll be happy to accompany you. Only, I have one condition."

I paused, waiting to hear what it was.

"I want to pay our way. I won't take 'no' for an answer."

"Well, I've already bought the tickets, but you can pay for anything else, if that's what you want."

"I do and I will," he said. "Now, what do I wear? I've never been to one of these shindigs."

"Well, it's a black-tie affair, but the good news is that

you won't have to rent a tux."

"I'm so relieved."

"But, do you have a dark suit? I think you'd look great in that."

I planned on wearing a long, black, ankle length dress, pearls, and high heels. Bucky was six inches taller so I had no concern I would tower over him at the party and looked forward to walking beside him into the room.

SATURDAY EVENING - MARCH 26, 1994

CHAPTER 27

A SWEET WEEKEND

When we arrived at the Country Club, Bucky was pleasantly surprised there was valet parking and a greeter at the door. I was eager to show Bucky where I had spent most of my leisure time the past eighteen years. Many of my friends and their spouses had already arrived and were mingling during cocktails before dinner.

Since seating was predetermined, I looked for printed guest cards with our names along with our table assignment. Lo and behold, when we arrived at the round table, we saw my dear old friends, Sandy and Mickey Garrison already seated. Beside them were Sgt. Ron, the State Highway Patrol officer, and his wife Sharon. Wes Hall and his lady friend, Sherri Bloom, completed the eight seats at the table.

I introduced Bucky to everyone and wanted to be sure he would be seated next to someone who shared common interests. That turned out to be Wes. I had no idea Wes was a ball player until he spoke up when I introduced Bucky mentioning a little of his background. Apparently, Wes played for a ball team sponsored by the Embassy, a downtown bar and grill where journalists gathered for lunch. I also hoped to catch Wes for a few moments sometime during the evening and ask him to investigate the Columbus, Ohio, abortion clinic.

Before dinner was served, we decided to walk around and glance at paintings to be raffled later during the evening.

"Sandy is a long-time friend," I said to Bucky as we strolled among the auction items.

"We sat together by the club pool while our children swam. She and her husband played couples golf with us on Friday nights and we used to enjoy monthly dinner dances together. Sharon and I remember each other from high school. We didn't hang out together but sort of traveled in the same circles. We had mutual friends who were involved in school and sports activities. I had no idea she was married to Ron or that he graduated from our high school a couple years ahead of us."

"They seem like nice people," Bucky said. "Like you," he smiled, looking at me. I smiled back with contentment.

"Ron is the Sergeant I just interviewed in my office about the arrest of Angel and her gang. Wes is the investigative newspaper reporter I spoke to on the phone. He sat in on the trials of Marcus and James. Sherri, who came with Wes tonight, looks familiar to me."

As it turned out, Sherri was the auctioneer for the evening. Everyone at the table also began walking around the perimeter of the dining room and through the foyer with drinks and appetizers in their hands looking at paintings which were lovely and pricey.

I wrote a bid for a painting of a Navajo Woman, painted by R.C. Gorman, a Navajo painter. He had named this lovely Navajo woman, Celestina. It depicted the woman sitting on the ground holding a large, wooden, ceramic serving bowl. The colors were brilliant, bold Southwest tones

Luck was with us: my bid won the painting. Because of its size, the painting needed to remain in the ladies' locker room until it could be transported by SUV. I would have to return for it another day, but enjoyed picturing how it would look above the mantel in my condo.

After the main course, but prior to Bananas Foster being served, I was able to corner Wes and briefly told him the story of Angel's abortion. He promised to pursue it at the end of the week. In the short term, he was going to be tied up in the sentencing hearing for Song, as was I.

The evening continued and was simply lovely. At one point, when excusing myself to go to the ladies' room with the other women at the table, I heard nothing but praises about Bucky; his looks, his demeanor, his personality, and the way he looked at me. It was very pleasant to hear.

While enjoying dessert, I suddenly realized why Sherri looked so familiar. I had seen a picture of her on the cover of a recent edition of a local monthly magazine. The article was a promotion for the dinner and auction tonight, and Sherri was teaching a ten-year old girl at the Sheriff's Ranch to play chess.

"How often do you volunteer at the Ranch?" I asked Sherri leaning closer to hear her answer.

"Every second and fourth Saturday. I played chess and bridge in college and decided chess would be a better choice. It only takes one opponent instead of three."

"Would you ever be interested in teaching chess to my guys at Casa Hope?"

"Of course, just give me a call and we can work something out."

We exchanged business cards and decided to have lunch soon.

At evening's end, Bucky returned me to my door and I invited him in for a hot nightcap which he was happy to accept. He chose Kalua in decaf coffee; I decided on the same.

Flipping the switch on the wall brought the gas fireplace to life. When I pushed back the patio curtains, we walked outside onto my deck which overlooked a lovely and well-lit circular pond.

Rhythmic sounds of the fountain and deep croaking sounds of the frogs lent an air of a tropic paradise to the moment. Positioned in the corner of the deck was a hot tub that could easily seat four people. We laughed and agreed to relax in it sometime soon.

"My sons like to sit in the tub with large, Puerto Rican cigars and solve the problems of the world," I said. "They didn't care if snowflakes were falling. It's been their New Year's Eve tradition for years."

We agreed on the early church service. Then, he took me gently by the shoulders and kissed me good night. I had been ready for our first real kiss all evening and wasn't disappointed. I felt a sense of serenity enfold me.

I'm really happy, went through my mind.

Then, re-entering the condo, I walked him to the door and closed it quietly behind as he walked to his car. I was very pleased with the entire evening and very impressed at how easily he fit in with my friends.

What a perfect gentleman he's turning out to be! As I leaned against the front door, I noticed my palms were sweating, my cheeks were flushed, and my heart fluttering.

Early the next morning, Bucky picked me up for church and explained he had belonged to this church for many years. He prepared me to meet his friends but couldn't really anticipate who would approach them. As it turned out, Judge Charles Lincoln was the first person we saw as we entered the double doors.

I was impressed with the friendliness of the greeters. They seemed to know Bucky, but he didn't stop for any formal introductions. Instead, he guided me through the crowd to where Charles and Darlene were standing. The four of us entered the sanctuary and Bucky indicated where I should sit beside Darlene. The men would sit on either side with us in the middle.

Bucky had been right. I thoroughly enjoyed the entire service.

Another perk, I'm beginning to understand the moral fiber of this man, Bucky Walker.

As we descended the steps of the church, Bucky asked if I would like to have lunch. But, I begged off saying I needed to complete some paperwork prior to going to the Pops concert with him later this evening.

Later that evening, Bucky arrived at my door right on time wearing a herringbone tweed sports jacket, black flannel trousers and black wingtip shoes.

"See you later, Jocko," I said as we headed out the door to the concert.

My season tickets were in the mezzanine section reached by an escalator in the spacious lobby. The concert began and was delightful. When the lights came on halfway through the concert, indicating a brief intermission, I suggested we step out into the mezzanine area and have a beverage. Bucky quickly agreed and told me he would get our drink orders.

"Tell the truth, now: Are you enjoying the musical selections, so far?"

"Absolutely. I don't know how I would like classical, but these pops tunes are great."

At the same time, Bucky appeared to be glancing around instead of remaining totally focused on me.

"The truth is, I simply don't see any other softball

players here this evening," Bucky said.

I laughed so hard my cranberry juice came spurting out of my mouth. Fortunately, it didn't hit Bucky's light blue Oxford shirt front.

I realized, then, that I needed to learn more about Bucky's past. Apparently, he had been quite a ball player in his high school and early adult years, meaning prior to age forty.

"I've recently received wonderful news: I'm going to be inducted into the Toledo Softball Hall of Fame in June," Bucky said. "I have two questions, Rosie: Would you like to attend the induction ceremony, and would you come to my first Senior softball game when the season begins?"

"Silly question. Of Course, I would! It'll be great to see you play and I'd be honored to see you inducted."

"I'll be honest," Bucky said. "The rules are different, and I'm a little nervous."

The lights blinked for all to return to our seats. He took my hand as we walked back inside, each thinking private thoughts. It wasn't long before the second half of the concert began.

How refreshing to be escorted this entire weekend by an honest gentleman with no secret agenda. I'd like to find out more about his plans for the future.

The finale concluded with the soloist's beautiful rendition of "I Left My Heart In San Francisco."

There was a standing ovation and the director thanked the singers, the orchestra and the audience for their attendance and applause. Then, he announced the next upcoming performance and encouraged everyone to consider getting tickets soon as venues were usually sold out early.

I led Bucky by the hand to an entrance at the stage's side.

As soon as we stepped through the heavy curtain, I spotted my friend, Carol, the soloist. Introductions were made and Carol invited us to a cast party at Katie's, a downtown restaurant. It was within walking distance from the Performing Arts Center. The three of us strolled down the street, arm in arm, discussing the performance.

"My husband, Jack, is holding a table for us," Carol said. "I can't wait to introduce you, Bucky. It's been awhile since Rosie and we could be a foursome."

Finally, we've made friends outside of Bucky's circle and my profession, I thought. *Now we have something of our own.*

MONDAY MORNING-MARCH 28, 1994

CHAPTER **28**

SONG'S SENTENCING TRIAL

Dr. Rosie slipped into the second row of the courtroom just behind Angel. She sat down and removed a legal pad from her leather briefcase so she could record any details for assessment later.

Angel was in street clothes, a white, button-down, long-sleeved blouse, tucked into black slacks, with black socks and black flats. She was seated beside her Attorney, Dan Singer, at a table in front and facing the Judge's bench. To her left was the uniformed female corrections officer, Verna Mitchell, with her holstered weapon. In the first row, across the aisle was Attorney Chickalette with his client, Song Lee. To Song's right sat another female corrections officer. On the far, right aisle, sat the Prosecutor, Laura Robinson and her Assistant Prosecutor, Joan Nichols.

Two armed male officers stood by the doors leading into the court room. The officers were stationed just in case relatives or friends of the victims decided to take matters into their own hands. That was particularly unlikely, however, on the part of Mr. Brook's 83-year old wheelchair-bound mother. In truth, Richard Brooks used to lead people to believe his mother was younger, so they would perceive his own age as younger. He'd always seemed to be trying to recapture his youth as he worked with college kids. Even so, students viewed him as a competent, but lonely man, no matter what his age.

"All rise!" Bailiff Bill Gorman commanded. Everyone stood until Judge D.P. Tucker entered through the door from his chambers, and seated himself on the bench. Then the Judge motioned for everyone to be seated.

"The State may proceed," he said in a clear voice.

His reputation precedes him. Rosie thought. D.P. is known to most as the 'hanging Judge'. She wondered how this would affect Song by having him assigned to her case. Few know that D.P. stands for "Dr. Phillip" which was his nickname after receiving his Doctor of Juris Prudence from Duke law school...Dr. Phillip Tucker.

"Your honor, may we approach the bench?" Prosecutor Laura Robinson asked as she stood up, displaying a confident mood.

She and Attorney Chickalette went forward out of earshot of anyone in the Courtroom, other than the Bailiff and Court Reporter, Sally Jacobs. Rosie decided to call her friend, Linda Willis, the school nurse at Roosevelt at the break. She wondered whether Sally Jacobs was related to the special education teacher, Lou Jacobs.

"Although a guilty verdict was obtained from this defendant, the victims' families want to be heard, your Honor," stated Prosecutor Robinson.

The Judge glanced down over his reading glasses, and answered in a soft voice.

"That will be fine."

It was protocol for the Prosecutor to request an opportunity for the victims' families to be heard. Judges always permitted this procedure even though they knew friends and families of the defendant hoped their statements would influence a judge to be more lenient during the sentencing phase.

The two attorneys returned to their seats, and Attorney Robinson called her first witness. A podium with a microphone was set up in the center aisle facing the judge. The court reporter sat prepared to record all testimonies which would be made available for D.P. to review at the conclusion of the hearing.

Rosie wondered if Judge Kate Brown, who had been appointed for Angel's sentencing hearing, would also review the victims' families' statements. They would not be asked to go through a second agony of speaking at both young defendants' hearings.

There was no swearing in by Bailiff Gorman. Judge Tucker simply asked the witness, Mrs. Young, to state her full name and relationship to the deceased, Bobby Young. He instructed Mrs. Young to speak clearly so the court reporter could document her statement. She had a hanky twisted around her left hand and her face was already streaked with mascara from crying.

"My name is Joyce Young. I am the mother of Bobby Young who was murdered for no good reason as he left a telephone booth down the street from our apartment," Tears well-up again in her eyes. "Bobby bled out on the frozen sidewalk before an ambulance could get there. Bobby had just called his grandfather in Tennessee to say he had signed an offer to play college ball. My son was a great athlete headed to Ohio State University with a scholarship to play football even though that dream is now done for everybody!" Her shoulders shook as she softly sobbed into her hanky. Collecting herself after a moment, she continued in a pained voice.

"Not only was he an accomplished athlete, but he was dedicated to his community and hoped to give back someday. You can ask anybody who knew him. He was humble. He was active in the church youth group. He was respectful of his teachers and appreciated his coaches. Now, I understand," said Mrs. Young. "that this young woman,

Song, was also looking at a bright future. She, too, was on a college scholarship and was making her parents proud. If your family is present, I am very sorry for your loss, but it is far different than ours. We don't know why Song suddenly became involved with a man like James. But, we do hope there will be severe consequences for her decisions. In my opinion, she should spend the rest of her life behind bars! An eye for an eye and a tooth for a tooth!" Mrs. Young stopped for a moment, then seemed to calm down as she continued.

"As a Christian woman, I have personally forgiven her. But, maybe, on her birthday and especially at Christmas, maybe Song will think of us, and think about the holidays we will be cheated out of spending with our beloved, innocent son." She bowed her head, then turned to return to her seat while wiping the tears out of her eyes.

Rosie glanced around and saw there were few dry eyes in the Courtroom. The person seated beside Mrs. Young appeared to be the age of a daughter or friend of Bobby's. The Court's Victim-Witness Advocate, Lisa Turner, sat directly behind Mrs. Young, and gently patted her shoulders. Angel never stirred from her position with her hands in her lap and her head down.

Attorney Robinson then called Margie Bennett to the podium. Mrs. Bennett was a tall, athletic woman with auburn hair and sunglasses. She drew close to the microphone, removed her glasses and introduced herself as the wife of the deceased businessman, Brian Bennett, who was gunned down as he waited for the bus.

"Sir, we have four children: Bill, a Junior in High School, Heather, a Freshman, Jeff in the eighth grade, and Patty, a fifth grader. They have lost their father, a good man, a great father who will never walk onto the soccer field for senior night, again. He will never see any of them graduate from high school or college. The girls will never enjoy taking Brian to their father-daughter dances, again, or walk them down the aisle. And, I will never enjoy those golden years of retirement for which we have been planning our entire marriage,"

Mrs. Bennett was not sympathetic toward Song in the least.

"Being the mother of two daughters," she said, "I would expect our own girls to face the same consequences, if they were to participate in such senseless slayings.

"Prior to this taking of Brian's life, our family always enjoyed the Christmas season, and now we will simply dread its onset and duration in the future. Two of our children have birthdays between Christmas and New Year's. This young woman and her companions have changed all our lives forever!"

Mrs. Bennett closed by asking the Judge to put himself in her shoes and think about how he would feel if his wife's life was suddenly taken without warning. She thanked him for his attention, turned her back, looked at no one, and walked out of the courtroom.

Judge Tucker asked for a brief recess stating that he had to participate in a conference call. Rosie's guess was that the testimonies had been so emotionally charged, he figured everyone could stand a break. Couple that with the fact that many people knew nothing about Judge Tucker's own marriage. Could Mrs. Bennett's words have brought back unhappy memories of his own?

Rosie's thoughts began to wander: D.P. is married to my friend, Penny. They met at school when Penny was working on a Psychology degree at Duke University. Rosie also knew from her private conversations with Penny that their marriage was still suffering after the loss of their fifteen-year old daughter, Kenna. She had struggled with Cystic Fibrosis and had recently passed away from complications when running a race for her high school.

Rosie felt her relationship was too close to the Tuckers to accept cases to be heard in Judge Tucker's court. Even though Angel's sentencing had been assigned to Judge Kate

Brown, this witness may have struck a chord inside Judge Tucker. Rosie decided to call Penny for a long over-due one-on-one lunch after she left court today. They all stood as the Judge left for his chambers. Rosie tapped Angel on the back and smiled as the corrections guard turned around and glared. She made eye contact with Angel, but said nothing, quickly removing her hand.

Taking a deep breath, she hastened to the ladies' room and encountered Wes Hall in the corridor. He reported that he had tracked down the abortion clinic. They agreed to have lunch at the Embassy Bar and Grill following the final victims' families' statements. A short time later, everyone resumed their previous positions in the courtroom.

Judge Tucker came back into the courtroom as everyone rose per protocol. He resumed sitting on the bench, then asked Ms. Robinson to call her next witness. Ms. Robinson called Mr. and Mrs. Pappas to come forward. Mr. Pappas kept his arm securely under Mrs. Pappas' elbow and led her down the aisle, assuming their places at the podium.

"We are the owners of the Greek carry out called Kali Mera," Mr. Pappas stated. "Our daughter, Sophia, worked for us to give us a break from long, sixteen-hour days. Usually, my wife and I would leave the store and pick up Sophia's four-year old daughter, Lily. We would take her to our house where my wife would feed and bathe our granddaughter. After a quick bite to eat, I would return to work with Sophia and we would close at ten. Once the supermarkets close, our last hour gets quite busy.

"The night our Sophia was shot and killed, I was delayed returning for the evening. Can you imagine my horror when I found her crumbled, lifeless body behind the counter?" He began crying softly as tears rolled down both cheeks which he didn't bother to wipe away.

Mrs. Pappas could barely maintain her balance as her husband told the tragic story of their only child's murder. Mr.

Pappas steadied his wife, then asked the Judge for "no mercy".

"Lily will grow up not remembering her mother, our sweet Sophia. Our own memories were cut short and include the vivid picture of her blood-splattered body in my mind. That is not how I want to remember her. It is not natural for your daughter to die before you. It is not the way God meant it to be."

Without saying another word, he respectfully turned his back and gently walked his wife out of the court room.

Rosie wondered if Mrs. Pappas was sedated in order to survive the testimonies of the others and then of her own husband. She sighed as the final family member was called to the microphone.

Last, but not least.

An elderly woman was wheeled forward by a young woman in a nurse's uniform who positioned the wheelchair beside the podium and handed the seated woman the microphone. Then, putting on the chair's brake, she walked to a vacant end seat in the back row. The elderly woman wore a black hat and long, black chiffon dress with jacket. In a distinct Scottish accent, she introduced herself.

"I am Sheila Brooks," she told the Judge. "I followed my son, Richard, to America after he graduated from Oberlin Conservatory of Music in Ohio.

"My husband died from pneumonia when our only son, Richard, was ten. Over the years, we have owned a successful business, and once I sold it, we were left well enough off to live comfortably. So, it was easy for me to leave Scotland and come to the United States where it seemed Richard had the best opportunities for a career. He married briefly, but divorced. He also had friends who came over and played music and sang old Scottish songs to me. I felt secure knowing my son was coming home at night.

"For his benefit, I never stopped hoping he would find another wife, someone sweet. For my benefit, I selfishly hoped to hold a grandchild before I died. I was after all, supposed to die first." She stopped, then began to weep before composing herself.

"During the time he was at the University working, I knitted hats to send to troops overseas. My women's group from church donated them to the men and women serving in the Middle East. Since his death, I have nothing to look forward to and have not mustered up any interest in music or knitting. So, you see? Richard's death affects many people in a widening circle. It is beyond a tragedy what has happened. So many suffer from this senseless act."

Mrs. Brooks continued and explained that she has a nurse companion, Jeannie, who fixes her dinner, bathes her, and helps her get ready for bed in the evening.

"But, now the days seem too long, and my thoughts are sometimes evil, for which I am ashamed. My thoughts often turn to revenge for the awful, pre-mature ending of my son's life."

Mrs. Brooks took only a pause before adding: "I feel sorry for the parents of the little gang of killers. Their loss helps bring my thoughts back to a more spiritual nature. For I know where Richard will spend Eternity which is more than anyone can say for them."

Jeannie came back down the aisle to push Mrs. Brooks out the exit in her wheelchair, the doors shutting quietly behind them. The poor woman's demeanor was just as sad as the other family members.

"The State has one more person to speak on behalf of the deceased, your Honor," said the Prosecutor, Ms. Robinson. "Although they had become part of the perpetrators' gang, April Chandler and Sam Strong were also viciously murdered. Having grown up in the Children's

Home, they have no family to speak in their behalf, but we have someone who will." She beckoned for George Emmanuel to step forward and address the Court.

Mr. Emmanuel slowly proceeded to the podium. He was beyond retirement age, but never stopped serving his regular customers at George's Evergreen Bar and Grill. He loved preparing Greek meatball sandwiches and other ethnic dishes totally unfamiliar to his Hispanic guests. His cane was evidence of their esteem. Carved pine with green, yellow, and red stripes, they had purchased it in Mexico for him.

"I, also, lived in the orphanage where Sam and April lived from the time I was five until almost twelve. My mother passed away and my father could not take care of me until he remarried. Some of the old nuns remembered me. Because of that, the nuns would allow Sammy and April to go out with me for ice cream and play a game of putt-putt golf one Sunday every month. They had no other visitors, unlike some of the other children. They became like family to me." Mr. Emmanuel paused.

"I provided all the children circus tickets, baseball tickets, Christmas trees and Christmas gifts. I kept a jug on the bar and my patrons contributed to these causes. Sometimes I attended events held at the Home and even at their schools. Sammy was in the band and April had several singing parts in annual plays. It was very noticeable how Sammy looked after this much younger girl, April. He allowed her to play with his hair and sit in his lap, so she could see the stage better or feel secure in the orphanage.

"I remember Sammy's graduation party and how sorry I felt for April to lose the only brother figure she had at that time. That event, for that reason, was bittersweet. Sammy kept in touch with me when he joined the service and to my knowledge, served our country well. As Sammy's term of duty came to an end, April was graduating from high school. She joined Sammy for the summer at Hilton Head Island and of all things, she found a job scooping ice cream.

I would like to think my influence subconsciously factored into her choice of jobs.

"I could see Sammy had a heart for younger kids. It made perfect sense that he chose to play his guitar and sing to them under the moss trees. Those kids visiting Hilton Head Island must have loved his music and his interactions with them.

"When the two of them returned to Toledo in the fall, they approached me for a job cleaning the bar after hours. I was more than happy to hire them. I was putting in twelve-hour days in order to supervise my other cleaning guys. If I wasn't on the premises, those guys would drink my liquor and replace the vodka bottles with water or just steal the top shelf alcohol."

George paused to wipe his brow, or perhaps his eyes, as he clutched his cane with his other hand. Then, he continued.

"I offered them an apartment above the bar where they could sleep days and stash their meager belongings. I owned the building and could do without the rent. Everything worked out fine for about nine months. Then, they began alternating shifts instead of working together each night. It seemed as if they might be sneaking other people upstairs.

"My shift was 6 pm until 6 am, and my partner worked days. He was the one who reported his suspicions to me. I had no choice, when liquor began disappearing, but to ask them to leave. They did not make excuses or deny the allegations. It broke my heart, but I never saw them again.

"When I cleaned the apartment, I found what appeared to be small weed pipes. I was saddened at the way our friendship ended and their new friendships began. But I was even more saddened to hear they were murdered. They never deserved to be killed like that. I just can't imagine they would ever have been involved in violent crimes. But, I thank you for hearing my story."

Mr. Emmanuel turned and with his head down, walked slowly back to his seat. An older woman seated beside him, patted him on the knee. A younger woman, dressed very professionally, sat behind them and put a reassuring hand on his shoulder. Rosie assumed they were his sister, Libby, and his daughter, Petra, who had moved in with him to fill the void after her own mother passed away.

Judge Tucker slammed his gavel.

"Court is dismissed for lunch and will resume at 1:30 pm this afternoon for the witnesses to speak on the part of the defendant." Bailiff Gorman then announced in a loud voice asking everyone to rise. When the Judge left the bench, the silence was thick and deep. Everyone filed out of the courtroom quietly with only a nod or a small wave here and there to others in attendance.

As they exited the courtroom, Dr. Klein noticed Lisa Turner, the victim's advocate, looking her way. She couldn't know at that moment Lisa was filing a mental note to contact Dr. Klein once this case was completed. Dr. Klein was known as one of the best resources for grief counseling and Lisa would be calling soon about the needs of everyone they heard speak today.

Rosie glanced back and saw Angel's attorney speaking softly to her with his hand on her shoulder. The corrections officer, Verna Mitchell, led her to a side door, and presumably back to her cell until court resumed this afternoon. Rosie headed to the Embassy Restaurant to have lunch with Wes and call Penny Tucker.

Wes was seated in a booth in the rear of the narrow bar area. He appeared to be reading the local news section of the paper. Rosie slid in across from him. A familiar server asked her for her drink order, to which she responded,

"Coffee, simply black as usual."

"Rosie, I'm pleased we can get together. I was dismayed to hear about Angel's abortion. The good news is that I was able to track the agency, although in fact, it no longer exists. By Ohio law, all records of minors were kept. Sure enough, a girl from Greenfield received services the year Angel would have been thirteen. Obviously, false names were provided by her stepfather."

"Do you have any more information about this man?"

"No, not yet, but I plan to find him, and then we'll nail him. Angel doesn't have to be afraid of him anymore. Maybe we can see to it that he's brought to justice."

"She doesn't need to fear him, you're right. The unfortunate truth is she likely will be behind bars for the rest of her life."

Wes and Rosie spent the remainder of their lunch together simply feeling frustrated and sad and angry at the man who had violated a child's body and her trust. Angry at a mother who failed to protect her daughter.

It was one of the saddest lunches Rosie could ever remember. Maybe the afternoon would be better with witnesses speaking about the good points of the defendant. There had to be something that somebody could remember.

MONDAY AFTERNOON- MARCH 28, 1994

CHAPTER 29

SONG'S CHARACTER WITNESSES

At 1:30 pm, everyone had again filled the courtroom seats. Bailiff Hall called the Court to order. Judge Tucker asked the Defense to present their witnesses.

Attorney Chickalette requested Song's parents, Dr. William Lee and Mrs. Naomi Lee, to step forward. They were short in stature, slightly graying, with an appearance of modesty and professionalism. Dr. Lee had founded a pediatric medical practice specializing in children on the Autism Spectrum in his native country of South Korea. He was well published and highly respected in the Seoul community.

Dr. and Mrs. Lee glanced lovingly at their daughter as they approached the podium. Their eyes glassed over with tears of remorse. As in the case of the Sophia Pappas' parents, Dr. Lee held his wife's arm to support her as he began to address the Judge without any prepared notes.

Dr. Lee began by described Song's childhood prior to leaving Korea to attend boarding school on Baden Island in the United States. She was a typical little girl who loved school, her friends, and her family. He remembered how much she enjoyed ballet and piano.

"We attended church together," he said, with tears welling up in his eyes. "She participated in Sunday School and the Children's Choir.

Very early on, we saw that Song had courage when she decided to learn to play the trumpet. She took private lessons for a year before leaving Korea to go to music school in the United States."

He then described the rest of their family by saying he and his wife had two younger daughters who never desired to leave home to pursue educational opportunities. They were always very protective of their girls. So when it seemed that older boys found reasons to hang around Song, they thought the Baden Boarding School of Music would provide a more protective environment than public education in the large city of Seoul. Another reason to send her was the fact there were private music teachers in South Korea, but no Christian schools.

"We truly believed our beautiful, thirteen-year old daughter would thrive academically and musically at a school that specialized in exceptionally gifted students," Dr. Lee explained. "Money could not buy a child's admission to this exclusive school of renown. Auditions took place in person and the guidance counselor, Mrs. Goodwin, interviewed both Song and us. She emphasized the importance of total commitment on part of the entire family.

"Dorm space was limited and the small ratio of teachers to students was outstanding. Never could we have foreseen the outcome of this very important decision to send Song, at such a tender age, to the United States of America.

"When Song notified us that Mrs. Goodwin had submitted a performance video and was able to get her a full music scholarship to the University of Toledo, we were thrilled, believing this to be a move forward. During Song's freshman year, we brought our other daughters, Kim and Emma to watch Song perform with the marching band at the homecoming football game." Dr. Lee briefly paused, turned and pointed to Song's sisters, both seated in the Courtroom with their eyes now glued onto their sister.

"After the game, we were introduced to Dr. Schuller, the band director." Again, Dr. Lee turned and held his arm out in the direction of a middle-aged man seated beside Kim and Emma.

"Dr. Schuller made great comments about our daughter's personal character and outstanding musical ability. According to Dr. Schuller, she was punctual, prepared, respectful, and always encouraging and kind to other students until her Sophomore year.

"After she was arrested, we immediately flew to Toledo. Dr. Schuller picked us up at the airport. He was very apologetic and offered to do whatever we needed to assist with our daughter. He recommended an attorney and took us to the Marriott Hotel. Before leaving us, he told us how Song had become distracted, and her moods seemed to fluctuate from being agitated to lethargic. He told us she had begun to separate herself from the other band members. In hindsight, he was sorry he had not requested an appointment with her.

"Your Honor, our daughter, Song, is solely responsible for her decisions. We must not blame James or even ourselves for this disgrace to our family. It is obvious, she must pay the penalty imposed by the Court and personally answer to God. We sincerely hope you will consider her past as presented today by those who love her and knew her, as you determine her future. Thank you for listening, Sir."

Dr. and Mrs. Lee both bowed slightly to the Judge, then turned and returned to their seats. It was apparent they wanted to remain as close to their daughter as they were permitted for as long as they were allowed.

Attorney Chickalette announced his next witness.

"Please come forward Dr. Thadd Schuller."

Dr. Schuller, a music director, had a Ph.D. in Sound Mixing from the University of Michigan. He was a tenured professor at the University of Toledo and Chairman of the

Music Department. One of his responsibilities was directing the marching band.

At six foot-two, he was lanky and well- dressed. He came forward and, although he didn't appear nervous, read from a written statement.

"I have known Song since she began her college career in September 1991. She was younger than most freshman but very talented academically and musically. She played several instruments and was a trained vocalist as well.

"She got along with everyone and stood out as a potential professional musician. Song performed with a quartet the department used to recruit students for the following year. "Song taught piano to girls majoring in voice. Passing piano comps was a requirement to graduate with a major in music. She was an encouragement to her students and her band buddies. Band members bond as if they are a family in a large university.

"In the Fall of 1992, the changes in Song were noticeable. She began to miss classes, band practice, and music lessons set up for her students. None of us could make heads or tails of the dramatic difference in her behavior and attitude.

"It saddens me to see what has happened to Song. I am sorry I did not identify the seriousness of her condition and the fact she was using drugs. Although she is not my daughter, I would like to apologize to her parents for not protecting their daughter from this ugly fate."

When finished, Dr. Schuller folded his paper and placed in inside his suit jacket, looked up at the Judge, then turned, and giving a brief glance in Song's direction, returned quietly to his seat.

"Your honor, if it is acceptable to the Court, I have two more witnesses to call forward tomorrow," Chickalette said.

D.P. Tucker, wiped his brow with his handkerchief, took off his reading glasses, and nodded in agreement.

"Court is adjourned until 9:30 am tomorrow morning."

Angel was ushered out by the jail guards. Her testimony would proceed tomorrow. Song's former roommate would speak first, and then final statements would be made by Angel.

Following those testimonies, the Prosecutor, speaking on behalf of the State, and the Defense Attorney, speaking on behalf of the defendant, would provide recommendations for Song's sentencing at that time.

I called Bucky to see if by chance he might be on campus today. He answered his cell phone with a loud, friendly welcome.

"Hello There! To what do I owe this honor?" I was glad to hear his warm voice after such a downer of a day.

"Hi! I have an unexpected two-hour opening in my schedule, and wondered if you would like me to come over to the Student Union for coffee?"

"I have plenty of time for you, Rosie. Park in student lot A off Brown St. Come up the steps and I'll be there to greet you. Be careful, the steps may be slippery this time of year."

"That works for me. See you in about fifteen minutes." I was delighted and proceeded to the parking garage. The valet brought her car around for her. I tipped him my customary $5 and he walked away with a wave and a smile.

As planned, Bucky stood at the top of seventeen steps that I carefully climbed, huffing and puffing right up to the last step. We walked hand-in-hand, not more than a quarter of a mile, to the Student Union. Bucky led me to the Faculty dining room because he said it lent itself to more quiet, private conversations. We ordered coffee and pecan pie with whipped cream. The student server knew Bucky by name and, in turn, was introduced to me as one of his baseball players.

"There's no more time designated for recruitment trips. This year's pre-season has begun, so, be forewarned, I'll have my hands full every day now except Sunday."

"Are you happy about the fruits of your labors? And, does this mean we can sneak in mid-week dates now that you're not traveling?"

"I think my efforts will produce a great team next year, and I know we will be very competitive this Spring. The young man who just served us is an excellent pitcher and hitter too. And yes, being local all week, although very busy, will create more time for us together."

I studied his profile and liked his strong face, but gentle manner.

The time passed far too quickly for us both. Bucky suggested I come to his office in the fieldhouse. I said I would love to, but really needed to get back to my own office and retrieve Jocko.

"I'll take a raincheck, though, and promise to drop by soon."

I happily savored the moment of this stolen time together. We had also solidified a plan for the first segment of our weekend. Bucky had invited me to an early Friday evening "Meet-and-Greet" event at the banquet area of the Student Union.

"It'll be Good Friday and the parents will be picking up their sons for a long week-end break.," I remembered him saying. "It'll involve the current team members and their families. One of our ball players is a music major and is scheduled to bring three members of his band to play classic smooth oldies as the attendees mingle and enjoy light appetizers. I'll introduce each member of the team and he, in turn, will introduce his parents or guests.

"Once everyone is seated, a four-course meal will be served." he continued. "Following the main course, the captains of the team will speak about what the team means to them and their hopes for the season.

"We'll be sitting with the athletic director and his wife and my assistant coach and his wife. It's not a formal event, so dressing in business casual attire is just fine."

What I savored most of all was the way Bucky walked me all the way down the steps to my car, held my door open, and gently kissed me.

It would not be the last time.

TUESDAY MORNING - MARCH 29, 1994

CHAPTER 30

ANGEL'S TESTIMONY

The third-floor hallway of the Court house was filled with professional-looking people simply milling around. Angel's testimony was of interest to many people. Present were family members, friends of the victims and representatives of the press. No one was present on Angel's behalf.

Judge Tucker entered at precisely 9:30 am. Everyone stood until he motioned them to be seated. The Judge then asked if the defense was ready to proceed. Attorney Chickalette stood up from behind a large rectangular desk, adjusted his suit coat button closed, then answered in a loud, firm voice.

"Yes, your Honor. I call Beverly Stanley to step forward."

Beverly was dressed in black slacks and a crisp, white collared cotton blouse. She appeared to be in her early twenties with curly, brown hair above her collar, and green eyes. She carefully withdrew a piece of white, legal size paper from her purse as she approached.

"Good morning, your Honor," she said in a quiet

voice. "I was Song's roommate for a full school year, and also three months in the Fall of 1992."

"I was also a freshman majoring in music at that time. I remember Song as shy and reserved, and I was a boisterous majorette, I've been told," Beverly said. "We shared everything together when we settled into our rooms for the night. Neither of us dated nor pledged sororities. I couldn't have afforded that, and Song showed no interest in clubs, whatsoever.

"I went home to Cincinnati the summer following our freshman year. Our housing lease was paid annually so Song stayed in our dorm room and taught private music students. I don't know if she took any classes. She had at least two friends who did not live on campus or attend college, named April and Sam. There were times when all four of us would meet for pizza. Sometimes, they came to a home football game to see us perform in the band.

"The last year we roomed together, I returned in time for band camp, and I noticed Song appeared more interested in her off-campus friends and community-type activities than in school things. She mentioned a guy named 'James' who played in a band, but she didn't exactly say where. But, she did invite me to go to a jazz concert in the park. I couldn't go with her, though, because I was getting ready for my first day of Fall classes.

"That was the beginning of the end, in my opinion. When I did see her, she complained about feeling so restricted by band commitments. She seemed lethargic and not interested in her new classes. I was getting suspicious of the influence this guy, James and her friends seemed to have on her. But I had no power or right to approach her about that.

"I know she has only herself to blame for her decisions. But I am here to say what a marvelous roomie and person she was before falling in love with James. I feel sorry for the victims and their families. I feel sorry for Song's parents. I am, so very thankful, the gang did not choose to murder her. I will always love you, Song." She looked over at Song directly when she spoke those last words.

Looking around, a few visitors in the courtroom were wiping their eyes as Beverly proceeded to a seat in the back row. Dr. Schuller was seated beside her, and put his arm around her shoulders, giving her a gentle squeeze. The Lee family had moved up and were seated in the row behind their daughter, directly across the aisle from Dr. Rosie.

Then it was Angel's turn to be called to the stand. She was wearing street clothes that could best be described as neutral in color, both casual and modest. Her blouse had a collar with buttons down the center with a vest matching her trousers. The Bailiff instructed her to place her right hand on the Bible and swear to tell the truth, the whole truth, and nothing but the truth, "…so help you God." She answered affirmatively, then was advised to be seated.

"Good morning, Angel. Please state your full name for the record."

"My name is Angel Morgan."

"Are you here today on your own volition? In other words, no one has forced or coerced you?"

"If you're asking if someone made me come here, the answer is no."

"There has been no deal or arrangement whatsoever concerning your own sentencing, right? In other words, no one has offered you a deal in exchange for your testimony. Right?"

"I am just here to tell how I know Song, and what kind of person I think she is."

"Is Song testifying at your sentencing trial?"

"No. Not that I'm aware of."

"How do you know the defendant?"

"We met through some new friends of mine."

"New friends? How long had you known them?"

"I had just met them at the 7-11 store on the corner of Monroe and Bancroft. I was going to buy a bus ticket to Florida. They were really nice and asked me to stay overnight at their house."

"And did you?"

"Yes. I bought them some beer and donuts because they asked me to, then we walked a few blocks to their house."

"What were their names?"

"I only knew them as Sam and April."

"Did they say it was their house?"

"No. They really didn't say. When we got to it, I could tell it was an abandoned house. They slept in the basement to be out of the cold. I guess you could say they were homeless."

"What happened when you got to the house?"

"We crawled through a broken cellar window and put our stuff down. Then we went to meet their other friends who were in a garage behind the house by the alley."

"Who all were there?"

"There were two black men and an Asian girl. The men's names were Marcus and James and the girl's name was Song."

"Is Song in the Court room today?"

"Yes."

"Can you point her out?"

"Yes. She is sitting right there." Angel pointed toward Song who was sitting at the rectangular table vacated by her attorney. Attorney Chickalette was standing with his legal pad open as he addressed Angel sitting on the stand next to the judge.

"You and Song became part of a 'posse' or gang. Six people were murdered in six days. Can you tell us how the first murder occurred and the part you and Song played in it?"

"Marcus and James asked us to go for a joy ride. James was driving and Marcus was in the passenger seat. Four of us were huddled in the back. There was heat in the car, so it felt comfortable on a cold night. Suddenly, without saying a word, Marcus just rolled down the window and shot a kid getting out of a phone booth. We didn't even know he had a gun! He jumped out and stole the kid's Fila shoes right off his feet and his letter jacket. We all just couldn't believe it! Then he came back into the car.

"We drove onto the interstate, then, and headed over the state line into Michigan. About the five-mile marker, James turned the car around and drove back to the garage. He turned off the headlights in the alley and backed in. I don't know why"

"Did you ask him why he shot the kid?"
"Yes. He said he was wearing a rival high school letter jacket."

"How did you and Song feel at that point?"

"Song liked James, until then. But her attitude changed when she saw the evil he was capable of. At that point, the two of us and April were terrified. I don't know how Sam felt."

"How was the second victim chosen?"

"The two men said they needed more drug and gambling money. We all went for a ride this time through downtown streets just after businesses closed. A man was waiting for a bus. He was well-dressed and holding a briefcase. This time Marcus was driving and James unrolled the window. He just aimed at the guy and pulled the trigger. Then he jumped out and grabbed the briefcase and off we went. Again, we hit the interstate and crossed the state line. Then, again, they turned around at the five-mile exit and headed back to the garage. Same as before."

"Did the men find what they wanted?"

"Yes. They took money out of the briefcase and left to play poker. They took Sam with them and said they would front him some money."

"The three of us girls stayed in the house next door. It had power. The owners were just away for the winter."

"We turned on the TV and saw the news broadcast of the killing of the businessman. There were two witnesses. They didn't say who. I noticed two young people ducking down when James shot the guy. They might have been community college students."

"At Song's invitation, April and I slept there instead of in the cold, damp cellar."

"Why do you think Song invited you both?"

"I think she was afraid to stay there alone not knowing when the three guys would return and who they might bring with them.

"Three guys?"

"I told you Sam had gone with them. He didn't seem

to enjoy getting high or gambling. He probably didn't feel as if he had a choice, once they told him to come."

"When did you see them next?"

"April and I left at dawn and went back to the rancid basement. We didn't see them until they came over and banged on the door."

"Describe what happened next."

Angel repeated what she had told Dr. Klein about the assassination of her new friends. Her head hung down and she made no eye contact with anyone. There was a hush in the courtroom.

"Where was Song when the shooting of your friends took place?"

"She'd been ordered out of the car too. My back was turned. I guess she was just standing there."

"What happened after you got up from your knees?"

"Marcus and James just laughed. They shoved me from behind toward the car. Song and I got into the back seat and didn't make a sound"

"Is it true, you moved into the house with them?"

"Yes, they told me to get my things and move over there."

"Did Song sleep in the same room as James?"

"No. Actually I never saw Marcus or James sleeping anywhere. They were in the garage mostly at night."

"So, there was time for you girls to escape. Why didn't you?"

"We had nowhere to go that we wouldn't be found. We had no money, no purses, no nothing, but a few clothes. The toothbrushes we used belonged to the couple who owned the house. And after they killed our friends, the guys sort of hunkered down with us for a couple of days."

"How would you describe Song's attitude at that point?"

"She kept whispering how sorry she was to have made such serious mistakes, and to have put me in this terrible situation. She felt terrible about disappointing her parents and the dead people."

"What did you say to her?"

"I told her she couldn't have known. Drugs do terrible things to your judgment. We both met Sam and April in such innocent circumstances. The four of us could not have known Marcus' and James' intentions."

"Tell us about your roles in the convenience store burglary and murder."

"The men again were in the front seat. They pulled into the parking lot and said they would be right back. We thought they were going to buy some Thunderbird wine or Non-filter Lucky Strikes. They didn't ask us if we wanted or needed anything. We saw one clerk inside."

"What were you girls talking about while they were in the store?"

"Basically, Song could barely choke back tears, so we weren't talking at all."

"So, then what happened?"

"Marcus and James came running back to the car. And off we sped toward the state line again. Five miles over the line, an exit, and a return to the highway coming south."

"What did the men say during all that time? Did they have wine and cigarettes?"

"I didn't notice. I don't remember them getting anything out of the car. They backed it into the garage and told us to make them something to eat at the house. There really wasn't much there to fix. Song's check from her parents hadn't arrived yet."

"Tell us how Song got money from home."

"She had a mailbox at the University, and they mailed her money twice a month, I guess."

"Had you ever been to the mailbox with her?"

"That afternoon they made us all go there for her to check. They were really upset the money hadn't come yet. That's what caused them to decide to rob the store."

"By the way, did they wear masks?"

"Not that I am aware of."

"They never intended to leave any witnesses alive, did they?"

"I never heard them talk about that. Song and I never knew ahead of time that they would rob anyone, let alone kill them."

"Tell us how the final murder came about, please."

"James had noticed a man talking to Song when she checked her mailbox again on Wednesday. He asked her who the guy was. She said his name was Mr. Brooks and he worked at the bookstore. Then, because James asked, she described how the man told her he might have a job for her and handed James his card. James and Marcus talked, then told Song to invite Mr. Brooks over on Christmas Eve."

"Go on."

"Mr. Brooks agreed to come over. We were instructed to lure him upstairs to the bedroom, which we did. We thought maybe they would rob him. Marcus and James were hidden in the closet. They came out with a gun pointed and strapped him to the headboard with electrical cords. They told us to grab our stuff and go to Mr. Brooks' car. As we closed the front door, we heard the shots. We knew he was dead."

"What on earth were you thinking?"

"I was thinking 'When will this nightmare end?' I don't really know what Song thought. We looked at each other and actually held hands in the back seat as the guys drove off."

"Soon after, all four of you were apprehended by the State Highway Patrol. Is that right?"

"Yes, Sir."

"How did you girls feel when the cops pulled you over?"

"Actually, I felt relieved the nightmare was over, and no one else would be killed."

"Was there any conversation between you and Song at that point?"

"Once the cops ordered Marcus, and then James, out of the car, Song and I squeezed hands quickly, then we were separated by two more officers."

Attorney Chickalette thanked Angel for her willingness to testify and told her she could step down. She took a deep breath and returned to her seat in the second row. At that point, a recess was called by Judge Tucker until 11 am. The final witness, Song Lee, would be speaking to the families of the victims and the Judge.

At precisely 11 am, Court was reconvened by the Bailiff. Attorney Chickalette requested permission for the defendant, Song Lee, to address the courtroom. Judge Tucker nodded his head forward as approval. Song approached the podium with her hands free, but her feet shackled. It was not noticeable through her, navy bell bottom trousers. She unfolded a piece of yellow legal paper and cleared her throat to begin.

"I am very sorry, your Honor, for the victims and their families," She said, "If I could trade my life for theirs, I would do so. I also apologize to my parents and all the people who have supported me through my life's journey. I am not making any excuses for my inexcusable choice of friends and unforgiveable conduct."

Song then addressed the Judge.

"I am ready to accept the responsibility for my actions and inactions. My inactions initially resulted from selfish desires for a relationship, and later, fear for my own life."

She fought back tears. "I failed to anticipate the dire consequences and suffering of so many victims," Song confessed. "I am very sorry for my deliberate actions to invite Mr. Brooks to the house. I should have, in fact, recognized the danger. I can't forgive myself and I definitely don't expect the families and their friends to ever forgive me."

Song, then, thanked the Judge for his time and tearfully returned to her seat beside her attorney.

"If there are no other witnesses to be heard, Counselor, the defendant should return to this courtroom to be sentenced next Tuesday, April 5, at 1:30 pm."

Court was dismissed with the sound of his gavel.

Dr. Rosie decided to check her mail at the downtown office and have a quiet lunch at the top of the building. She did not invite anyone to join her, electing to carve out some time to settle her mind and her emotions. She ordered mushroom brie soup and water with lemon. It was early enough that the dining room was nearly empty. Then, she began reviewing all notes she had taken the past two days. She felt real compassion for the parents whose children preceded them in death, not the natural course of life. It's natural to assume children will plan their parents' funerals, not the opposite.

Angel's testimony was compelling and certainly did not characterize Song as an evil, drug-crazed killer. Although the victims' families and friends certainly evoked much empathy from all present, it appeared that both Angel and Song were also victims as well. The difference, of course, was that they had choices along the way and made poor decisions.

Dr. Rosie wished Bucky could have been in the Courtroom with her since it was an open hearing, and because it is nearly impossible to describe the proceedings to someone who is not present. It is like viewing an extraordinary sunset over a body of water, and attempting to depict the beauty of it to an absent friend. She looked forward to being with him on Friday.

Beckoning to her server to bring her usual cup of freshly brewed chicory-flavored coffee, she waited with many thoughts going through her head. She decided to walk to the county jail to check on Angel's mental state hoping she would be willing to converse. Of interest would be how she felt after testifying about the horrendous happenings of that week. She wondered if Angel slept without nightmares, thinking, "Recapping them could easily bring them on."

When Rosie arrived at the jail, Angel had not been transported to her unit yet. She was seated in the interview room with a lunch tray of tomato soup (not bisque) and grilled cheese. Her head was bowed, and she showed no indication of wanting to taste her soup or take a bite of the sandwich.

As Rosie entered, Angel looked up with tears in her eyes. She spoke without being questioned. "I can't believe all the hell those parents must have gone through."

"You didn't hear them speak at Marcus' or James' sentencing hearings? asked Dr. Rosie.

"I was not invited to attend those hearings. I only testified at their trial. They decided to be tried together in front of three Judges. They really didn't have another hearing, I don't think. The Judges conferred for several hours, ruled them guilty and imposed the sentences the following day."

"When you testified, did the defense attorneys cross examine you?"

"Yes. One was a little harsh, the other I remember as almost apologetic."

"How do you feel about their sentences?"

"I don't know. Basically I feel numb. I wonder why one of them got the Death penalty and the other got Life. If I get life, it's the same sentence as James and I never shot anyone. It seems I should have a lesser sentence, particularly since I cooperated. Not that I don't deserve Life in prison, but it seems strange that James will share the same fate."

"I understand," Rosie said.

"Song never held a gun either. I think she was just eighteen when this all came down. She started college early. Super smart and talented girl, ya' know. Come to think of it,

James wasn't even eighteen yet. Maybe that is why he got Life without parole instead of the Death penalty."

"Well, Angel, your childhood struggles, abuse and so on, should factor into your sentencing. If you think of more details you would like to share with me, it would be helpful."

"Some memories are too painful. I was abused in JDC a couple of times too. Sexually, by someone I thought I could trust."

"I am so sorry to hear that. Can we talk more about that?"

"There was a janitor who worked there for about a year. He mopped the kitchen and dining area at night. We were permitted to buy candy and soda from the canteen when we earned a little money. My chores included putting clean silverware away after the dishes came out of the dishwasher. I stacked the plates for breakfast which was cafeteria style.

"The janitor's name was Chester Clark. He was white, short, fat and wore a green apron over his jeans. I remember he wore slip-resistant black shoes. Chester would strike-up conversations with me and seemed interested in my situation. One night he shoved me into a broom closet and took advantage of me. When he released me, he handed me a Snickers bar and a Coke he had in his apron pocket. I swore I would never go back there on nights of his shifts. But one night, he swapped with Kristy who was a nice lady. My friend, Ellen, and I snuck down to get a Coke and a bag of chips. Chester saw us, and Ellen ran. He grabbed me by the back of my neck and there we were…off to the races, or should I say the broom closet, again."

"Oh, Angel. I am so sorry. I have several questions. Did you tell Ellen?"

"Yes. I did. He threatened me not to tell, but I figured if I didn't tell other employees, that didn't mean Ellen. I needed to tell her so she would never get abused by him. I would have hated that. She was a virgin as far as I knew."

"Did he get fired?"

"He did leave very suddenly. They never said if he quit or was fired. After that, Kristy seemed extra nice to me when I did chores on her shifts."

"I need to be leaving now, but I'll be back on Friday. Are you okay?"

"I'll be here, Dr. Rosie. You're the first person I've told about Chester. But being in JDC was truly less dangerous than being at home under my mom's supervision. Chester was the only one who abused me in all the five years I spent at Juvie. I think Kristy may have guessed, but I never told her details. I always wondered if Ellen told an adult what I said, but I never asked, and she didn't offer any info."

Feeling it was enough for the day, Rosie drew the interview to a close and made plans for the next time they would talk before saying good-bye.

She left and walked swiftly to the parking garage. Looking into her wallet, she only found a twenty and thought the attendant would jump out of his shoes when she handed it to him, saying, "Keep the change and have a great week."

She couldn't wait to get home and begin looking into this new tragic episode of Angel's life.

LATE TUESDAY AFTERNOON - MARCH 29, 1994

CHAPTER 31

CHESTER WHO

Dr. Rosie's trusty companion was waiting in the foyer as she entered her condo. Patting the top of Jocko's head, she put her briefcase and shoulder bag on the entryway table before retrieving her phone from her purse. Then, attaching Jocko to his bright red leash, headed out the door again since he was eager to get outside. As they walked around the complex, she put in a call to her investigative reporter friend, Wes.

"You aren't going to believe this, Wes."

"Nothing you say ever comes as a surprise to me, Rosie. Been in the business too long, as have you."

She told Wes the story Angel had just shared and asked him to locate Kristy Delaney to discover what she knew about Chester. She also hoped he could find Ellen Prince to confirm the story which would help Angel's situation. Wes thought it all sounded likely to have happened. He also commented that he didn't think Angel would have made up the broom closet scenario.

"I'll start by checking out a list of area sex offenders," he told her.

"Maybe I should call Paulette Hunter at the Juvenile Detention Center," she said. "They had established a relationship, and it seems feasible that Officer Hunter could shed some light on this situation."

"Yeah, I'd appreciate if you would, Rosie. By the way, maybe we could have lunch on Thursday. That will give me all of Wednesday to pursue leads, and let you know what I find."

"Sounds like a plan," Rosie said before they finished their call. Later, Rosie looked in her appointment book and found Officer Hunter's phone number. She called, expecting to get a message machine, but Paulette Hunter, herself, picked up the phone.

"Hi, Paulette This is Rosie Klein. Do you have a few minutes to talk?"

"Oh, hello.! Yes, I'm between staff meetings. To what do I owe this pleasure?"

Dr. Rosie explained she was looking for information on a man named "Chester" who worked in Housekeeping when Angel was at the institution. She needed his complete name and the reason he left the job.

"His last name was Clark, and he was fired for falsifying information on his application. They hadn't required a background check at the time of his hiring because he said he just completed a tour of duty in the Marines, and he passed a drug test.

"Angel's story is probably correct, then," Officer Hunter continued, "Except for the length of time he was here before getting caught. After he completed his three-month probationary period, our office did find that he was listed as a sex offender. His parole included the stipulation that he not be near or employed by any place where minors gathered. Obviously, that would include a residential juvenile detention center," said Hunter. "When it was discovered, he was immediately let go."

Dr. Rosie asked if she might have contact information on Ellen Prince. Officer Hunter indicated she would look and get back to Rosie first thing in the morning.

Rosie continued walking with Jocko until they again reached her condo door. Unlocking the front door, she released Jocko from his leash and watched him bound into the living room.

"Animals sure do enjoy the simple things in life," she smiled. Seeing that Jocko had run to his water dish, she realized the walk had made her thirsty, too.

WEDNESDAY MORNING - MARCH 30, 1994

CHAPTER 32

CATCH HIM IF YOU CAN

Rosie arrived at her Summerhill office at 8:45 am. Jocko simply loved Wednesdays and seeing Ruth. She always had a treat waiting for him along with a pot of coffee for his mistress, Rosie. Sure enough, there were bagels, coffee, and chocolate crème cheese sitting on the coffee table in Rosie's office.

"Hey, there! Good to see you Ruth, it's been a busy few days," Rosie called out. She began filling Ruth in on the developments of the past couple days. The phone rang loudly, calling Ruth away in the middle of her story. It was Wes confirming lunch at Bob Evans. He was a breakfast kind of guy and knew Bob's offered Eggs Benedict all day long.

"It was pretty easy to track Kristy Delaney down," Wes said. "She still works three shifts a week at the JDC. I'm fairly certain I'll have information about Chester's whereabouts and Ellen's, too, by lunchtime."

"You're terrific, Wes, I really appreciate your focus on this. I'll see you at noon. I've got a few details to fill you in about too."

No sooner did she hang up the phone, than another call came through. It was Paulette Hunter. Officer Hunter said Ellen Prince was living with a family in Rossfield, employed as an Au Pair and attending Bowling Green. She had taken the liberty of calling Ellen and asking if they could speak with her about Angel.

"I was happily surprised when she agreed to meet us. She's waiting to hear where and when we want to see her. She prefers evenings when the family won't require her services and she has no classes. That's suits me, too."

"Does this Thursday evening work for you? I'm offering to drive."

"Sounds great," Officer Hunter agreed. "We can meet after my shift at the JDC. I'll be standing outside at six on whichever night you pick. That way, you won't have to park your car downtown. Then we can head over to her house."

At noon, Wes had a booth waiting for them when Rosie arrived at Bob Evans. She had imbibed so much coffee already, she felt like floating away. So, for lunch, ordered her standby, water with lemon. Unlike Wes, Rosie ordered a grilled chicken, cranberry and pecan salad. He commenced to tell her what he found out about Chester Clark and Kristy Delaney.

"Chester is back in prison for parole violation. Not only did he falsify information to work in the Juvenile facility, he was working at a daycare from noon till six when they found out, and living in an apartment across from an elementary school. Three violations! Before all this, he served ten years for sexual assault of a teen-aged step-daughter and a nine-year old neighbor boy.

"Kristy Delaney still works at the JDC but has been promoted. Now, she's a line cook and the young women love her. She did find out about Chester's broom closet antics. It was after he was fired and presumably back in prison. The information did not come from Ellen. It came from a tearful, younger girl who couldn't hold back the story. Similar MO as with Angel except this little girl didn't work in Chester's area. She was simply lured there by his offer of candy and soda. During her one incident, she was able to get away from him, so it wasn't rape, but it was assault. The child was recently released to a foster family. I don't think there is reason to drag her into this mess. Do you?"

Rosie then told him exactly what Angel had shared with her. After discussing all angles of the case, they finished lunch and parted ways.

Rosie headed back to the office to fetch Jocko and return long overdue calls. She filled Ruth in on everything that happened over the past few days. Ruth said she and her husband knew George Emmanuel. They would stop in his bar after the Mud Hen games and have a beer and a Greek meatball sandwich. That beat the price and quality of baseball concession food.

"George is a tender hearted, old guy who just lost his wife, Katie, after fifty-two years of marriage. He never allowed her into the bar, said it was too rough an atmosphere for her."

"Really?"

"Yup. The merchant marines would come in when their ship was docked on the river. A burlesque place was three doors down the street."

"Oh, my goodness. I know that corner," Rosie said.

"Yeah, the Emmanuels also had a cute, dark eyed, little girl with long braids," Ruth said. "Her name was Petra and she would skip into the bar after Greek school on Friday night. The day partner would give her a ride home after his shift because George worked nights. The last I heard, she finished a Ph.D. in Spanish and works in a Christian half-way house for guys who served time for alcohol or drug charges."

"I'll bet the guys are mostly Latino."

"Yup. Some are from Puerto Rico. Petra moved in

with George to help him grieve after Katie passed."

Later in the day, Rosie told Ruth she was leaving to drive Jocko home, then meet Officer Paulette Hunter at the JDC at six. When she explained the purpose of the meeting, Ruth offered to take Jocko home, but Rosie said she would do it since he needed her attention for a little while.

Dr. Rosie pulled up to the JDC just as Officer Hunter was exiting. They greeted each other, agreed to go by first names, Rosie and Paulette, then headed over to Ellen's house.

"What exactly is your interest in her?" Paulette asked Rosie as they started to drive.

"I'd like verification of Angel's assault by Chester on two separate occasions. I would also like to know what kind of a young woman Angel was."

"You're right to track her down. I can tell you how Angel came across, but it may not reflect her true feelings and attitude. She may have known how to 'play the game', so to speak."

"I don't expect to keep Ellen long. Do you have time for dinner?"

"Actually, I'm famished. An officer called off, and I didn't get a lunch break this afternoon".

"Are you married, Paulette?"

"Divorced. No kids. Didn't heed the red flags. Oh well, not much harm done other than my bank account. You?"

"Widowed. Two kids, college age. Just met a very kind, gentleman. Baseball coach at University of Toledo. He's widowed, too. We were introduced by his best friend, Judge Lincoln."

"Oh. I've heard about Judge Charlie. Word has it, he's

the most eligible bachelor in town.

How about an introduction, Rosie? A double-date, perhaps?" she smiled, but Rosie thought there might be some seriousness in the request, too.

They approached the house where Ellen lived; porch light on, curtains drawn back.

"Apparently the adults are University professors and have two little girls who need supervision before and after school," Paulette said.

The two women walked to the front door, and Paulette rang the doorbell. A young woman, medium tall with short brown hair, opened the door wide, nodded and smiled. She identified herself as Ellen.

"I remember you, Officer Hunter." She smiled. "The family has gone out to dinner and I'm able to invite you in." She took both women's coats and hung them in a small closet.

Dr. Rosie and Officer Hunter sat on the sofa, while Ellen sat across from them in a recliner. Paulette proceeded to lead the discussion. She asked Ellen what she remembered about Chester Clark some years ago.

"I remember he was a big old, fat, white guy who cleaned the floors and tables in the dining area. I didn't much care for him, but never really knew him, either."

"We primarily want to know how you feel about Angel, and if you can describe your relationship?"

"Angel took me under her wing. I was three years younger, scared, but smarter, if you don't mind me saying so. I could understand a lot of what was going on."

"Why were you locked up, Ellen?", asked Dr. Rosie.

"For shoplifting. Can you believe it? We were living

in the United States while my dad completed his Ph.D. in Political Science. We're from Vienna, Austria. I got in with the wrong kids at my school and wanted to be accepted. So, we would hang out and go do things for 'fun'. That's typical for a fifteen-year old girl, right?

"My parents tried to help me but had to return home because time on their visas ran out. By then, I was in juvie and couldn't go with them. So, they left me here and returned to Austria. That's where they live now. I know they've forgiven me for my mistakes. It was actually my dad that got me this job with the Donovan family."

"Can you tell us more about the incident with Angel?" Officer Hunter asked.

"No one liked this Chester guy. When Kristy worked, she played pop music and gave us soda and brought us cookies from home."

"Nice," Rosie said.

"It seemed like Angel got stuck working more when Chester was on duty. One night, he chased us, and I ran. A little later Angel came back with her shirt ripped in the front. When I asked her about it, she said Chester had grabbed her for dropping the mop on his foot. But once we were alone, she confessed he had shoved her into the broom closet and forced her to have sex with him. She said it happened once before and wanted to be sure he didn't catch me. She was really upset the last time and said she thought he was going to choke her to death. She made me promise, on my honor, not to tell anyone."

"Did Angel get along with the other young women?" Officer Hunter asked.

"Absolutely! We called her our 'Defender'. She was bigger and stronger than most of us girls. The older ones understood not to bully us or call us names. I guess you might say she got along best with the younger girls. I really believe she gave herself up to Chester just to protect me."

"Did you hear about the murders Angel was involved in Officer Hunter?"

"I couldn't help but hear about them. When I saw her picture, I couldn't believe it was really her. I was so sorry I never returned to visit her once I was released from JDC. Maybe it might have made a difference in her future. From talking with her, I knew she had nowhere to go when she got out. I don't know what else to tell you."

"Well, you've been extremely helpful, Ellen, thank you very much. Here is my card," said Dr. Rosie. "If you think of anything else that might be important for Angel's case, please give me a call."

Ellen took the card from her hand and asked her to please say "Hi" to Angel for her.

"Be sure to speak to Kristy, too. She'll tell you what a good, hard worker Angel was in the kitchen and dining room whenever it was her turn.

Paulette and Rosie agreed to swing by the JDC and get Paulette's car, then meet for a burger at Johnny Rocket's and compare thoughts about the interview with Ellen. Rosie also wanted to get home early enough to chat with Bucky about the Friday Meet-and-Greet event. More and more lately, he wasn't far from her mind.

Sure enough, there was a message on Rosie's answering machine. She returned his call thinking she would just discuss details about their date. But he had more on his mind.

"I've been thinking, Rosie. I'll be going to my church's Good Friday service at three o'clock on Friday. The service is held at that time to honor the hours Christ suffered on the cross. I'd really like to have you with me. Care to go? Then we can go from there to the Meet-and-Greet. I need to be there a little early to help place name tags on the tables."

"I'd love to go with you, Bucky. I'm honored that you asked. That time is special to me as well. On another topic, I've had quite a day. How has your day been?"

"Mine was just fine, but I thought of you and wondered what might be happening with your case."

"We'll have plenty of time to talk about my entire week, if you're interested. Right now, I'm exhausted mentally and physically."

"I understand. I'll pick you up at two-thirty on Friday, okay?"

"Wonderful! I'm really looking forward to seeing you." Rosie smiled to herself when she put down the receiver. Being with Bucky brightened everything.

GOOD FRIDAY - APRIL 1, 1994

CHAPTER 33

MEET AND GREET

As Friday afternoon approached, I began to speculate whether the baseball player who was a music major in school might know Song. He would have been a Junior when she was a Sophomore. While she played a brass instrument, he played a string, upright bass.

I vowed to ask Bucky if it would be appropriate to ask him about knowing Song, and if so, at what point in the evening. Then, I decided to put all thoughts of this trial and Angel out of my mind. It would be the first weekend I was not scheduling time to review materials or connect with professionals related to the case.

Bucky picked me up at the agreed upon time and gave Jocko a scratch behind his ears with a pat on his head. As we drove to church, I asked him about the appropriateness of asking the ballplayer if he knew Song.

"His name is Sean Simmons and he's one of my Senior captains. It's fine for you to ask him; maybe he'll remember her", Bucky said.

Once again, we met Judge Lincoln and Darlene at the doors of the church. This time they were handing out programs and greeting worshippers entering the vestibule. Many people were dressed in costumes depicting the attire of the early Christians. The service depicted the last supper of Christ with his disciples, the arrest of Christ in the garden of Gethsemane, the betrayal by Judas, the suffering and crucifixion. It also showed the anguish of those who knew and loved him, and the burial in the tomb behind the stone.

Rain began to fall as everyone exited the church. We said good- bye to friends and headed toward The University's Student-Union.

"It almost always rains this time of day on Good Friday. Have you ever noticed?", Bucky asked.

"I can't honestly say I have, Bucky."

"It's not the end of the story, you know. Wait till you see the celebration on Sunday. That is, if you would like to accompany me."

"I can't wait," I replied, feeling happy that he was continuing to include me in the parts of his life that obviously held real meaning to him.

Inside the Student Union's cafeteria, the tablecloths were dark-blue, and napkins were gold representing school colors. The combo musicians were setting up instruments and wore shirts in school colors. Bucky escorted me over to introduce me to Sean Simmons, his musician ballplayer. Sean shook Coach Bucky's hand and bowed slightly as he shook mine. Then, Bucky asked to be excused, politely wanting to give us some privacy, saying he was needed to set up name tags on the welcome tables.

"Where are you from, Sean?"

"Actually, I graduated from Sylvania High School. I wanted to play ball locally so my parents could see the games. They sacrificed so much to help develop me into the player that I am, it seemed like the least I could do to repay them."

"That shows me they raised a fine, grateful young man. They must be very proud of you. Will they be here this evening?"

"They should be arriving any minute. Both are employed by the Sylvania Fire Department. My dad is a Captain and my mom is an EMT. They work a twenty-four hour on/forty-eight hour off schedule. It's kinda crazy. On her days off, my mom is a substitute teacher and my dad plays guitar in a band at Fairway Christian Church. Oh, and I sing and strum along with him."

"Wow. Thanks for sharing. Sounds like great family bonding." Then, I decided to ask the question uppermost in my mind.

"I wonder if you recall Song Lee, a music major and band member here?"

"I remember her very well. As a cute little Asian girl, she stood out immediately. I can't believe what happened to her," he seemed genuinely concerned as he spoke. "Both newspaper and television reports portrayed her as a violent, calculating killer. Number one, she doesn't seem to have a violent bone in her body to me. Number two, if she's calculating anything it's the timing of her steps to the beat of the rhythm."

"Her demeanor in the Courtroom was very poised and respectful," I added. "I assume she is dedicated to her parents and is extremely remorseful for disappointing them."

"Oh. There is one last thing," Sean said. "I knew Mr. Brooks too. Song would never have deliberately harmed him. His poor mother is left alone now. Music students used to see him pushing her on campus in her wheelchair. We all feel really bad about what's happened."

"Thanks for talking with me about it," I said. "Enjoy your evening, Sean, and best of luck for your season."

Bucky and my eyes met across the room. I walked over to join him at our designated table. Another couple arrived and Bucky's eyes were diverted to them. It was his assistant coach, Luke Matthews, and wife, Julie. She's a professional tennis instructor whom I recognized immediately since I had taken some drill classes from her at Toledo Indoor in the past.

In their early forties, the Matthews had three small children at home. Luke and Julie met at Ohio University where they were both physical education majors. Bucky was a graduate assistant there and had brought Luke on board when he received his appointment as head baseball coach at Toledo.

I found it interesting that Bucky had also met John Lazarus at Ohio University.

Ohio University certainly breeds successful men, she thought looking around the table of interesting people.

The Athletic Director, John Lazarus and his wife, Martha, joined us at our table. Bucky introduced me and described me as a "murder doctor". Everyone laughed, then he explained that I was participating in the Angel Morgan/ Song Lee cases.

Abruptly, the laughter ceased. Every citizen within forty miles of Toledo remembered exactly who the six gang members were, and the names of all their victims.

Then the questions began.

"How in the world do you do it, going into jail and deciphering the truth from the lies?" John asked.

"Martha used to be a magistrate for my friend, Judge Lincoln", Bucky interjected.

"It was hard enough separating the sad, sometimes ugly, divorces I dealt with from my family life. I can't imagine hearing murder testimonies all day, let alone viewing remains of corpses. I think I could remain objective, but I certainly would not be very joyful for John to come home to." Martha explained.

"It's definitely a challenge, Martha," I agreed.

Salads arrived and dressing and rolls were passed around the table. The combo began playing soft elevator music, mostly to please the parents of the players.

I turned to Julie and identified myself as one of hundreds of tennis students Julie had taught.

"I don't expect you to remember me. I was in one of this winter's 3.5 doubles groups and the 4.0 singles. Once the snow subsided, I returned to simply running and walking my dog, Jocko, but I certainly enjoyed your instruction."

"You do look familiar. I thought it might be from seeing you on the local news stations. Now that you mention it, Rosie, I recall observing your great ground stroke placement. Have you ever been involved in sports psychology?"

"Yes, I worked with a professional indoor soccer team and taught visualization to the offense and goalies."

"Neat. What did you have them envision?"

"I would suggest they see the net as wider for the offense and ask the goalies to see the ball as larger. It was intended to build confidence."

By now, the athletic director and coaches were listening to our conversation.

"Have you worked with athletes in individual sports," Julie asked.

"Yes, in tennis, bowling and golf. I made it my teaching method to emphasize self-talk after observing what physical and mental habits they displayed. Then, I would link words to their habits. For example, if the player was struggling with the serve, I might have the player say 'get the toss up' before each serve. Have you noticed MacEnroe's mannerisms before his serves?"

"Yes, now that you mention it," Julie said.

"Well, if a golfer was swinging too quickly or not following through, I would say to think 'slower and finish' before the golfer set up to take a shot.

"Once I worked with a professional golfer who asked me why he could sink a six- foot putt for par but would miss it for a birdie. My answer was a challenge to him which he didn't take well. I said, 'You don't see yourself as a winner, and you sure don't want to be a loser. It takes birdie golf to win a tournament. A par avoids a bogey commonly known as the kiss of death.'"

Everyone laughed.

What a great audience for these examples, I thought. At that point, the main course of chicken, rice, and broccoli was served, and conversation turned to food, the team, and everyone's hopes for the season.

"I'd like to announce something I think rather important, " John said. "At least it is to my family and me." This got everyone's attention.

"I'm retiring at the end of this school year, and I'm recommending Bucky as Athletic Director in my place. That is, Bucky, if you are interested in assuming that position?"

Bucky looked at me with obvious surprise. He'd never said anything about being dissatisfied as Head Baseball Coach. With his natural enthusiasm, I knew he felt strong bonds to his players.

John looked at Bucky in anticipation of some response. No one broke the silence until Bucky finally spoke.

"I'm honored you have such confidence in my leadership ability. The role of Athletic Director requires leadership and administrative abilities. If this appointment were to go forward, then I will recommend that Luke become Head Baseball Coach. I have all the confidence in the world in his abilities and dedication to our young men."

"Well, Luke. What's your position in all this?" John said.

"On behalf of the team, I can say we would miss Coach Walker tremendously," Luke said looking directly at Bucky with deep sincerity.

"Thank you very much, Luke. Being head coach has not been a popularity contest and I'm grateful that's how you feel," Bucky responded.

"If you accept the promotion, Luke, it will definitely be better for the guys." John said."If it's okay with you John, I suggest the three of us meet in the morning and take a look at all these possibilities," Bucky said.

"I'm for that one hundred percent, but I'm still announcing my retirement this evening."

Someone caught Bucky's attention from a corner of the room to indicate that it was time for him to begin the introductions of the team and parents. After opening remarks, he called up his Captain, Sean Simmons, first. Sean was handed the microphone and proceeded to introduce himself and his parents.

On behalf of the team, Sean thanked the Athletic Director, Head Coach and Assistant Coach for their time and commitment. The rest of the Meet and Greet involved each player standing in his place. stating his name, year, position, his parents and their hometown. Applause of appreciation thundered through the room after each one.

Then, Coach Walker stepped to the microphone and asked John to say a few words. His words were heartfelt and appreciated by the audience. But, when John announced his intention to retire at the end of the year and to recommend Coach Walker to succeed him, the players didn't know whether to clap and congratulate their coach or weep silently in their seats.

An awkward silence followed until Sean Simmons initiated a round of applause. No one mentioned who would be named head coach, but many of the guys whispered among themselves betting it would be Luke as the logical choice.

On our way home, I looked over at Bucky's profile and admired his strength.

"How do you think the event went, Bucky?"

"Better than I could have expected. How do you feel about it and the people you met?"

"I can't get over the fact of how small a world we live in. How many times have we been now with people either from our pasts, or with whom we share a lot in common?"

"For example, Rosie?"

"Well, the way we met, for one. I've worked professionally with your best friend, Judge Lincoln for a long time. Yet you knew him, too, before we met."

"True," Bucky responded.

"Then I unknowingly placed Wes, a softball player, at our table at the blind auction. You had things in common to discuss."

"True, and he was very interesting."

"Then, tonight," I continued, "We sat at the table and I recognized your Assistant Coach's wife as someone who I played tennis with at an indoor facility. Who could have imagined we would be connected in the future?"

"Well, you definitely make a good point, Rosie. How about a quick nightcap at Alfie's for old times' sake?"

"Only if drinks are on me." I cheerfully responded.

"You drive a hard bargain, girl."

Before dawn on Easter morning, Bucky pulled up in front of my door. He had told me to dress casually because it was going to be an outdoor, amphitheater type service at a Methodist campground. I wore shoe-boots, black jeans with sequins on the back pockets, a jean jacket and a turtleneck sweater. Jocko looked mournfully at the two people he loved, wondering why he wasn't included.

Bucky saw his mournful look and it occurred to him we could take Jocko along. Jocko was delighted to be included. Once we were seated on wooden benches, he obediently laid in the aisle beside me and never made a sound. Watching Jocko's quiet manner, triggered a thought. My mind went back to the nineteen days of my husband 's hospitalization a few years back.

At the time, I couldn't understand why God hadn't answered my prayers in the manner I desired. Not only didn't my husband regain consciousness from the coma, but quite the opposite, he passed away. Continuing to reminisce,I I thought of how Bucky had entered my life and how I was feeling happiness again. It made me realize God's plan for my life was still unfolding

Jesus is alive and dwells in me, I thought.

At my suggestion, we picked up Chinese food and headed to Stoney Creek State Park. Sitting at a picnic table on the bank of the creek, we shared sweet 'n sour pork, pepper steak, vegetable egg rolls, and fried rice. The climax to the meal was opening the mystery fortune cookies.

"This year will bring blessings beyond your wildest dreams," mine read.

"Look no further, your future is brightening in front of your very eyes,"Bucky's fortune read. We laughed together. Jocko made sure there were no leftovers.

"Have you hiked here before, Rosie?"

"Not for a long, long time. It's very serene, and I've always loved the sounds of a babbling brook. So, let's do it."

With Jocko busily sniffing everywhere, we hiked across a narrow bridge. A small sign nailed to a tree had an arrow pointing to the left, saying, "One Mile". We followed the trail along the creek and were surprised to end at the parking lot where Bucky's vehicle was parked.

Arriving back at my condo, we kissed good night, and I entered the door feeling happier than I could remember in a long time. I begged off doing anything the remainder of the day, yet felt the need to call my family and wish them a Happy Easter. Even before that, however, I felt a need to take a nap, given that we had gotten up at the break of dawn for the morning service.

The phone rang and I opened my eyes to accept the call. It was my son, Christopher, calling from Florida to wish me a Happy Easter. He and his wife, Bridgette, and their two children were spending Spring break at Ormond Beach. My deceased husband and I owned a three -bedroom condo there and I had happily gifted the week to Christopher and his family since I didn't want to go there alone with all my past memories.

"How's the weather down there, Chris?"

"Just great, Mom. Josh and Beth have collected shells on the beach and plan to make jewelry to sell to their friends. Bridgette and I have been just chilling and the kids, well you know. They're just like energizer bunnies.. Can't thank you enough for offering to let us stay here."

"My pleasure. I'm swamped up here with a murder

case that's finally coming to an end." We talked for awhile.

"Okay mom. Got to take this tray of lemonade out to the pool. Everyone is waiting. Love you."

"Love you too. Tell the clan, Yaya loves them."

I decided to watch the final round of the PGA golf tournament and anticipate a call from my second son, Stephen. California time always posed a challenge as far as communication goes.

At 7 pm the phone rang.

"Is this a good time to chat, Mom?"

"Yes, of course. Any time you call is an exceptionally, good time to chat."

"The boys are down for a late afternoon nap. It has been a hectic weekend with the annual Easter Egg hunt in Sausalito yesterday. How's your weekend been? Is Jocko still alive and kicking?"

"Jocko has a new friend. He's the baseball coach at the University of Toledo, and they are attached at the hip. I should say 'at the leash'. Ha."

"And how exactly might Jocko have come to obtain this new friend, Mom?"

"Can't fool you, can I, son? He's my new friend and I hope you and Faith can meet him soon."

"Well, don't take this relationship too seriously, too quickly. Learn by example like your son, Stephen. You've always applauded me for not being a trial-and-error kind of kid."

"Nothing to worry about. We're becoming fast friends and have been introducing one another to different ways we each like to spend time. He's never been to any Pops performances until recently. Now he likes them."

"Did you tell him I'm a musician and a professor out here in California?"

"Why of course, Stephen, that was the first thing out of my mouth. When might you guys be coming back to Ohio? Do you plan to attend your class reunion this summer?"

"Too soon to tell. Depends on the kids' activities and summer camps. I'll let you know. Is there still room in your condo for the four of us?"

"If you're hinting about whether Bucky stays here with me, the answer is 'no', he doesn't. So, if you want to stay here yourselves, the answer is 'yes' with a capital Y."

"Can't get anything by you, Mom, can I? Well, got to go. We can talk soon, okay?"

"Absolutely. Love you guys."

"Love you too."

MONDAY MORNING - APRIL 4, 1994

CHAPTER 34

ADRIAN COLLEGE REVISITED

Bright and early Monday morning, Rosie coaxed Jocko into the backseat of her car and headed for Adrian, Michigan. March had gone out like a lamb with daffodils and tulips springing up in many places. She figured her interview with Joel Baker, the missionary son and friend of James Abraham, could be held outdoors. Jocko could help break the ice.

In her travel bag, Rosie had a tin of homemade chocolate chip cookies, a dozen Snicker bars, and twelve-quart size bottles of Gatorade. She figured these treats would make Joel popular when his roommates returned from Easter break. The cookies weren't really homemade, but the bakery said they were fresh. She could see they were large and chewy.

Just as Rosie pulled up to his college building across from the chapel, Joel was exiting his dorm. He had told her he would be wearing an Adrian beany by which she could identify him. No other students were around.

Rosie opened her window and waved.

"Hi Joel. I am Dr. Klein. This is Jocko. Thank you for taking time to speak to me about your friend, James. I'm also grateful for the opportunity to re-visit the campus I grew to love when I attended Adrian. Sorry you couldn't spend Easter weekend with Mrs. Barlow's family."

"It's okay. I felt a responsibility to keep the dorm safe from locals who might vandalize or burglarize it while the students were off campus. I want to thank you, Dr. Klein, for your interest in this really bizarre case. I never saw any of this coming. James was a mild-mannered guy who never posed a threat to anyone. I understand he was well loved back home in his village. I know he was loved in our small Ohio community and by our family."

"I understand he was going to return home soon. Was he packed up and ready to return to Zambia with your parents and sisters?"

"Yes. I remember sitting at the foot of his bed as he packed a duffel bag with American souvenirs for his family. I told him I would see him soon when I would be back home in Africa for the summer."

"Please tell me about your relationship with James."

"We were like brothers, not just in Africa, but in Moss Creek, too. I've got older brothers, so here, I got to be like an older brother to James. In Africa, from the time we were ten, when short-term missionaries brought us sports equipment, we rode bikes and played soccer together on the farm. We milked cows for my dad and fished in the river that separated our farm from the village."

"So, James went to public school with you and your sisters?"

"Yes, and my mother taught about eight of us Bible stories and songs on Wednesdays evenings. James could speak, read, write, and sing in English from the sixth grade. For the younger kids, we used Lucy, a local translator who knew Tonga and English."

"James made friends easily and seemed to adapt to our extraordinarily different culture," Joel's voice choked up. "I'm heartsick about the path James took and the senseless slayings of the victims. I simply can't believe James was capable of such violence. My entire family viewed him as a very caring, sensitive soul who had a fervent desire to serve the Lord through his music."

Perhaps, it's time to lighten the tone of our conversation. Rosie thought. *This poor guy lost not only a good friend but sort of a little brother.*

As they began walking, they passed through the oval, arched walkway into the empty stadium.

"I just loved attending football games here when I was a student. Mostly, I was interested in the half time band performance and cheerleaders," Rosie reminisced. "Back then, I never envisioned myself being a psychologist. The girls of my generation were expected to become secretaries, nurses, or teachers. How about your mom, Joel?"

"My mom met my dad when their parents were missionaries in India. They were both eight years old and away from their parents in a Christian boarding school. The next year, my mom's family moved back to the States, so she and my dad wrote letters. He, and his parents, returned to Toronto Canada. Every summer, both families spent a week at a Christian camp on Lake Huron in Ontario Canada.

"After high school, my dad went to college to become a Pastor and my mom toured the United States with a large, Christian choir. After two years, they couldn't stand the long-distance relationship and got married."

"Wow. What a sweet love story," said Rosie.

"Instead of pastoring a church, they became missionaries. They raised six of us in Zambia. My older siblings were raised in Lusaka, the Capital where my parents taught English as a second language. My two younger sisters and I have been raised on a farm, some four hours distance from the Capital."

"What do you plan to major in, Joel?"

"I would like to pursue a major in Bible studies with minors in Computer Science and Journalism. Not sure how I'll combine those skill sets but I'm confident the Lord will direct and guide my steps."

"I can surely understand," she thought for a moment. "Would you like to write James in Lucasville State Prison?"

"Oh, man, I would really appreciate that opportunity."

"I'll get his address for you. I can tell you one thing, be sure to use white paper and send it in a white envelope. That's what prison rules require you have to do."

Joel patted Jocko's head and thanked Dr. Rosie for the cookies, candy, and drinks. She told him it was her pleasure, and just to call her 'Rosie' from now on. They hugged briefly. Rosie watched him shuffle down the path to his dorm with his head down and his hands in his pockets.

Then, getting back into her vehicle, she headed for the nearest Starbucks to use the bathroom, purchase some strong, black coffee and head for home.

MONDAY AFTERNOON- APRIL 4, 1994

CHAPTER 35

ANGEL'S TAKE ON THE HEARING

On Monday afternoon, Rosie stopped home long enough to walk Jocko and make sure his red bowl was full of fresh water and his soft, gravy-like food was mixed with harder nuggets. She changed into a more professional-looking outfit of slacks and a blazer over a button-down collared shirt.

Just after the clock tower struck one, she arrived at the county jail. Officer Jordan was devouring his peanut butter and jelly sandwich at the visitation window. She handed him her shoulder bag per custom.

"Sorry to interrupt your lunch, but could you please ask Angel to bring her homework with her to the interview room?"

Jordan brushed the crumbs off his mouth and chin and just smiled.

"Gladly, Dr. Klein." Then, speaking into the voice monitor he said, "Hey, Verna, have Angel Morgan bring her paperwork to the interview room." Then hitting the button beneath his desk, he unlocked the door.

Angel arrived with paperwork in hand.

"She ate her two donuts this morning, a bologna

sandwich, and canned beans for lunch," stated Verna Mitchell.

This corrections officer seems to really care about Angel instead of judging her for her actions, Rosie thought. She decided to mention that she had noticed her concern to Officer Mitchell when the opportunity presented itself.

"Thank you for letting me know, Officer Mitchell. And thank you for caring about her."

There it was. The opportunity had just presented itself.

"Hate the sin but love the sinner, commands the Bible," Officer Mitchell responded as she closed the door and left the room.

"How are you feeling today? Have you really eaten lunch?" Rosie asked.

"As well as can be expected, I guess. Seems like I'm having fewer nightmares. No appetite for jail food. If there is anything good about my time here, it's that I've lost twenty pounds over the past fifteen months. Sometimes, I stick half a sandwich in a plastic cup and when they return for the tray, they think I ate it all."

"If it is okay with you, Angel, I'd like to go over the sentences you've completed?"

"Fine. I didn't know how to answer them, but you said to say the first thing off the top of my head, so that's what I did."

"Let's look at some of your responses. For example, you said, 'I regret getting into trouble since the age of eleven and doing drugs since the age of nine.' Is that true?"

"Yes, Dr. Klein. When my mother moved us to Indiana to avoid being charged with neglect, she stashed some marijuana and pills in my pillowcase. She figured if we were stopped, the cops would never think to look there."

"Wow, Angel. What was your reaction to that?"

"We stayed at a cheap motel with flashing neon lights that kept me awake all night. About three a.m., I decided to try the pills to see if they would help me sleep."

"Did they?"

"No. Just the opposite happened. I could have danced on the ceiling. My eyes were bugged open and my legs were twitching so hard I was afraid it would wake my brothers. We were all in the same bed."

"What happened next?"

"We were off and running when the sun came up. My mom didn't miss the pills or maybe she forgot what she did with them. Besides, she reached for the bags of marijuana and was satisfied to have them."

"What kind of trouble did you get into at the age of eleven?"

" I was hungry and so were my brothers. Next to our bus stop was a Dollar Store. I told the boys to wait outside and I walked to the back of the store where the coolers were. I grabbed a package of bologna and stuffed it into the elastic waistband of my jeans. On the way back down the aisle, I noticed some packages of cheese crackers. I grabbed six little packages and put three in each of my side pockets. I didn't realize there were large mirrors on the ceiling and that the clerks up front were able to see what I was doing. By the time I reached the front checkout counter, a large man grabbed my hooded sweatshirt from behind. He whirled me around and tilted my face up toward him."

"What did he do next?"

"Well, I started to cry. Then he asked me what I thought I was doing. For once in my life, through my blurry eyes, I told the truth. I said my brothers were standing outside and we had nothing to eat at home."

"Angel, you felt a tremendous amount of

responsibility for your brothers, didn't you?"

"Someone had to protect them. Our mother was useless."

"What did the store manager do?"

"He said he felt sorry for us and he didn't call the cops. Instead, he gave me a loaf of bread to go with the bologna and a can of Pringles. Then he found a jar of peanut butter and grape jelly to go with it. After that, he put the stuff in a bag and added a half-gallon of milk."

"What a blessing."

"I hate to admit it, but what I saw was how easy it was to con grownups. I guess I didn't really appreciate what he'd done for us. It started me on a path of stealing by being more careful. Now I knew if I was caught, they wouldn't get too angry at a starving little girl with two younger brothers." She hesitated a moment, then asked a question.

"Dr. Klein, if they had called the police, do you think they would have put me in jail and maybe I would have learned a lesson, or somehow we could have been rescued from our situation?"

"Angel, I don't know, but I do think you needed someone to talk to about right and wrong. You said you cried yourself to sleep at bedtime. Can you tell me why?"

"I was scared, frustrated, and most of all felt in secure and very unloved."

"The statements that had to do with your mother show how much you wanted her to love and protect you. To this day, even though she caused you to suffer, you still say you wished for a relationship with her?"

"Yes. She won't have anything to do with me now because she says I have become a horrible person. I wonder if she knows she helped me do that."

"Angel, I am so very sorry. Your mother is clueless as to how her behavior influenced your behavior. You did say your goal was to become a beautician. Did anyone help you develop that goal? Did anyone know it was your goal?"

"I think I told a teacher or a counselor in Juvenile Detention. But I couldn't pass my GED, so my future looked limited."

"You said you feel a little scared but feel good because you are sober. Can you explain that to me?"

"I'm scared I might die before I'm thirty years old."

"How do you foresee that happening?"

"The Prosecutor could recommend the death penalty to the Judge like he did for Marcus. Or I could be placed in a dangerous prison where you can get murdered by an inmate or an officer if you refuse to be a sex partner."

"Angel, with your life story, I can almost guarantee the Prosecutor won't recommend the death penalty. And I doubt you will be in such danger in the Marysville Women's Reformatory."

They sat for a moment in silence."Do you have suicidal thoughts?" Dr. Rosie asked quietly.

"No. I used to think I would like to die and go to heaven. But once those guys shot our friends and spared me, I realized how desperately I wanted to live. Plus, by now, I've done such bad things, I don't think God or Jesus will let me into heaven. Do you think if I help some women in here, God might forgive me?"

"Angel, as soon as you asked for His forgiveness, God gave it to you. You are already forgiven. Let's talk about being sober. You answered that you feel good because you're sober. Do you mean you feel proud or happy, or both?"

"I know I'm not sober by choice. I never was clean

or sober in the outside world. I would like to believe I've changed and have the strength to be sober on my own, but I'll never know. I guess I'm happy, but don't have much to be proud about. Maybe I'm proud of how I tried to protect and take care of my little brothers," she looked at Rosie.

"You know what I mean, Dr. Klein. Not happy about my circumstances, but happy to be facing reality straight on, without being high on drugs or booze."

"You described yourself, Angel, as trustworthy, sweet, helpful, and outgoing. I can tell you are helpful, and it was sweet of you to take care of your brothers. They certainly trusted you. Would you say you were helpful and trustworthy in other situations? If so, would you share examples?"

"Sure. Let me think. Sometimes, I stayed after school to clean the blackboards for my homeroom teachers in junior high. Then they would give me a lift home and stick Snickers bars in my pockets for me and my brothers. One nice teacher stuck a jar of grape jelly in my pocket. I remember one week-end, we had nothing to eat but bread, jelly, water, and Snickers bars."

Oh my gosh. Here I left Snickers bars for Joel and his friends knowing they were a treat to be remembered, not the entre of the day. How wise the teachers were but no one turned in her mother. Hm! Maybe her life would have turned out differently if they had taken that step, Rosie thought while looking at this young woman whose life was the result of such childhood trauma.

"You said you don't get along with most women, and men are nothing but trouble. Yet you say you would like to be married, need love and affection, and a lot of support. How would you try to find female friends, and a husband, with the attitudes you expressed about men and women?"

"I know more about the kind of friends I should make.

They can't be on drugs or alcohol.

"I could find them in church or maybe even school, and I have so much love to give Dr. Klein. But, friendships need to be a two-way street, don't they?"

"That is true, Angel. Good thinking. I see you also mentioned sports and dancing as favorite hobbies. How do those activities make you feel?"

"Dr. Klein, I played basketball in JDC and it reduces stress, big time. Football I just like to watch. Dancing makes me smile and feel free," Angel turned her neck and sat a little straighter.

"Do you need to stretch or have a break, Angel?"

"No. I like talking to you. Somehow it gives me hope."

"Thank you. I do have a couple of things less pleasant to talk to you about. You wrote you hate talking about the times you were raped. Will you talk to me about them for a few minutes?"

Angel paused, then looked directly at Rosie.

"Yes. I have been told that talking about it is the best way to heal, but I haven't trusted anyone till you."

"When was the first time you recall being raped?"

"I was nine. It was just before my stepfather was arrested and we moved in the dark of night to Indiana."

"Did you tell your mother or a teacher or anyone?"

"No. But just before he was arrested, a lady from Children's Services was at the house on a complaint filed by an anonymous neighbor. She asked if I was beaten and I said 'yes'. That was the truth. She asked if I had bruises. I said not right now. She asked if I was molested. I said no, just hit with a belt. That was a lie. She left her card and told me to call her the next time he hit me or my little brothers. Now, I wished I'da told her the truth, but I was afraid."

"Do you remember the lady's name?"

"Yes. It was an easy name, like Ginny North, I think."

"Why does that seem like an easy name?"

"I had a school nurse that used to give us sweatshirts when it was cold and made sure my Mom treated our head lice. Her name was Ginny."

"Okay."

"North is a direction and I tend to remember directions. We were always on the run, it seemed."

"Why did you lie to Mrs. North?"

"My step-dad threatened to drown my brothers, if I ever told anyone. He didn't warn me not to say I was being hit."

"Tell me more."

"In Indiana, my teen-age step-uncle, Troy, dragged me into the woods about every Saturday for a whole summer. He stopped when school started because he was afraid, I might tell my teacher. My mom's boyfriend, Roger, was the one who took me to Columbus for that terrible, painful procedure. I bled for three weeks after that. I wasn't sure if it was his baby or Troy's. The nurse at that place gave me a box of sanitary napkins, but my underwear was still a mess. I had to steal a new pack of underwear. Talk about being scared..."

"That is terrible, Angel. Who else lived in that house, and in what part of Indiana was it?"

"It was called Centerville, Indiana; not too far from the Ohio border. It was a little town but had its own department store, Dollar General. We lived in an old, two story farmhouse, with a big front porch. There was my mom, my brothers, her new boyfriend, Roger, who she found at the farmer's market, his brother, and their father who had us call him Grampa. We all lived there together. Grampa never touched me. He was just an old alcoholic who drank beer from the time he got up till he passed out at night. Oh, and old Grandma who had dementia and remained in her room staring out the window all day."

"What happened to that family unit?"

"They were all busted for selling marijuana at the local movie house. Grampa was not arrested but they wouldn't let us stay with him because we were not blood relatives. My brothers and I went into foster care. You hear bad stories about foster care, but for us, it wasn't so bad. They kept the three of us together, which is rare from what I've heard. We were first took in by the Kesslers. They were a nice couple.

"Mr. and Mrs. Kessler home-schooled us, thinking we wouldn't be there long enough to adjust to public school. They had already raised their kids who came for dinner on Sundays. It was the only normal family we'd ever known. Two parents with kids who graduated from high school. All of them went to church and everyone worked for a living except the Mom who homeschooled us.

"When I was fourteen, my mom somehow got out of jail. I think she gave the authorities the name of a big wig drug dealer, and it reduced her sentence a lot. The Kesslers were right to think we would be with them only briefly. I was very disappointed when Mom came to get us. Then she took up with a new guy and we all lived together again, still in Indiana."

"You ran away at fifteen, correct?"

"Yes. She grounded me to my room for like the tenth time. Each time it was for yelling at her boyfriend, or not cleaning up after the animals, or not having the laundry done for the boys to wear clean clothes to school. Sometimes, I couldn't even find any clothes without holes or ones that were two sizes too small. One time she locked me in my room for twenty-one days except for fifteen minutes, three times a day to pee and eat."

"Did you run away during the school year?"

"It was springtime, so I didn't finish the ninth grade. I knew enough not to be homeless in Indiana or Ohio in the cold weather. I stuck it out, for as long as I could. But, I was feeling like hitting her back, and I knew it would be the end of me if I did that. And once again, her boyfriend would chase me around when she went to the grocery store. Once the bedroom door got torn off the hinge, and he told her it happened because I slammed it. She saw me as disrespectful and 'violently inclined'. Those were her words."

"You mentioned when you are angry you feel like hitting someone. Do you think your anger comes from back then?"

"Yup. I started hitting my pillow, but then began hitting the wall. Once I put my fist through the drywall. There was a picture hanging near the spot. I moved the picture over to cover the hole in the wall."

"Angel, you did a great job of describing Song to Judge Tucker and the spectators in the Courtroom. I will be doing the same for you. That is my designated role, you know."

"I know, Dr. Klein, but I want to speak for myself, too. I heard there won't be any victims' families there. I'm glad because I felt horrible hearing all the hurt we caused them. I don't blame them for hating us. Me."

"Are you going to write your statement down, Angel or just speak it?"

"What do you think I should do?"

"It's up to you. Some defendants write down notes to help them not to forget what they want to say. Others just talk to the Judge as if no one else is listening."

"I would be glad to read what you write, if you go that way. You can even practice with me."

"Okay. My hearing is next Tuesday. Can you come back on Friday?"

"Yes. That's what I was thinking. I won't tell you what to say. It needs to come from your mind and your heart."

"I get it. I have been thinking about it for a long, long time."

"Okay, then, I'll see you on Friday." Dr. Klein rose as did Angel and they hugged briefly. Dr. Klein opened the door to let Angel out. Officer Mitchell led her down the hall. Dr. Klein sat back down to collect her materials and her thoughts. She got up and walked out of the building with just a simple wave at Officer Jordan.

She had a lot to think about.

MONDAY, LATE AFTERNOON - APRIL 4, 1994

CHAPTER 36

ROSIE CONSULTS WITH SINGER

Rosie decided it was time to get together with Danny Singer and informally share everything she had collected about his client, Angel. As she approached the elevator doors in his office building, she made a call to his receptionist.

"Hi, Becky Joy. This is Dr. Klein. Is Attorney Singer available to meet with me? I'm in the building and would like to bring him up to speed on everything I've learned about his client, Angel Morgan."

"Oh, hello Dr. Klein. He's been talking about getting together with you. His staff meeting is just about over. I would say to come up. I'll buzz him to give him a heads up."

"Thanks, Becky Joy. Will I be seeing you at Bailiff Gorman's charity golf outing?" Rosie asked while pressing the elevator button.

"Yes. I'm scheduled to play on Danny's team with Attorney Jim Flannigan and Patrick Kirkland."

"Well, last year you nosed me out, Becky, for 'longest drive on the fairway'. This year, it's only fair you leave that honor to me. Ha!" Rosie said, as the elevator doors opened.

"Only if you let me take 'closest to the pin'. I can't believe how accurate your approach shots are," Becky responded.

The elevator doors opened on floor seven. As Rosie exited, she walked straight into Attorney Jim Flannigan. He took her by both of her shoulders, looked her straight in eyes, and said, "So, Rosie how are you doing?" Without waiting for her reply, he continued on.

"I heard through the grapevine that you're dating someone! He'd better treat you right or I'll get my Irish mafia guys after him!"

"Nice of you to ask," she smiled back, "And to offer protection. I'm doing quite well these days. I have Jocko to keep my life secure and structured. Dogs have so many more needs than cats. And, yes, I was recently introduced to a great guy by Judge Lincoln. He's the University of Toledo's baseball coach."

"Okay, then. The legal community needs to protect our girl. Keep that in mind. And don't let us over burden you with cases."

"I appreciate the concern, and the referrals. I have many more expenses now. See you soon."

"Right," Attorney Flannigan got on the elevator and waved as the doors closed.

Becky was sitting at her desk. She seemed to be gazing at a picture of her two-year old, son. "Has he had a golf club in his hands yet?"

"Not yet, but soon. Attorney Singer told me to send you right in when you arrived."

"Thank you, Becky. You do such a conscientious job."

Danny Singer stood up from his chair and came around his desk to greet Rosie. He beckoned to a chair at a small, round table. "Would you like some coffee? I can have Becky bring it."

"That sounds great. I just spent time interviewing your defendant, Angel, and could use a pick-me-up. Black please."

Becky brought the freshly brewed coffee and Rosie thanked her profusely.

"I'm ready to prepare my report for Judge Kate, if you want it. Otherwise, since there won't be a jury, I'll take the stand and you can lead me through my findings."

"That might be a good idea. Let me think about it. You are only educating the Judge. Have you found a great deal of information to help mitigate her sentence?"

"It's unbelievable. Her abuse began at three years of age by her mother. There was a brief agency intervention. The family unit remained intact. Then at age nine, her older sister left to live with her paternal grandparents. They were unrelated to Angel who had two little brothers to take care of while her mother drank and attached herself to different men. She suffered abuse when her mother or the men friends found her behavior unacceptable, usually due to something she did or did not do for her brothers."

"Wow. Have you verified her version of these events?"

"Absolutely. I enlisted the help of Wes Hall. He tracked down the abortion clinic in Columbus, Ohio, where her mother's boyfriend, Roger, took her to abort his baby." Rosie paused and looked him straight in the eyes.

"Daniel, she was only thirteen years old. Wes found the clinic closed but the State of Ohio mandates a record of minor girls be kept and the time frame Angel gave me matched a case he found listed."

"Oh, my gosh. These are the type of facts Judge Kate will see as relevant in her sentencing. What more?"

"She and her brothers were in foster care for about a year. The adults had gotten busted for drugs. Unfortunately, once her mother was released and rehabbed, supposedly, they were reunited. The foster parents were Christians and very good to them. I'm hoping to speak with them before I testify. Who knows? Perhaps they will want to come and tell the Judge how desperate this little girl was."

"Any idea where they might live? If you need help, my investigators can get on it."

"That's okay, Wes is searching for them"

"They were all living in Indiana. Angel told me they fled there when she was nine to avoid Children's Services in Ohio. She ran away from home in the ninth grade to get away from this Roger guy and his teen-age brother. The brother was chasing her around, too. By then she used drugs and alcohol to numb her feelings."

"After she ran away, she stole a Mercedes. Then she was arrested, and you know most of the rest."

"I thought I knew her case very well but, based on what you're telling me, I knew very little of the whole story. Is there any more about the five years she was in Juvenile Detention?"

"Funny, you should ask. Again, she was sexually abused. It was by a staff member who turned out to be a registered sex offender working there. I've followed up and he's now in prison for violating parole and re-offending."

"You certainly do a thorough job, Rosie."

She simply nodded at the praise. Angel deserved a thorough job.

"I need to get home and walk Jocko. Admittedly, it's more for my own good today."

"You do just that. I think your testimony will be powerful and will touch this Judge's heart."

"Thanks, Daniel. I am going to prep Angel on Friday. I assume you want me to go first on Tuesday."

"That's what I have in mind. I know the victims' families won't be testifying. Do you want her brothers and sister to validate the horrendous childhood they experienced?"

"Yes."

"How about if I call you tomorrow? Will that give them enough time to arrange coming to see you?"

"I'm not sure. They feel badly they've never stayed in touch while she was in Juvenile Detention. But, I also believe they'll do what they can to influence the Judge toward leniency."

Attorney Singer opened the door and escorted her to the elevator. They agreed to speak again in the morning. Meanwhile, he would relay all this case information to his assistant attorneys. Or so he said.

Dr. Rosie hailed the valet. a young, college student named Ace. A law enforcement student in classes on Friday, she only saw him when she came downtown on other days. Today was one of those days. Ace quickly fetched her car and gratefully accepted her more than generous tip.

Rosie called Ruth to ask a favor.

"Ruth, would you call Angel's brothers and sister and see if they could possibly come and testify at her sentencing hearing on Monday?"

"Sure thing, Boss Lady. How has everything else gone for you today?"

"Simply, super. And your day?

"Fine, considering my circumstances. By the way, you had an interesting call. It's not urgent. I think you are about to be appointed to another case. Attorney Flannigan called. You didn't happen to see him on the street today, did you?"

"Not exactly. Try, in the elevator on the way to speak with Danny Singer."

"I figured as much. Go home, Rosie, and play with Jocko. I will let you know what the siblings say. What time do you want them?"

"I would like to meet them at my downtown office at 9 am That will give us time to prepare and walk over in time for the 10 am hearing. Also, that way I can pay for their parking in my building's garage."

As I pulled out of the parking garage, my cell phone rang. I answered it and heard the voice I was growing to love.

"Hi Rosie, it's Bucky. Can you talk?"

"I'm driving home. Can you call me back in half an hour? I'll forgo the grocery store and hustle straight home."

"Sure. But I was wondering if I might come over and

walk Jocko with you?"

"That would be terrific. I'll see you at my condo at five, okay?"

"I'll bring some steaks since it sounds like your pantry is low, and I need to use them before the "best by" date. How does that sound?"

"Sounds super. I have potatoes we can bake and Romaine for a Caesar's salad. See you."

I wondered if Bucky has something else on his mind, other than walking Jocko and using his steaks before the expiration date? No sooner had I hung up the phone, then it rang again.

"Hey, Rosie. The three kids want to speak with you prior to the Tuesday hearing. They don't want to risk having trouble on the highway and running late. I told them your calendar is open on Thursday. We could ask Dr. Siefer if you could use the downtown office that day. And, yes, they do plan to participate in the hearing."

"Thanks, Ruth. You are the best. Go home and attend to your husband and your cats, Lily and Sophie."

Bucky knocked on the door and rang the bell simultaneously. No verbal response from Jocko but, through the window, Bucky could see his tail wagging vigorously.

"Well, well, well. Look what the cat dragged in. Oh, Bucky, so sorry. I was just speaking to Ruth and telling her to take care of her cats. Ha."

"Where should I put the steaks and the wine and the watermelon?"

"I'll put the steaks in the refrigerator, and we can carve the watermelon when we get back from walking Jocko, okay?"

"Sounds good."

"You certainly didn't need to bring wine and watermelon. Watermelon is known to cleanse the pallet, right?"

"Always refreshing after a hearty meal."

I attached the leash to Jocko's harness and opened the sliding patio doors.

"Do you always leave the house open when you walk the dog?"

"Are you kidding? Jocko is not simply a service dog. He's my protection against any and all intruders should they be lurking upon our return. Human or otherwise. Ha."

"Okay, what was I thinking, Rosie?"

Conversation was light and the exercise and fresh air refreshing. Upon returning, I lit the oven for the potatoes while Bucky turned on the grill and poured the wine.

"It looks like I will definitely be offered the Athletic Director's position. Apparently, the Board of Directors was already in the loop and just waiting for the announcement and notification of my interest."

"Wow, that is good news! How do you feel about all the new responsibility and leaving your coaching position?"

"I look forward to the challenges of the job but I'm also nostalgic about leaving my team. It's also difficult to recruit new players while not being the one to lead them. There's a sense of personal abandonment for some guys. It happened to me in college. I looked forward to playing for a coach who left for a coaching position at a larger university. My freshman year was okay. Then the new coach brought in his own recruits and even some transfers from his prior college. My classmates and I assumed new positions known as 'the bench'."

"Wow. You really do empathize with your team's feelings. All because you've been there, done that. At least your current players will know the new head coach. Only the recruits won't, right?"

"Correct. We'll just have to cross that bridge when we get there. By the way, have I invited you to our opening game on Saturday, April 9th?" Bucky looked at me and I noticed his eyes were smiling.

"I don't recall an invite. What time and place?"

"It's a home game. 1:30 pm. with the national anthem and introduction of players. Game time, thereafter. I'll expect to see you in the front row behind the dugout. Okay?"

"You mean, you won't be introduced? Only the team?"

"Standard operating procedure, Rosie," he said. Then, he reached for my hand.

I could see something was on his mind. He didn't say anything for a moment. I could tell he wanted to ask me something important.

"Rosie, are we exclusive, at this point?" His look was questioning while emotions played on his face. His eyes were looking intently into mine.

"Bucky," I chuckled. "I thought you would never ask."

We gently kissed to seal the deal. My heart was full.

Looking outside, I realized the fountain was flowing.

"Let's make a wish and throw coins in the fountain," I said smiling at him. "It's sort of a tradition around here."

"Let's make a wish for our future," he said, reaching into his pocket for coins. He eyed the distance from my balcony to the enclosed area of flowing waters.

"Think I can make it?" he said, referring to the distance. But I had another answer.

"You already have."

The rest of the evening was leisurely and passed far to soon for both of us.

TUESDAY AFTERNOON - APRIL 5, 1994

CHAPTER 37

SONG LEE'S SENTENCING

At 1:30 pm, Rosie took her seat in the courtroom, third row behind Assistant Prosecutor Laura Robinson. Song was seated next to Attorney Chickalette to Rosie's right, in the front row. Angel had not been permitted to attend Song's sentencing today.

The young Asian woman was dressed in street clothes. Her head down, hands in her lap. Officer Verna Mitchell sat beside her in full uniform with her service gun holstered. Song's parents, Dr. and Mrs. Lee, were in the row directly behind them. So close, they could whisper encouragement, if desired. Directly across from Rosie were Dr. Schuller, the music director at the University of Toledo, and Beverly Stanley, Song's prior roommate.

Rosie noticed the court reporter, Sally Jacobs, looking up as if to inquire if and when she should begin recording. Local television reporters, and Wes Hall from the newspaper, were seated along the back rows. Cameramen were not allowed into the proceedings but were lurking just outside in the hallway. Two officers were stationed at the doors to maintain control of the courtroom.

While reporters were permitted in the courtroom, they would not be permitted to interview Song. Cameramen were not privileged to see or hear her. At the end of the hearing, she would be escorted by Officer Mitchell through a side door. Her lawyer would most likely make a public statement on the steps of the courthouse.

Finally, it was time to begin.

Judge Tucker entered the Courtroom and Bailiff Gorman instructed everyone to rise. The Judge seated himself, then asked everyone to be seated. Hitting his gavel on the bench's wooden block he called out:

"Court is now in session."

"Attorney Chickalette, is there any reason to believe that this defendant does not understand the charges against her?" Judge Tucker inquired.

"No, your honor. She stands perfectly competent to enter her pleas."

"Attorney Chickalette, is there any reason to believe that this defendant did not know right from wrong at the time of the offenses?"

"No, your honor. She understood right from wrong and although she did not wield a weapon, she accepts her role and responsibility in the commission of these murders."

"All right then, this Court will proceed with sentencing of Ms. Song Lee."

Judge Tucker asked Ms. Lee to stand.

"Miss Lee, has your Attorney advised you of your right to a fair and impartial trial before a jury?"

"Yes, your Honor."

"Did you decline to allow a jury to determine your guilt or innocence?"

"Yes, your Honor, I did," her voice was strong.

"Did you willingly plead guilty to one count of aggravated murder?"

"Yes, your Honor," Song responded.

"Did you willingly plead guilty to one count of conspiracy to commit murder?

"Yes, your Honor," Song responded.

"Did you willingly plead guilty to four counts of aggravated robbery?"

"Yes, your Honor," Song's voice wavered as she began openly weeping now.

"Did you willingly plead guilty to six counts of obstruction of justice?"

"Yes, your Honor," Song stated, her voice no longer strong, as the weight of the counts of violence continued to be intoned.

"Then let the record show that Miss Song Lee has willingly pleaded guilty to the charges brought against her."

"Miss Song Lee, this Court, on behalf of the State of Ohio, accepts your guilty pleas to all charges against you for which you have pleaded guilty."

Song stood silently and respectfully looked at Judge Tucker. Murmuring began throughout the courtroom.

"The Court has taken into consideration the statements of the families and friends of the victims as well as the statements made by you, your family and friends.

"In the matter of the conspiracy to commit murder and aggravated murder of Mr. Richard Brooks, for which you have willingly pleaded guilty; the matter of the aggravated robberies of Richard Brooks, Bobby Young, Brian Bennett, and Sophia Pappas, for which you have willingly pleaded guilty; and six counts of obstruction of justice to include the murders of Sammy Strong and April Chandler, for which you have willingly pleaded guilty; you are hereby sentenced to 30 years to life in State Prison for conspiracy to commit murder and aggravated murder; 20 years for each count of robbery; 10 years each on six charges of obstruction of justice. The sentences on each charge will be served concurrently and will begin immediately. Court is adjourned." Judge Tucker pounded his gavel.

No one has ever attached last names to Sammy and April until now, Rosie realized at that moment. They simply were referred to as 'the orphans'. Not even their friend, George Emmanuel, had mentioned their last names.

Bailiff Gorman stood and remained still as the courtroom emptied.

Officer Mitchell allowed Dr. and Mrs. Lee to embrace their daughter who was sobbing uncontrollably. Attorney Chickalette whispered something to his client.

More than likely he's assuring her he'll see her later for a debriefing interview, Rosie thought.

Officer Mitchell led Song by the elbow out the side door. The local news station commentators grabbed their notebooks and phones and rushed out to the hallway. Wes Hall glanced at Rosie nodding his head toward the hall. She assumed they would agree to meet for coffee at the Embassy. She wanted to ask him for one more difficult favor. She wanted him to find Angel's foster parents in Indiana.

Wes was waiting at their usual and customary booth which provided the most privacy in the grill. Ordering coffee, they decided to split a piece of the infamous peanut butter pie.

"Okay, lady. What did you think of the hearing?"

"I guess it was exactly what we expected. It's not as

though the Judge has any latitude on imposing sentence once the defendant pleaded guilty as charged."

"He has to play by the play book, but it's sad to see a young, vibrant, talented woman waste away in prison for the rest of her God given days," he thought a moment. "Although, he didn't say Life without parole, did he?"

"No, he didn't, and now we face the exact same future for Angel. These young women have been led to believe it's better to accept a deal to spend the rest of their lives locked up then to get the Death Penalty. But to me, it's a kind of death either way. What would you do under their circumstances, Wes?"

"If I was Song, with no prior record and no past drug use, I would have opted for a jury trial. They might have returned guilty pleas on lesser charges that don't mandate Life in prison."

"You definitely have a point, there. My girl, Angel, had a history of skirmishes with the Court system and drug and alcohol uses underage. Of course, she also was a pathetic, sad, child, which is what I plan to bring out, in her behalf, next Tuesday."

"Oh, I heard from my sources, that Dr. Lee has been offered a teaching position at the Ohio State School of Medicine. They are working on moving to the United States to be supportive of their daughter. They plan to visit her as often as permitted which I think may be every other week-end."

"Wow. That's terrific news for the Lee family. It leads me to my final request of you, Wes"

"Okay. Let me hear it. What are friends for? Just remember you owe me one, Rosie."

"Let's find Angel's foster parents, Mark and Ann Kessler, and let them speak about her early sexual abuse. The

Court messed up bigtime in Indiana when they reunited her and her brothers with their mother."

"I'll start with Children's Services of Indiana. What was the town again, Centerville?"

"You got it. Thank you so much."

They enjoyed a refill on coffee and split the pie right down the middle.

"On a lighter note, how's it going with your new boyfriend, Rosie?"

"Delightful. He's dedicated to his team and to God, and he's recently let me know that Jocko and I are high on his list too."

"You deserve this second chance on love! Did you know I didn't meet my main squeeze, Sherri, until I turned forty-two?"

"No. I didn't know that. Does she enjoy baseball or softball with you?"

"Never misses a game. We plan to get married at the Botanical Gardens of The Rock of Gibraltar in September. It is called a site wedding, Rosie."

"Interesting. Why at The Rock?"

"It'll be beautiful. We plan to walk across the border to Spain and spend a week on the beach at the Costa Del Sol. Can you believe the border is the International landing strip that separates the British territory of Gibraltar from Spain? Americans are welcome in both countries. Slight problem is the exchange of money. Spanish euros but English pounds."

"I think it sounds wonderful. Be careful, though; the streets are narrow there and the monkeys are extremely aggressive, I've been told. They steal purses off ladies' shoulders and will grab food out of your hands. One of the tourist highlights is the hotel where Churchill planned the English strategy for the war. There's a large veranda with rocking chairs there. He was known to spend mornings in a chair with his tea and his cigar."

"Thanks for the graphic description, Rosie. You know, we could make it a double-wedding," Wes had a glint in his eye.

"No thanks, Wes. But, if we're invited, we might consider renting a motor scooter. I understand that men in suits and ties toss their briefcases in a basket on the back and tool to work on them. We could put Jocko in one. Anyway, congratulations. Speaking of Jocko, I need to get home to my trusty companion. I want to make arrangements for Angel's siblings to see her before she is transported to State Prison in Marysville."

Rosie stood up to leave.

"I'll follow up for you, Rosie, and find Mark and Ann Kessler. See ya' later. Oh, I'm picking up this tab, but don't think for a minute, you don't owe me."

Rosie breezed into the Summerhill office and put a quart of no sugar added-peanut butter and chocolate ice cream on Ruth's desk. Ruth was just hanging up the phone. Her eyes widened and she began to speak.

"Thank you, Boss, but this means you need something from me. "

"I need to get ahold of Officer Jordan to make arrangements for Angel's brothers and sister to visit her before she's transported to prison. Oh, and I need to find out James' address at Lucasville so Joel can write to him. I promised Joel when I met with him at Adrian College the other day that I would secure the necessary information. He can write, but I know it's doubtful Joel could every visit James in prison."

"I'll make my other calls from home," Rosie left

calling over her shoulder:

"Please let me know what Angel's siblings say about Thursday."

THURSDAY MORNING - APRIL 8, 1994

CHAPTER 38

FINAL SIBLING INTERVIEWS

"Thank you for participating in your sister's sentencing hearing. I've arranged with Officer Jordan for you to visit her right after lunch. How is your time schedule today?"

Greg, the older brother of Angel's siblings, answered for the three of them while everyone was sitting in my downtown office at the beginning of our meeting.

"We're fine with that arrangement. We took the entire day off in order to come to Toledo. You don't need to pay for our parking. It's our privilege to be here, Dr. Klein."

"Okay. Let me brief you on what will happen. First, let me tell you about a few things you will be asked. Did your sister take care of you when you were small, and if so, in what ways?"

"The answer to that is, definitely, yes!" Mikey said.

"She cooked if the gas was on in the house and the stove would work. There were times she just opened a can of chicken noodle soup, added warm water, and we ate it, 'cause that's all we had. Sometimes, she would wrap cheese in a piece of toast, and we'd dunk it in coffee for breakfast."

"Dr. Klein, I was out of the house by the time my sister was nine," Amber interjected. "From my early childhood experience, I can tell you, our mother spent her time intoxicated, lounging around the house with men, or sleeping."

"How many times, were you kids separated from your mother by authorities in Ohio and Indiana?"

"The boys weren't born yet, the first time Angel was removed from the house," said Amber. "The night the neighbors reported that Angel was wandering outside alone in a diaper, I was at my paternal grandparents' house. Children's Services, then, left me with my mother and placed Angel in foster care. She was probably about three years old."

"Unfortunately, as soon as our mother cleaned up her act, Angel was returned. There was some rule about not splitting us up. What they should have done is place both of us in foster care.

"Soon after that Mom found a new man and we moved to a new neighborhood. She married him for the appearance of stability and proceeded to have our little brothers. I was seven and changing their diapers, but only if there were any clean diapers to use. Some days they ran around butt naked and peed in corners of the living room.

"I doubt Angel remembers much of that though, she was only a few years older than Greg. I do remember she sucked her thumb all day long, and Mama slapped her hands. At night she wrapped herself up in a tattered blanket and rocked back and forth on the filthy floor in the bedroom that all four of us kids shared.

"My grandparents began having me come visit them most weekends which put the burden on Angel for the taking care of the little guys as everybody grew older."

"Amanda, why didn't Angel go with you to visit your grandparents?"

"They weren't related to her. We had different fathers.

Our Mama had four kids with three different men. The boys' father was Antonio Rossi," Amanda explained. "We don't have a clue who Angel's father was. We just know our Mom called him 'Morgan'. My own father was a loser, but at least his parents took care of me in his place. I guess they didn't think Angel was their responsibility."

"Greg, can you tell me what you recall happening after Amanda left the house? I know you were only about five years old, right?" Rosie asked.

"We started going to this church on Wednesday nights. Angel was with the big kids for Bible study and games, but we got to sit with her in the children's church service. One night just as we were coming home in the church bus, it went round the corner to our house and we saw lots of blue lights. The cops were at our house.

"That stands out in my memory because when we walked in the front door, we saw our dad on his knees with his hands handcuffed behind his back. The cops were searching everywhere for drugs."

"Wow, that sounds like a scary time. Do you remember it, too, Mikey?"

"Yes, I was actually really small and sort of a daddy's boy. I didn't get hit like Greg and Angel did, just mostly ordered around. I was told to get dad's cigarettes or his beer and get them fast. That kind of thing. Sometimes, I was even told to get his belt so he could punish the older kids."

"Did you see him beat them?"

"Oh, yeah, lots of times. He beat them on the back or butt so the school wouldn't see marks on their arms or legs. But, he never, ever punched them in the face like he did our mom." Mikey's voice wavered as he thought of his disturbing memories.

"What stands out for you about your time in Indiana, Greg?"

"The family group we lived with was very weird. Mom's new boyfriend, or so-called husband, Roger, and his teen-age brother, were nasty, hostile guys."

"How so?"

"They were cruel to their own animals, mean to their old father, and disrespectful to their mom who clearly had dementia. We didn't call it that as kids, of course we didn't know what she had. Back then, we sort of just thought she was old and sick."

"This is difficult to ask, but were you aware your sister was being sexually abused by your mom's boyfriend and maybe his brother, too?"

"Yes," Mikey spoke quickly.

"Mom would take Greg to the store and leave me and Angel behind. Supposedly, she was told to watch over me. But Roger would make an excuse to take her for a little ride in his truck. One time when they came back, she wasn't wearing any underwear, there was blood coming down her legs, and she had a bloody lip. She hurried to the bathroom, then stayed in our bedroom until Mom got back. After that, he took her for a ride whenever Mom would go to the store, but I never saw blood anymore."

"Did you tell anyone?"

"No. If they came back and she had any cuts or bruises, there was always some excuse like they would say they were walking along a creek and she tripped over a stump or something."

"Do you remember Roger ever taking her for a long ride and I mean overnight sometime?"

"We all went to Ohio one time for some doctor's visit. We dropped Angel off and went fishing at Lady Lake. When we picked her up, she seemed a little out of it. She slept most of the way as we drove back to Indiana."

"Well, I want to thank you all for sharing some very painful memories. It helps a lot since they coincide with what your sister has told me. That means, you have validated the information."

"You are welcome, Dr. Klein. We wish we could have intervened before she got herself into this terrible mess, but we're very grateful that you took her as your client, " Amanda said. "Do you think we could see Angel, now?"

"Of course. As I've mentioned earlier, I've arranged for you to visit your sister after lunch. Let's go catch a bite to eat first, okay?"

"That is so nice of you, Dr. Klein. Thank you for all of it."

THURSDAY AFTERNOON - APRIL 7, 1994

CHAPTER 39

SIBLING VISITATION

Officer Jordan checked photo IDs of Amanda, Greg, and Mike, then, asked them to place their belongings on a conveyer belt and step through the metal detector. After everyone retrieved personal items, they entered a large visitation area where Angel was already seated. She smiled broadly when she saw them walk into the room.

I'm thinking they brought her in first to lessen the shock of seeing their sister in full prison garb, Rosie thought.

Angel stood up and reached out her arms in greeting. All three siblings encircled her and hugged her while everyone wept. It was a sweet homecoming of sorts. Rosie's eyes were brimming with tears.

If nothing else good comes out of this case, at least this, itself, was well worth it, she thought.

Taking seats that were connected to the metal table, they all tried to talk at once, then Amanda began speaking.

"We are so happy to see you, Angel. I'm really sorry not to have come to visit you much, much sooner."

"Well, it's not exactly like I attempted to contact you, either," Angel said through her tears.

"We've told Dr. Klein how much you mean to us, and

how much we appreciate the sacrifices you made in taking care of us as little boys." Greg said.

"I didn't really sacrifice anything, Greg. I had nothing to sacrifice," Angel said. "We were all in it together, and taking care of you the best I could, comforted me in more ways than you could imagine."

"I'm sorry I was the favorite and didn't get hit like you did," Mikey said. "You took beatings in my place when I created mischief and I really regret it now."

"Please don't feel that way, Mikey. If this is God's plan for my life, what I put up with through those years, has made me stronger, physically, mentally, and spiritually. I am more patient now. I know I can persevere. I just pray God has forgiven me for being part of a crime spree that's resulted in the premature, horrendous deaths of six innocent people."

"No doubt about that." Amanda said emphatically. "Our Pastor emphasizes the grace God provides to those who believe. Grace to be courageous and face your Goliath with confidence." The boys nodded and smiled at their sister trying to be comforting in some way.

"Tell me about your husband and kids, Amanda. Is he good to you and are they cute?"

"He's a good Christian man. We met when a group of us from Cedarville Bible College went on a mission trip to an Apache Boarding School and Reservation in Arizona. We both have hearts for the American Indians, particularly the children."

"Our own kids are two years apart, five and three. Our five-year old, Paul, will start Kindergarten in the fall. He graduates from pre-school in May. Can you believe he knows how to read and write his name already?"

"Wow. I would say he has a much stronger foundation for learning than we did. How about your three-year old?"

"Rebecca is precocious. She likes to draw, and dance, and be read to. I work part-time in a local hardware store to get me out from under the kiddie's shenanigans. Phew."

"They know we're their uncles, and now they'll get to know they have an aunt. You!" Mikey said. "Aunt Angel," he smiled as her eyes teared-up again.

Angel questioned Greg and Mikey about their lives.

"We've just graduated together from a Fort Wayne, Indiana vocational high school. We live in an apartment together in South Hampton and are going on to Owens Community College. Every other weekend we go home to our spiritual parents' house in Indiana. We were blessed to spend our junior high and high school years with Mark and Ann Kessler. Remember them? We lived with them for a year before Mom got us back.

"Then after you ran away, we were removed from her permanently and reunited with the Kesslers. Mom was sent to prison."

It was a lot to take in and Angel grew quiet. She looked down briefly to remember her own mother's face. Everyone sat in silence, then Amanda reached for her hand and held it.

"We were taken to visit her, but didn't understand anything about her sentence," Mikey continued. "We heard she did two-and-a-half years for possession of cocaine, got an early release, and never tried to gain legal custody of us back again."

"Is Mama back in prison?" Angel asked.

"We don't really know," Greg answered.

"Can you believe she disowned me once I moved in with my grandparents for good?" Amanda said.

"Yes, I truly can believe it," Angel said.

Officer Mitchell entered the room.

"It's time," she said quietly. "I have to take Angel back now." Angel stood obediently.

She's come to respect Verna Mitchell for all the kindness the officer has extended to her, Rosie reflected. How tragic this young woman didn't get this kind of love before now. They all embraced. They all wept. They all promised to stay in touch with Angel and visit once they received instructions.

"We will definitely be in Court on Tuesday to support you and say whatever we can to influence Judge Kate," Amanda said.

"You'll be in our prayers and those of our prayer warriors. Do you know what that means, Angel?"

"No. Can't say that I do."

"We belong to groups of Christian people who pray daily for the needs of others, whether they're Christian or not," Greg said.

"Well, right now, especially, I can use all the prayers I can get. Please thank your 'warriors' for me, okay?"

"I'll be back to see you in the morning, Angel," Dr. Klein promised.

As Angel was led away, her siblings watched and there was sadness in their eyes. Then, turning to leave, they looked over their shoulders once before proceeded out of the secure area to the lobby, everyone walking in silence.

"Thank you, so very much, Dr. Klein," Amanda said. "We don't know how we would have gotten to see her without your help."

"It's hard to see her this way," Greg said shaking his head in disbelief of his poor sister's fate. Rosie escorted them to the parking garage where she handed their parking tickets to the agent in the booth and paid.

"I'll see you all again right here at 8:30 am on Tuesday morning."

"Yes, you will," Mikey waved.

FRIDAY MORNING - APRIL 8, 1994

CHAPTER **40**

FINAL PREP WITH ANGEL

Rosie met her business partners, Larry, Steve, and Debi for breakfast at Debi's favorite restaurant, The All-American Pancake House. They usually met the first Friday of the month to discuss marketing strategies, but had delayed their April meeting because it fell on Good Friday.

Now, it was the second Friday of the month and Rosie had many marketing ideas to discuss beginning with the aspect of opening a fourth office. Dr. Steve managed the North office while Dr. Debi co-managed the Summerhill office. Only Rosie and Larry leased space downtown from Dr. Siefer with the option to see clients at the North office or Summerhill office as well. While her work could include criminal cases, Larry limited his Court-appointed work to the allocation of parental rights, known as child custody, which involved Family and Juvenile Courts.

"How's the Angel Morgan case coming? Steve asked.

"Her sentencing hearing is on Tuesday. Fortunately, the victims' families and friends presented their statements to Judge Tucker for the Song Lee sentence hearing so we won't have to repeat them. Judge Kate has the witness transcripts to review prior to recommending her sentence for Angel."

"So, who will be testifying on Tuesday, Rosie?" Debi asked.

"I will. Then, Angel has a statement for the Judge meant for the victims' families to hear, too. They'll be present, but won't be called to speak. Danny Singer hasn't told me whether I precede Angel or not, but I'm meeting with him this afternoon."

"How is Angel feeling? How are you doing with all this drama?" Larry asked.

"I'm fine and actually heading over to see Angel after breakfast. I want to encourage her to share what is on her heart and help reduce her anxiety as much as possible. She's going to read me her statement."

"Are you satisfied with your investigation? Are there many mitigating factors involved in Angel's case? Larry asked.

"I've had fantastic assistance from Wes Hall. Know him? He found the abortion clinic Angel was taken to by her father. He found her siblings. Basically, Wes is my right-hand man in all the background investigations."

"Yeah, actually, we know you've found a new, right-hand man Rosie." They laughed.

"How's Bucky, anyway?" Debi asked. "Does he golf?"

"He has not taken the time to learn to golf yet," Rosie smiled. "But, to answer your questions about mitigating factors, this young woman was really abused by her mother from a very early age, as well as by the men in her mother's life. She was made to feel worthless and ashamed, then expected to give up her childhood and take care of her little brothers. She never finished high school and at one point things got so bad, she ran away, stole a car, then spent five years in the Lucas County Juvenile Detention Center where she suffered more abuse. This gang was the first group after juvvie that made her believe they cared about her. Obviously another lie."

"Wow. What a story! She was victimized for sure,"

"I think we should table our marketing meeting for a more appropriate time, don't you guys?" Steve said. "With all this ahead of you, Rosie, you have enough to think about."

"Yeah, let's eat and listen to Rosie talk about something more pleasant, like her new right-hand man," Larry said. "What's his name again?"

Later, Rosie was able to take her coffee into the visitation room along with a bottle of water for Angel. Officer Mitchel brought Angel from her cell and smiled at Rosie. She was carrying pages of notebook paper and a pencil. Rosie stood and gave her a hug. Angel responded by putting her head on Rosie's shoulder.

"Good morning, Angel. Did you enjoy yesterday's reunion with your siblings?"

"Much better than I could have ever expected. I thought the boys hated me for abandoning them when I ran away. I didn't realize they had a nicer life with foster parents who loved them."

"They definitely received love, and now they're able to give love to others, like you, Angel. Would you like to read your statement to me?"

"Yes, I'd like that. I wrote it over about three times. Do you want me to stand up?"

"Just do whatever makes you the most comfortable for now." Rosie watched her stand, envisioning the judge in front of her. The paper in her hand trembled slightly.

"I am Angel Morgan, your Honor. I thank you for the opportunity to speak here today. I am not here to make excuses for my terrible actions. I am here to say I am glad to have been able to testify in the trials of Marcus and James. I know it doesn't change things that they were the shooters and I never held a weapon. I am not asking for sympathy. I should have found a way to escape and lead the cops to their hideout. I didn't, and I will regret that forever. Maybe some lives could have been saved."

Angel paused. She closed her eyes and shook her head. She took a deep breath and continued reading.

"To Mrs. Young, I am here to say how sorry I am about your son, Bobby. I know the bond you shared was priceless and your hopes and dreams for his future were shattered. To Mrs. Williams and the kids, my heart goes out to you as well. To Mr. and Mrs. Pappas and little Lily, no words can ever express how terrible I felt when Marcus and James returned to the car after shooting Sophia. I was a coward not to run. And to Mrs. Brooks and everyone touched by these senseless slayings, I understand why you can't forgive me. I will do better in the future and try to scare girls straight that I meet in prison. When they see what happens when someone like me makes poor choices, they might stop and consider what they are doing with their lives. I accept my responsibility in what has happened and am so, so sorry. Thank you for listening."

Rosie sat speechless as did Angel. Rosie broke the silence.

"Angel you have written an outstanding testimony. Identifying each victim's family and personalizing your condolences was a great idea. You will be fine on Tuesday."

"Dr. Klein, please pray for me in church this Sunday. I know you have a direct line up to the Lord."

"Actually, Angel, each of us has a direct line up to the Lord through Jesus. Spend time this weekend with him yourself. He is your friend. Trust him. He has a plan for your life even when you don't see him or think he hears you."

"Someone else once told me the same thing. I believe you, Dr. Klein."

As Rosie left the jail, she crossed paths with Danny Singer who was coming to see Angel.

"Hi, Rosie, I was going to call you to postpone this afternoon's conference. Can we do it on the phone? After I speak with Angel, I would like to get on the road. My son has an away track meet and I'll have plenty of time to talk from the bleachers. His events will be an hour apart. You know how high school meets go."

"That works fine with me, Danny. I can use the time at home to finalize my comments. Can I fax you questions you might want to ask me?"

"Okay. Fill me in on your opinion this afternoon and send the fax to my office. I'll be working tomorrow morning for a while."

Later, when Singer called her from his son's meet, she explained the detailed factors that portrayed Angel as a victim more than a criminal. She told him Angel's brothers would testify to the childhood abuse they all endured.

"It validates Angel's allegations," Rose said.

He suggested she bring the young men to his office Tuesday morning. Later, Rosie faxed him questions pertaining to each category: Childhood rape and abuse, post abortion trauma, PTSD, family dysfunction, alcohol and drug abuse, poor academic achievement, youthfulness, and mental impairment.

"Will I be testifying before or after Angel?"

"I think it is more powerful for you to testify right after her brothers. Don't you?"

"I agree. Then the hearing can culminate with Angel's apology and unspoken plea for mercy from Judge Kate" Rosie said. Still, two questions were nagging her.

"May I ask you two questions, Dan?"

"Of course, what are they?"

"Why didn't you take Angel's case to trial? Is it true she was offered a deal if she testified against Marcus and James?"

"Let me answer your second question, first. It's true she was offered a deal by Matt Murphy if she testified as State's witness. My responsibility was to save her life. Matt took the death penalty off the table in exchange for her testimony and guilty pleas. Your first question of why not take it to trial after that was because she pled guilty which, of course, negates a trial. The trial phase has to do with guilt or innocence you know."

To Rosie, it seemed Attorney Singer sounded a bit exasperated. He may have been insulted she had questioned his professionalism, but decided to proceed and let the chips fall where they may.

"I'm sorry, Dan. I respectfully disagree. With my testimony of the mitigating circumstances surrounding this young woman's life, no jury would have opted for the death penalty. In fact, they may have convicted her of lesser charges. It possibly would have meant half her life behind bars, not perhaps two lifetimes."

"Maybe so, Rosie, but it's water over the dam now, isn't it? And besides, you must admit she failed to take any steps to prevent further bloodshed after the first unexpected murder."

SATURDAY MORNING - APRIL 9, 1994

CHAPTER 41

CALL TO THE KESSLERS

The Kesslers weren't difficult for Wes to find since Greg provided their phone number. Upon calling, he told the couple to expect hearing from the psychologist assigned to Angel's case.

Ann Kessler answered on the third ring. Her voice was cheerful and her "hello" was inquisitive.

"Good morning, Mrs. Kessler. This is Dr. Rosie Klein. Thank you for being willing to share your recollections of Angel." Rosie had a legal pad in front of her along with a cup of her favorite locally brewed Boston Stoke coffee.

"My husband and I feel so badly for that young woman," Ann Kessler said. "All of this was avoidable. The authorities missed the boat. But, out of her misfortune came her brothers' blessings. They were returned to us after their mother was arrested, and they're great men, now."

"I've met them, Mrs. Kessler, and I agree with you. What was Angel like the year you had her?"

"She was insecure and timid. She had not been taught basic hygiene. We created a chart and she marked on it each time she brushed her teeth, took a shower, washed her hair, made her bed, put her dirty clothes in the hamper, fed our animals, dried the dishes, and got dressed for school in the morning.

"By the third quarter that year, her reading was only one year behind grade level, and the teachers found her very pleasant to have in class."

"Sounds like you helped her make great progress. What was your impression of her mother?"

"She was a self-centered, undisciplined, fearful woman. Her husbands had beaten her and the kids. Her abuse toward the kids was more mental and emotional. That is, she withheld affection, called them names, and never complimented them for anything."

"Well, I certainly believe you've validated the details that Angel and her brothers have expressed, Mrs. Kessler," Rosie said. "Basically, I don't have any further questions at this time."

"Please, Dr. Klein, just call me Ann."

"Okay, Ann. Please call me, Rosie. Please tell Mr. Kessler that Angel wants you both to know how grateful she is that you raised her brothers."

"Okay, Rosie. I will tell Mark. He'll be happy to hear it. Once Angel is settled in prison; we would like to put money into her account for incidentals."

"That is very thoughtful, Ann. One last thing, how did you happen to adopt the boys?"

"Well, one reason is, we knew they would be driving soon, and believed it would be much easier for them to prove identity and residence, if they had our last name. They also needed to be our legal sons to put them on our automobile insurance. We love Greg and Mikey. We wanted them to know they had a permanent home with us even after the age of eighteen. The system kicks kids out once they become of age and if they have no stability, well, that's when troubles can begin again."

"That is truly awesome, Ann. I want to thank you and your husband for sharing your lives,"

"Be blessed Rosie."

Another call came in just as I hung up the phone. It was Bucky calling to give me final instructions as to how and when to get to the baseball diamond.

"Hi there, Rosie."

"Hi, Coach."

"Just a heads up to tell you the game won't start now until two-thirty. The team we're playing is stuck on I-75 around Dayton. The driver of an eighteen-wheeler fell asleep at the wheel and overturned. Thankfully, no other vehicle was involved, but the truck's cargo of automotive parts is spread all over the highway. They're being detoured through two-lane, central Ohio farmland. Too bad, so sad.

"Even so, I sure would like to see your smiling face in the stands before the anthem," Bucky said. "Look for Judge Charlie and Darlene. They plan to sit with you. After the game I'm gonna make you an offer you can't refuse."

"Really? Well, let's hear it."

"The team briefly gathers in the locker room. Once we shower, we leave the premises as a team. Then the guys go to one of the local players' house for a pasta dinner. The coaches and guests gather at the Riverside Inn to socialize and dissect the game. Even though it's Saturday baseball and not football, the traditional event is known as the Monday Morning Quarterback Analysis"

"Interesting. I'll take you up on the offer! What does 'The Monday Morning Quarterback Analysis' entail?"

"Coaches and players too, look back on the 'play by play' recap of the game. After the fact, it's easy to see what plays could have worked if they were utilized, why plays didn't work, or how the batting lineup might have been structured better."

"Sounds intriguing. Okay, I'll see you in the first row behind the dugout wearing my University of Toledo ballcap. Maybe I can get Darlene to cheer your guys on exuberantly."

"That'll be fun, Rosie. She's too modest to boast about being a college cheerleader, but, maybe if you let her know you were a dancing Rockette for the basketball team, she might give you a high-five."

"You think?"

SATURDAY AFTERNOON - APRIL 9, 1994

CHAPTER 42

OUT TO THE BALL GAME

I called my friend, Linda, hoping we could meet for a quick brunch before the baseball game. Linda answered with a rather slow, sleepy "Hello?"

"Hi there, girlfriend. Would you like to meet me at First Watch for Eggs Benedict Florentine?"

"Sure, what is the occasion, Stranger?" Linda's voice was perkier now.

"Not nice! I've been preoccupied with the Angel Morgan case. Remember?"

"Not to mention your new main squeeze. Tell the truth, girlie."

"You will come, right?"

"In a jiffy. I'm half-way out the door. Oh, are you buying, Rosie?"

We both arrived at the restaurant at the same time and greeted each other with a hug. The hostess seated us and took our drink orders.

"I was thinking," I began the conversation. "I could use some help with my abortion support group. You are absolutely the best one to co-lead. Being a nurse with an emphasis on mental health, your input would be extremely helpful to these sad women."

"Interesting proposition, but you know I have a full-time job at the high school, and don't even have much time off in the Summer."

"Well, I'm shifting the group to every other Saturday morning. Of course, I will pay you. Does that work for you?

"I would love to do it, Rosie. When do we begin?" Linda was smiling widely now.

"We begin the second Saturday in May because Mother's Day is on the second Sunday. Some of my women have symptoms of PTSD and, having aborted, makes them particularly sad around Mother's Day. Even having more children doesn't erase the pain of losing a baby."

"What kind of symptoms are we talking? Flashbacks? Nightmares? Anxiety? Depression?"

"All of the above, Linda! Some suffer a lot on Mother's Day, some suffer more during the month their infant would have been born."

The server took our meal orders, and our moods changed as did the conversation. I told Linda that I had socialized with the owner of the indoor tennis complex where Linda and I had been doubles partners until my husband passed away. Then the cost of belonging to the tennis club, let alone the cost of court time or lessons, became no longer feasible.

"How's your tennis game now?" I asked her.

"Funny, you should ask. I met this really, neat guy. He plays in the mixed, Round Robin on Friday nights. Last night we went out for pizza which is weird since the group usually orders in after we play."

"Be careful, Linda. There are gigolos who seem to be successful and prosperous when truly they're in debt up to their eyeballs."

"Thanks for raining on my parade, Rosie. I get what you are saying but I don't believe everything a guy tells me. You know I've learned the hard way. Catching your fiancé cheating the week before your wedding is a lesson and a half."

"Let's not allow losers guys to disrupt a good meal and a sweet reunion of great friends."

Following breakfast with Linda, I had no problem finding Judge Charlie and Darlene at the stadium. The opposing team arrived late, but no one was injured following the traffic problem. After the anthem was sung, the game was fun. Toledo trailed 3-0 until the last inning. They were the home team and in the bottom of the ninth had runners on all three bases.

"The team wins when the bottom of the line-up hits the ball," Bucky had once told me. With three runners on base, the bottom really came through. That's because Sean Simmons stepped up to bat.

"Ordinarily, pitchers are not thought to be strong hitters," I had been told. But Sean was the last batter in the line-up and he knew exactly how the rival pitcher threw the ball. He knew how "to take a pitch" which meant allowing the first pitch to go by without swinging. With patience and accuracy, he hit the ball on the sweet spot, and it cleared the right fielder's head, rolling all the way to the outfield fence.

As Sean rounded third base, that base coach waved

him on and yelled: "Slide! Slide!"He slid into home. The throw by the short stop was wide and took the catcher off the plate. With a grand slam, Sean was hero of the "bottom of the ninth." Toledo won 4-3 and the crowd went crazy! The best part was that Sean's parents were in the stands sitting right beside me.

The evening also went well. The Monday Morning Quarterback analysis was quick and easy. It usually was when your team won Bucky told me. While I listened, I could sense a bit of nostalgia welling up in Bucky's voice as he told them of his future plans.

"Moving on to another position like this one is what any coach strives for," Bucky told the crowd. "But that doesn't make it any easier when you love the job you're leaving. Yet, there's a season for everything," he said, quoting the well-known verse.

I made a mental note to remind Bucky of that when we had a quiet, private moment alone. But that wouldn't be tonight.

We were both driving in separate vehicles, so I was careful not to drink more than a celebratory glass of wine. In the past, I had found out the hard way that drinking and driving absolutely don't match.

After the meeting, Bucky walked me to my vehicle, kissing me lightly on the mouth as we agreed to part ways for the night. Jocko needed to be walked and I needed to prepare for Court on Tuesday

"I have an idea for tomorrow after church, if you're interested, Rosie"

"Well, why don't I get home and get comfortable and you can call me to discuss this mystery?"

"Fine. Drive carefully, and I will call you in a little bit

I hadn't been home long and had just spread my court materials out on the dining room table when the phone rang.

"I would like to take you canoeing. We can pack a picnic. What do you think?"

"Aren't you inviting me to church?"

"Well, you are absolutely invited to church. Dress casually and bring a change of shoes, a sweatshirt and hat."

"You got it. Plus, I will pack our lunch. Cheese, crackers, grapes, apples, and chicken salad on rye, ok?"

"Sounds delightful. How about I bring the drinks and we stop for ice cream on the way home?"

"I'll be ready, Bucky."

"See you in the morning."

I wondered when I should muster up the courage to tell Bucky about my most horrendous lapse of judgment and most humiliating night of my life.

Maybe tomorrow.

SUNDAY AFTERNOON - APRIL 10, 1994

CHAPTER 43

THE MYSTERY DATE

"Jocko wanted to know why he wasn't invited. He could smell my brownies baking."

"What did you tell him?"

"I simply said there are no dogs allowed in canoes. He laid down and put his paws over his eyes. I gave him a treat without expecting him to "sit". Maybe I need a second dog or a cat to keep him company."

"Was the treat a taste of warm, fresh brownie?"

"Under the circumstances, it would have been cruel, not to share them, wouldn't it?"

I handed the cooler down to Bucky who was seated in the back of the canoe. Bucky took my hand and helped me step down into the canoe.

"You paddle in front, I'll be in charge of directing our course."

"Should I be nervous? Do you have references? A captain's license to operate this vessel?"

"It's not like I take just anyone on this mystery trip. The weather is perfect, and so are you.

"Flattery will get you everywhere." I placed the paddle across my lap as the current began carrying us down the river. I trusted Bucky to keep us centered. I actually trusted him with a lot more than that, I had begun realizing lately. He had become the source of my happiness.

We paddled some and chatted about the birds and fish, and turtles on the bank.

"We're pulling up on shore just around the next bend. We can lunch there."

"All this exercise has given me an appetite." I joked.

Stepping carefully into the shallow water, we pulled the canoe up onto the shore. Bucky lifted the cooler out of the boat and led the way to a shaded area. I carried the two seat cushions and followed Bucky to where he was arranging everything at the base of an immense rock. I was amazed at the number of initials engraved on its sides. One couple had encircled their initials with a heart.

How often has this man come here, and how many women have shared his lunch? I wondered, a slight misgiving grabbing hold inside me.

"What do you think, Rosie? Should we engrave our initials on the rock?"

I laughed out loud, unusual for me these past couple of years.

Bucky was looking into my eyes. I was hoping that the light crow's feet on each side of my brown eyes wasn't too noticeable. Nor could I know what he was thinking as he smiled at me. If it was something like: "What is it I don't know about this fabulous woman?" I would have to tell him the truth soon.

"I am always up for making history," I said. "Even the waves, should they flood the area, will not diminish the engraved testimony of our lunch together. I think we should also put the date beneath our initials."

"You are the most creative woman I have ever

known. That's a fabulous suggestion." He took a well-used pocket knife out of a leather fanny pack at his waist and handed it to me.

"I think you should have the honor, Bucky," I protested. "It was your idea."

"I'll go first, Rosie, but you have to add your John Hancock too," he said as we both laughed. I loved to see him relaxed. It made me feel calm and included.

Bucky carved "ABW" which stood for his legal name, Albert; his nickname, Bucky; and his surname, Walker. He handed the knife to me.

"Your turn."

I etched a plus sign, then the initials "RAK" beside his engravement.

"R is for Rose; A is for Anne; and K is for Klein," I said. "Did you know my middle name is Anne with an E?" I asked while handing the knife back to him.

"Is that right?"Bucky carved a circle around our initials.

"This masterpiece is encircled because it's meant to be never ending. Hopefully, just like our love." He turned to face me and cupped my hands in his. Then, looking directly into my eyes, he took me by surprise.

"I am declaring my love for you, Rosie Anne with an 'E'." He smiled and looked directly into my eyes.

"Why Albert, I'm overwhelmed by your declaration. Rest assured, I feel the same! I love you, too, and am so excited about building a future together."

He leaned forward and kissed me long and gently on the lips. I returned his kiss, then laid my head on his shoulder, feeling very happy. Yet I knew I must now tell him my dark secret. But when? Should I ruin the moment and speak of it? If I didn't start soon, the moment would be lost.

It was lost.

"Come this way," he said, leading me to the picnic food.

We perched on top of the rock facing the river and shared the grapes, cheese, crackers, hard boiled eggs, and chicken salad.

Birds in the trees were calling to each other and we listened with delight. Happiness, and warmth of the sun made the moment feel peaceful and happy.

Too soon, Bucky broke the silence saying we'd better head back since he'd only rented the canoe for two hours. Paddling against the current would take much more effort and time, he explained. I suggested we hold the brownies for the perfect ending to our adventure until we were back at my condo. I suggested that brownies topped with ice cream and served with freshly brewed coffee would be a great way to end the day. Jocko would like the idea, too.

Bucky offered to change his shirt and run into Churchill's to pick up some Bordan's ice cream. There was a sale advertising two cartons for one. We agreed that Elsie the cow on the front was the cutest ad we'd ever seen.

"So, what are your favorite flavors, Rosie?"

"Vanilla for the brownies and coffee for the freebie. Okay with you?"

"We are a match made in heaven," Bucky said in amazement. "My absolute favorite flavor is coffee."

After putting on my special coffee blend, Highlander Grog, I suggested we sit out on the deck. The reclining chairs were quite an improvement over "the rock" and aluminum canoe seats.

It's now or never, I finally decided. *If I don't tell him now, he'll think I've hidden it from him.*

"I must tell you about my sordid past," I began, waiting a moment so he could see this was important, and difficult to say.

"My business partners, Steve, Debi, Larry and I used to meet one Wednesday night a month. Usually, we had dinner at Mancy's, but one evening someone had a conflict. So, instead, we met at the North office. No one thought to bring food, so we settled for a few peanut butter crackers from a basket provided to clients.

"The meeting lasted two hours and my drive home would have been about forty minutes. But a couple I recently met at Alfie's, named Natasha and Nick, invited me to join them at Creekside Landing for a few drinks. That was my first mistake. Instead of going straight home, I decided to get to know my new friends.

"Upon arriving I caught sight of them and joined them at the bar. It was lady's night and the dance floor was totally jam-packed. The band played loud Beatles music and I could barely hear Nick and Natasha. They handed me a Cuervo with lime. We toasted and I began to sip in my usual ladylike fashion. Nick corrected me and showed me how to down the tasty little drink. I downed it. It felt warm and smooth, so I suggested to buy them the next round. Then, they suggested since I paid for two of them, they should buy me another. This made three Cuervo shooters on a basically empty stomach, and a stressed soul. We topped it off with a fourth and then proceeded to the dance floor as a threesome.

"Soon after, I thanked them, excused myself and departed for home. As I turned left out of the parking lot, I realized I couldn't see the road quite clearly, but rationalized I was sitting really low in my black Honda del Sol sports car. It was only a mile and a half to my condo in Summerhill.

"Then, I saw the flashing, red lights behind me.

Needless to say, I was recognized and when I couldn't pass the breathalyzer test, they arrested me and took me to the Summerhill police station, not even a quarter mile from home.

Bucky could see the strain on my face and must have realized I was baring a painful memory. He reached for my hand in support, for which I will be forever grateful.

"I wept. Unbeknownst to me, the police scanner was on and many of my attorney friends could hear my pleas. I had been scheduled to testify as the State's expert witness in five days from then. But, my car was impounded and I was told to call someone to pick me up or I would be transported downtown to the Lucas County Jail. That would have meant I would be incarcerated with the woman I was going to testify against.

Now, tears were slowly making their way down my cheeks. Bucky was quietly listening.

"I wept and pleaded. My son was living in Water Springs with his wife and son. No way was I going to call him in the middle of the night to come and fetch his drunken mother. I called someone I was dating casually, and he came and drove me home. The next morning my partner, Larry, retrieved my car. That night seemed like a nightmare. In retrospect, it was a miracle I was arrested before I could have hurt anyone or myself.

"My driving rights became restricted to work matters only. Fortunately, the Judge recognized the fact that I could be working from 7:00 am until 11:00 pm six days per week. However, the law still prohibited me from driving the first two weeks. Two days later, I was still able to testify as the expert witness in the murder trial. My son's best friend, Chad, was home on leave from the Marines. He drove me to Court and sat through my testimony in the first row. To the jury and those unaware of my awkward situation, it appeared Chad was my bodyguard. Even my colleagues suspected he was protecting me. They knew, in the past, I had been stalked and my life was threatened both on the phone and in writing.

"After my riveting testimony, a recess was called. In the corridor, Attorney Chickalette approached me. As the defense attorney on the case being heard, he was not the least bit pleased that my opinion failed to support his client's plea of Not Guilty by Reason of Insanity.

He looked me straight in the eyes that day and said, 'Your voice was loud and clear very, very early Thursday morning.'

"Two emotional states overwhelmed me: One being shame, and the other extreme gratitude. Chickalette could have destroyed me on the stand through his cross examination. He could have questioned my credentials and provided the jury with reason to doubt the veracity of my findings. But, instead, he chose to be discrete and not bring our personal lives into play. I have never forgotten how very professional he was that day."

"Rosie what a nightmare," Bucky said with real concern. "Thank you for telling me all this. I know it was hard for you to do. But I have to say that not everyone would have heard the police scanner. If Charlie had, he would have told me; and it didn't make front page headlines."

"Do you think less of me considering my poor judgment?"

"Oh, Rosie, not at all. The fact that you see being arrested as a positive thing that may have saved your life and the lives of others, shows me how wise and insightful you really are."

Bucky wrapped his arms around me and whispered softly:"It's time to move on. We don't need that kind of excitement for sure. This coming season of our lives will not be boring. It willbe fulfilling, to say the least."

What a relief not to carry such secrets into our new life together, I thought, then I laid my head on his shoulder, and cried.

MONDAY AFTERNOON- APRIL 11, 1994

CHAPTER 44

THE GOLF OUTING

I left my clubs at the golf drop off and tipped the caddy two dollars. Then parked my car, changed my shoes, grabbed my hat, and walked to the clubhouse with a couple of other golfers. Seated at the check-in table were Bailiff Gorman, Bailiff Wendell, and Judge D.P. Tucker.

"Welcome to my outing, Rosie!" Bill Gorman said. "Here's your goodie bag of balls, tees, and drink coupons. If you want to buy 50-50 chances for a week on the Island of St. Maarten, Oliver here, is ready to take your money."

"Thanks, Bill. I absolutely plan to do that. I've heard the beaches are magnificent and the restaurants on the French side are outstanding. I'll take ten tickets, Olivere, and I want to select my favorite numbers."

"Well, well, well, if it isn't my favorite sports psychologist," Oliver Wendell announced loudly. "But, you can't do that, Rosie. However, if you tell me your absolute favorite number, I'll make sure it's among the dozen tickets you purchase."

"Number seventeen, please," I said

"No problem! Give her a dozen tickets with at least one of them ending with the number seventeen, D.P"

"Here you go, Rosie," the Judge said. "Might

one presume you want to win this holiday week for a honeymoon? Rumors fly easily around our legal community, ya know."

"Judge, I think your source of information provides you fake news," I said, folding the tickets into my pocket.

Bucky approached me at the table giving me an opportunity to introduce him to the 'Three Amigos', as they were known.

"Bucky, I'd like to introduce you to Judge D. P. Tucker, and his Bailiff Bill Gorman. Also, here to take your money is Bailiff Oliver Wendell. I might warn you not to believe a word they say about me." I looked at him as I laughed.

"By the way, Bucky is sponsoring the sixteenth hole. That's *his* favorite number, and he would appreciate one ticket ending in sixteen, okay Oliver?" Everyone laughed.

At this point, I ushered Bucky over to the hotdog stand. He purchased hotdogs and diet cokes with ice without having to ask me what I drank.

"You're quite a detective regarding what I drink aren't you?" I asked.

"Haven't you figured out yet that I'm the strong, silent type?" he smiled at me. "But I see everything."

Bill Gorman's clubs were positioned in the golf cart behind the driver's seat with my bag right beside them.

"Why don't you slide in and I'll drive you out to the sixteenth hole,"I asked Bucky. "Since Bill is signing-in the participants, there's plenty of time for me to drive you out before the shotgun start. Hang on to your hat," I said pressing the accelerator.

It was a beautiful afternoon for a ride in a golf cart. There was a slight breeze, sunny skies, and wildflowers in bloom. We reached our destination almost too soon.

"Okay, here we are," I said. Bucky got out and was met by Jewel Fields, Judge Kate Brown's Court Reporter.

"Jewel, this is Bucky Walker. He's the hole sponsor and will help you sell chances on winning a new Cadillac.

"Good luck, Bucky, this is a par three hole. Players will buy a chance from either Jewel or you, but she's prettier, so you've got some competition to sell the most tickets. Even so, if anyone hits the ball into the hole, he or she will win the car. All the money from hole sponsors, fifty-fifty chances or hole-in-one chances goes toward Bill's charity."

I hopped back into the cart and announced I would see them later. Arriving back at the clubhouse, I noticed Bill beginning to speak to the golfers about the rules of play. Oliver and D.P. were waving to me They, along with Bill, were my teammates.

"We're relying on you, Rosie. Long and straight is the name of the game," D.P. said.

I became lost in thought for a moment being grateful that Song Lee's sentencing hearings were over. Playing golf with the Judge might have been termed a conflict of interest, but I knew there would be no discussion of that case today, especially with Angel's sentencing scheduled for tomorrow. The tournament was certainly a good way to relax my mind a little.

Bill finished his announcements and hopped in the cart beside me.

"We literally only have a few yards to our tee, and we're beginning on Hole One so we'll finish on number 18. That's the benefit of helping run this whole thing! When we're done, would you mind helping me post the scores as I collect the score cards from the teams?"

I heard a voice call to me.

"Hey, girl! Let's make a deal. You take longest drive on the front and I'll take it on the back. No reason to be greedy, right?" Becky Joy yelled to her from Dan Singer's cart. I recalled that Dan, Jim Flannigan, and Patrick Kirkland were very competitive in the courtroom just like on the golf course.

"Once I win on the front, I guess I can slack off on the back side," I shouted back.

"Not on your life, Becky," D.P. replied. "We intend to win, and Rosie is our winning ticket."

Jim Flannigan and Patrick Kirkland laughed.

"Becky's job depends on her performance for our team, so she's highly motivated to beat you, Rosie."

Everyone bought a chance on hole sixteen. No one won the Cadillac, but Bucky received many handshakes of appreciation for sponsoring the hole. His baseball team's opening game win was sports news reported in the Toledo Blade. Those who followed local sports were delighted to congratulate him.

The day passed pleasantly and without any major incidents including the weather.

Upon filing into the dining hall, all winning teams were posted along with the winning ticket for the week in St. Maarten. I came out a winner in several respects. I not only won for the longest drive in the fairway on the front side, but my lucky number seventeen won me the week in St. Maarten. Following a four-course meal, people began mixing and the teasing began.

"So, Rosie, when are you going to St. Maarten, and who do you plan to take with you?" Matt Murphy asked. Matt was not a golfer, but he and his wife loved to travel and take cruises to Islands of the Caribbean. Matt was also known as a straight shooter. He didn't drink, he didn't smoke, and he didn't laugh much. He was, however, ambitious and determined to win high profile cases in order to earn the title of Lucas County Prosecutor.

"Hi Matt. Yet to be determined. I'd like you to meet my boyfriend, Bucky Walker. Bucky and I were introduced by Charlie Lincoln. They were classmates. Bucky's not a golfer yet, but he is a sportsman. His passion is baseball."

"Nice to meet you, Bucky. I believe I've seen your name in print. Aren't you the baseball coach at the University? I teach Ethics at the law school."

"Pleasure to meet you. I am the coach, and Rosie is right, I'm not a golfer yet. But after sitting on the sixteenth hole for four hours, the sport has definitely got my interest."

"Well, that'll give you and Rosie more in common. I've heard tell, she spends every waking hour away from her job and her dog, Jocko, on the course," Matt joked.

"Let me introduce my wife, Cindy. We love to travel particularly on cruises. Don't we, sweetie?"

"Absolutely," Cindy said. "We don't share many interests in common, though. Matt is definitely not a shopper," she laughed.

"I noticed Ruth left a message from you, Matt, on my desk. I'll give you a call tomorrow if you'll be available."

"Good idea, Rosie. No sense mixing business with pleasure today."

I noticed my teammates, Bill Gorman and D.P. Tucker, beckoning from across the room. Bucky and I joined them in front of the awards table. It was time for the prizes to be distributed. Everyone, especially the winners, enjoyed the evening until it drew to a close.

Bill Gorman expressed his sincere appreciation to the golfers, and all sponsors, thanked everyone for supporting the cause, and bid everyone a good night.

I suggested we go back to my condo, walk Jocko, and chat. It was a beautiful Spring evening. Bucky smiled at me.

"That's a terrific idea."

Would it be too soon to bring up the trip to St. Maarten? I wondered. What's the worst that can happen? He says no, still too early in the relationship, or could be that his new position as athletic director will warrant a lot of his time this coming year.

Back at the condo, we found Jocko sitting in the foyer anticipating our return. I put my purse down and checked Jocko's water bowl; not dry, yet, felt no compulsion to refill it until after the walk. Attaching the leash, all three of us slipped out the back patio doors. It was one of those evenings when the moon and the sun were both visible in the sky. The North star was the first symbol of peace to manifest itself.

"What is your schedule in the summer, Bucky?"

"It depends whether my job as Athletic Director kicks in before September first. Usually, I'm on a ten-month contract with two months off in the summer. But, I'm guessing the Athletic Director position is a twelve-month job."

"Okay, I was thinking about the St. Maarten deal. I would like to go in November. If you're Athletic Director, is there any chance you could take vacation time around that time?"

"First of all, Rosie, are you asking me to go with you?"

"No. I was asking you to babysit Jocko...just kidding. Of course, I'm asking you to go, that is, if you would *like* to accompany me."

"I would love to come with you. November works well. My job is more demanding during basketball season. Football is winding down by mid-November."

"That sounds great, Bucky. I'll contact the timeshare owner tomorrow."

"Rosie, allow me to pick up the cost of the airline tickets and rental car."

"Oh, my gosh. That is so sweet of you! You won't have to ask twice," I smiled, holding his shoulders and kissing him on both checks European style.

TUESDAY MORNING- APRIL 12, 1994

CHAPTER 45

ANGEL'S SENTENCING TRIAL

Rosie sat quietly in her downtown office to gather her thoughts and pray for guidance before walking over to the courthouse. She wasn't as stressed as she would be if she were testifying at trial with cross examination, and with a jury hanging on her every word.

The news media began gathering early in the corridor outside Judge Kate Brown's courtroom. Hers was the more spacious room because she was the presiding judge. The extra space allowed for more spectators and news reporters. They filed in between several officers who stood on either side of the doors. Most reporters preferred the backrow seats so they could exit quickly and be the first news station to leak the scoop of the day.

Dr. Rosie quietly seated herself behind Angel who, once more, was positioned in the first row with Verna Mitchell on one side and Attorney Singer on the other. Suddenly, Wes Hall slipped in beside Rosie. She was relieved to see him and welcomed his support. What she didn't know was that Attorney Singer had requested him to testify on his conclusive evidence regarding Angel's abortion. Angel's three siblings, Greg, Mike, and Amanda, sat midway back in the center section.

Judge Brown's Bailiff, Oliver Wendell, announced the opening of the session in his rich baritone voice.

"Please rise." Everyone complied.

The Judge took her seat on the bench. "You may be seated," Bailiff Wendell intoned. The Court reporter, Samantha Ryan, was a very competent, elderly woman with a Court Reporter School of her own. Rosie assumed a few students were in the courtroom taking shorthand in their laps for practice. It would not violate any ethical standards since Court testimonies became public record.

Attorney Singer stood and announced the name of his first witness.

"Greg Kessler, please take the stand." Greg walked up to the witness stand and was sworn in by Bailiff Wendell. Attorney Singer, then, began his inquiry.

"Please identify yourself by name and by relationship to the defendant, Angel Morgan."

"My name is Greg Kessler. I am Angel Morgan's younger, half-brother."

"Please tell the Court about the time you lived together."

"We grew up together along with my brother, Mike, until Angel ran away. Our last names are different because my brother and I were adopted by our foster parents when we were placed in their care after our mother was arrested. Our biological father was in prison at that time. So, the Kesslers thought it would be easier for us to carry their name. They said it would help us once we needed legal identification such as drivers' licenses and voter registration cards. They also did it because they loved us."

"Is your sister here in the courtroom today?"

"Yes, sir, she is," Greg pointed to Angel. "She's sitting at the table there."

"Let the record show, the witness is now pointing to the defendant.

"Do you have any other siblings?"

"Yes, I do. We have an older sister, Amanda, seated beside my brother, Mike." Greg pointed toward them. "

Amanda left us when she turned twelve, and at that point she was raised by her grandparents."

"Why was she the only one to leave your parents?" AttorneySinger inquired.

"For two reasons, she had a different father and when she turned twelve, she was permitted to live with her grandparents. She had been spending weekends with them as long as I can remember. We were only six and five years old when she moved away."

"Did that change your lives?"

"Yes, Angel then became our pseudo-mom, and she was only nine years old. She fixed our simple meals, got us off to school in the morning, and made us take a bath a couple of times a week."

"Where did you live and who else lived with you?"

"We lived with my dad and our mom at first. They treated me and my brother okay when they were sober, which was only in the afternoons. They stayed up all night drinking and using pot, so they slept most of the day until we came home from school. They were usually having coffee by then to get their day started. By supper, they basically ignored us, and ordered Angel around like a slave girl."

"Was this the pattern every day?"

"Most days. On Wednesdays a big blue church bus picked us up after school. We went to this Baptist church and ate snacks, played outdoor games, ate more snacks, heard Bible stories, played indoor games, ate supper, and were driven home. It took the pressure off Angel."

"Why did your mother move out of state?"

"She moved to avoid being arrested. My dad was in prison. We moved to Indiana. Mom found a new boyfriend, Roger, and we lived in the country, outside of town, with his family."

"Who moved?"

"Us three kids and our mom. We had no more contact with Amanda once she left to live with her grandparents. I was six and Mike was five. We had just started school and enjoyed the church activities."

"What school did you go to in Indiana?"

"We didn't. They kept us on this rural property and made us play only in the back of the house?"

"You mean you were home-schooled?"

"No, sir. The whole family sat around smoking pot and drinking all the time. Well, maybe the grandparents didn't use drugs. It seemed like Roger's mother had dementia or something. His father walked with a cane."

"Do you recall having any fun with Roger or taking any little trips?"

"Just once. We drove to Ohio to take Angel to a doctor's appointment. We dropped her off and went fishing at a little lake. Didn't catch anything though, and I don't remember having bait on the hook. Maybe we had some bread."

"What happened next?"

"We went back to pick Angel up and drove back home to Indiana. She and my brother, Mike, slept in the back seat, and I sat up front with Roger."

"How old was Angel at that time?"

"Thirteen."

"One last question, Greg. When, and why, were you permanently removed from your mother?"

"It happened when Angel ran away. Angel couldn't take it anymore. Roger kept taking her into the bedroom and locking the door when Mom went to the store with Roger's mother. Sometimes, Roger's kid brother would drag Angel into the woods by her ponytail. She used to come back crying. As far as being taken from Mom, I think Mom was arrested for shoplifting or something, and it led to something bigger. One day they just came and took us and placed us with Mark and Ann Kessler. He was a pastor and she did hom-school us to catch us up to grade level. The Kesslers didn't want us to forget our mother so they used to take us to visit her in prison twice a year, on Mother's Day and on Christmas."

"Thank you for speaking with us today. You may step down," the Judge said. Attorney Singer walked to the table to check his notes.

"Your honor, I would like to call Amanda Howard to the stand."

"You may proceed," Judge Brown said.

Amanda approached the witness stand. As she passed the first row, she waved a small 'hello' with her left hand to her sister, Angel.

"Good morning. For the record would you please state your full name and your relationship to the defendant."

"My name is Amanda Howard and I am Angel Morgan's older half-sister."

"How old was Angel when you were placed in the custody of your grandparents?"

"Angel was nine years old. Our brothers were five

and six at that time."

"The Courts do not like to split siblings. Why were you allowed to leave and what prompted you to do so?"

"I did not have the same father as Angel or the boys. I also did not have quite the same experiences they did. I spent weekends with my paternal grandparents before the boys were even born. It was Court-ordered visitation."

"What experiences are you talking about?"

"The boys were both treated okay when their father and our mother were sober, but Angel was treated like a slave girl, and often beaten into submission. They were smart about one thing, though, they didn't want my grandparents seeing any bruises or hearing about any abuse. So, instead of on me, they vented their frustration on her."

"Tell us about your sleeping arrangements, and your daily routine when you lived with Angel and the boys."

"Angel and I shared a twin bed. The boys had their own beds in another room. Our clothes were strewn on the floor. We had no washing machine. There was a lamp on the floor in our room, but no table. We laid on the bare tile floor to read. The boys would come in and I would read to everyone. The school library was our only source of material. Even at nine years of age, Angel couldn't read for herself.

"There was never food to eat, let alone cook," Amanda continued. "The school would feed us breakfast and lunch, and if we were lucky, we had peanut butter and jelly for dinner. On Fridays, the school nurse would send me home with a loaf of sliced, white bread. In the summer, we were very hungry. I hate to admit it, but we stole food from stores."

"The school was aware of your situation?" Attorney Singer asked. "Why didn't they turn your parents into Children's Protective Services?"

"My mom had a history of temporarily cleaning up her act or running with us to avoid arrest. I think the nurse felt as if she was protecting us by keeping us nearby."

"Once you moved permanently to your grandparents' house, did you tell them the truth?"

"Yes. But my grandparents and I moved to another city, and so did my mother and the kids. In fact, she moved them out of the state once her husband was arrested."

"Thank you for sharing, Amanda. You may step down at this time."

"The Court will take a twenty-minute recess," Bailiff Wendell announced, "All rise."

"Rosie, may I see you in the hall?" Singer whispered to her.

"Of course, Dan. Just let me step into the ladies' room first," she replied.

She ran a brush through her hair, and reapplied her lipstick, trying to calm her emotions. Then, she stepped into the corridor and joined Attorney Singer at the end of the hall.

"I am thinking of calling Wes Hall to the stand to validate the abortion clinic info. What do you think?"

"Sounds like a great idea. It would support Greg's history of events nicely. In the past, I have protected my sources. But, in this case, Dan, it may be just what we need to prove Angel's victimization.

"Let's just keep it in mind following your testimony. I'll call you next."

"I'm ready."

Everyone filed quietly back into the courtroom and resumed their same seats. Judge Brown hit her gavel and said, "Court is in session. Please call your next witness."

"I would like to call Dr. Rosie Klein, your Honor."

Bailiff Wendell proceeded to swear Rosie in as an expert witness.

"Please state your name, your title, and your role with this defendant," Attorney Singer requested.

"I am Doctor Rosie Klein, Forensic Psychologist. I was appointed by the Court to evaluate the defendant, Angel Morgan, in respect to the mitigating factors of her life. The purpose is to provide the Court with factual information, to assist in the defendant's sentencing for the crimes for which she has pleaded guilty."

"Exactly what factors did you consider?"

"I looked at school records, medical records, childhood and adolescent family circumstances, police reports, witness statements, and arrest reports."

"How did you determine their relevance?"

"When evaluating a defendant, it is not sufficient to simply take the word of the defendant for the background information provided and version of the circumstances leading up to the alleged crimes.

"In addition to reviewing these records, I have interviewed Angel Morgan on eight separate occasions. With the information she provided, I located and spoke with her siblings, employees from the Juvenile Detention Center, school personnel, and Wes Hall."

"Why did you speak to Wes Hall?" There it is. I let the cat out of the bag by naming my source.

"I asked him to look into abortion centers in Central Ohio to see if there was a record of a thirteen-year old girl being brought in for an abortion in the year Angel described being taken to a doctor's appointment."

"And did Mr. Hall provide you with information in that matter?"

"Yes, he did. The center was closed now, but by Ohio law, the records of minors must be recorded and saved. He found a case that closely resembled the abortion described to me by Angel Morgan."

"What conclusions if any, did you come to, based on Miss Morgan's forced abortion?"

"In my evaluation of Miss Morgan, I concluded she suffers from Post-Traumatic Stress Disorder (PTSD), directly resulting from an abortion at the age of thirteen. To this day Angel describes symptoms associated with PTSD. She has flashbacks, intrusive recollections of the event and multiple rapes, nightmares, and depression.

"There is another diagnosis that coincides with PTSD," Dr. Klein continued. "It is known as Post Abortion Syndrome. Often girls and women who have aborted their babies, begin to suffer about it much later in life. This is known as the 'sleeper effect'. It is a grief reaction coupled with anger. For some women, it suddenly hits them that they were victims. Anger turned inward results in depression even to the point of suicidal ideation or suicidal attempts."

"What other factors did you find to be relevant."

"Her short-term and long-term memory are intact but her reading achievement is less than sixth grade level."

"What exactly does that mean?"

"It means, for example, she cannot read and comprehend the newspaper which is written at the sixth-grade level. Standardized test results are not valid when the test taker does not read and comprehend the items."

"I see. Is she retarded?"

"No. Her intelligence appears to be average, but her body of knowledge is limited due to her impoverished environment. All of this affects her reasoning and judgment. Although her chronological age is twenty-two, her mental age is approximately fifteen and her social development is less than that."

"What are the ramifications of these findings, Dr. Klein?"

"In my professional opinion, these findings point to her flawed decision-making ability. This is not unusual for young adults who have grown up in abusive, restrictive environments and then incarcerated throughout their late teens."

"Did Miss Morgan experience other trauma beside the abortion at the age of thirteen?"

"Her mother was abusive in many ways. She beat Miss Morgan, and called her names.

She was an alcoholic and drug addict. She spent time in and out of jail but upon her release, the family was always reconciled with no intervention

"Her stepfather threatened to drown her brothers, if she told anyone what went on in their family. From the time Miss Morgan was nine, she was expected to clean the house and take care of her little brothers. Often there was no food and the house was totally littered with dog and cat feces. She reported to me that at the age of eleven, she stole food from a store and the manager felt so sorry for her that he did not call the authorities. This would have been an opportunity for the family to be investigated.

"Her mother allowed her husband and boyfriends to beat and sexually abuse Angel. As a young teen, there were multiple sexual assaults at the hands of her mother's then-current boyfriend, and his younger brother. After that, Angel lived in a loving foster home for about a year. Then, once more, her mother was released from prison and the kids were sent back to live with her. This, along with cruel punishment at the hands of her mother, resulted in her running away at the age of fifteen. "

"Why run?"

"Her problem-solving skills were flawed by this time. From her mother she had learned two things: to run and to lie. She was taught to avoid consequences by running and to lie to avoid responsibility for actions. That is why the family bounced around, and no one in authority knew the real family issues."

"We know Miss Morgan spent five years in Juvenile Detention Center. What did she tell you happened to her in the Juvenile Detention Center?"

"She told me an employee raped her on two separate occasions."

"Did she tell anyone about these assaults?"

"In the detention center, another resident knew about it. I spoke to that resident, Ellen Prince, and she believed that on one occasion, Miss Morgan even protected her from this man by telling Ellen to run while allowing herself to be caught by the perpetrator. It turned out he was a registered sex offender, who, as a janitor, had not been subjected to a background check. He was later arrested, unrelated to this matter, for violating parole."

"Finally, Dr. Klein, in your professional opinion, did Angel Morgan's traumatic upbringing impact her decision to join this gang, and if so, how?"

"In my professional opinion, Angel Morgan's history and background seriously impaired her perception and reasoning. Her deep-seated need for love and approval made her vulnerable to the attention extended to her by this group of young men and women. She did not foresee the path their actions would take. For example, her thinking is very concrete. If someone uses the term "joy ride", she views that term as going for a drive for fun. Most likely, three others of the six took the meaning the same as Miss Morgan. She could not begin to comprehend the purpose of the "joy ride" or anticipate consequences of their actions."

"You mentioned she learned at the hands of her mother to run away when in trouble. Do you have an opinion as to why she didn't run away from this gang once the unexpected killing occurred?"

"Yes. She feared for her life. If she had any idea of running, she dismissed it after her two friends, who were also members of their own group of six, were murdered at the quarry. She was ordered to get down on her knees along with these two friends, and when her life was spared, and theirs were not, she told me she believed God was alive and had saved her for some reason."

"Does she have any clue what that reason might have been?"

"She felt she was supposed to testify for the State of Ohio in the trials of the shooters."

"Anything else?"

"Miss Morgan will address the Court on that matter herself."

"Thank you, Dr. Klein. You may step down."

Rosie returned to her seat and took a deep breath. Her role and function were completed. Now it would be Angel's turn to speak on her own behalf. Rosie put her head down and said a quick, silent prayer.

"Your honor, I would like to call Angel Morgan to the podium."

Angel moved slowly into the aisle, then stepped

up to the microphone. She carefully unfolded her written statement and looked up at the Judge. Her voice was clear and steady as she addressed everyone, including the victims' families who were seated behind her

"I would like to thank you, your Honor, for this privilege today. First, I want to apologize to the families of the four innocent people who were killed by Marcus and James." Angel proceeded to express sincere sympathy to each of the victims' families just as she had practiced reading to Dr. Rosie.

"I will always regret not doing something that could have prevented the last three murders. Second, I would like to tell my story, not for sympathy, but so you know the truth from someone who lived through it all. Maybe, by hearing my story, those in this Courtroom, in schools, and in police departments, will watch for the unspoken suffering of little girls who are being threatened, so they don't have to continue to go through all the abuses they suffered.

"In terms of my case, I didn't know the men were going to shoot anyone when they told us to get in the car for a "joy ride". I thought they were bored, high, and cold. There was heat in the car. I was really shocked when they shot the boy near the phone booth for his shoes and letter jacket. I suddenly knew what violent men I was involved with.

"When we got back to the abandoned house, April and I sat hugging each other on a mattress on the cellar floor. We were scared but we thought that was the end of it. Then the next day, we were back in the car cruising through downtown, and this time, James shot the second victim and stole his briefcase. We were in shock! Later, when we got back to the garage, they started smoking pot, drinking, and acting suspicious and kinda of scared like maybe somebody would tell on them.

"The next morning, they banged on the window and Sam, April, and I were ordered into the car. That's when they took us to the quarry and they shot Sam and April point blank in the back of their heads. When they didn't shoot me, I rolled into a little ball and cried. Then they ordered me back into the car. They said Sam and April had leaked our names to the cops. I knew it wasn't true. How could they? We didn't have any phone. This left Song and me totally terrified.

"Song was very smart. She was pretty and kind to me. She invited me to stay with her in the house next door. It had heat and lights and running water. Somehow, they knew the people were in Florida for the winter. That's why the men were staying there, even though they mostly hung out in the garage behind the vacant house.

"The day after they shot Sam and April, the guys made Song go to her mailbox at the University to pick up a check from Song's parents in Korea. She told me they would send one every month for her spending money. But, on that day, no check came. Next thing I knew, the four of us got in the car, again, and went to a convenience store. They said they could get some money. I had no idea they would shoot the clerk.

"Before we knew anything, we heard a gunshot shot and out they ran. Every time they committed a crime, they drove onto the highway and headed into Michigan. Up a few miles, then they would turn around and drive home. The car was kept in the garage facing outward.

"The last horrible act was on Christmas Eve. Song checked the box again and this time, her check was there. Then, the guys saw her talking to a man. They asked her who he was, and she said he worked for the University. That got them to thinking. They told us that they wanted to have some fun. They thought it would be 'nice' to invite him over for a party and that Song should invite this man to the house. When he agreed to come over, we went along with the idea that maybe we could have some fun and it would be kind of like a party.

"When he got to our house, we invited him in and made him comfortable in the living room. Song and I drank wine and ate cheese and crackers with him.

"But, I'm so ashamed, the wine made us do things that were wrong. We asked him to come upstairs to our bedroom. Marcus and James were hiding in the closet, which we knew, but thought they were just going to scare him. But, instead, they came out and tied him up with electrical cords and ordered us to take his car keys and leave. We were kind of knowing by now they weren't going to just rob him, but didn't know what to do. I just wanted to get out of there.

"We were on the front porch when we heard the gun shots. Then, Marcus and James came running downstairs, and we all jumped into the car, and James drove us away. That night we were arrested, and, honestly, I was relieved. I thought maybe this time the nightmare was really over and I was safe at last.

"I am totally responsible for my actions, and I do not ask for, or deserve, your forgiveness. I will live with shame and deep regret the rest of my life, for however many days God has planned for me. If there is any way in prison that I can save someone's life, I pray for the chance to do that.

"Perhaps, someone arrested for petty crimes will see the serious consequences of my stupid choices. Maybe they will not make the same mistakes if I tell them what I have done. I am so sorry for everything I was a part of. Thank you, your Honor, for listening."

Angel kept her head down and slipped back into the seat between Officer Mitchell and AttorneySinger. There was silence in the Courtroom.

After a moment, Angel glanced over her shoulder toward her brothers and sister. Amanda nodded her head and smiled.

"Attorney Singer, if the testimony on behalf of Miss Morgan is complete," Judge Brown stated, "Court is dismissed. It will re-convene this afternoon at 1:30 pm at which time I will impose sentence on Miss Angel Morgan."

TUESDAY AFTERNOON - APRIL 12, 1994

CHAPTER 46

THE FINAL VERDICT

Court convened at 1:30 pm just as Judge Brown had specified. Bailiff Wendell asked the defendant to rise at which time Angel Morgan stood with her arms down and hands folded in front of her. Samantha Ryan was recording the hearing so a transcript would be available to authorities.

"Miss Morgan, did you know you could have had a trial with a representative jury?"

"Yes, your honor, I did."

"Were you aware you could have requested a trial with a three Judge panel?"

"Yes, your honor I knew that."

"Did you voluntarily waive your rights to a trial?"

"Yes, I did."

"Did you accept the plea agreement without coercion of any kind?"

"Yes, I did."

"Do you understand the charges against you?"

"Yes, I do."

"Have you had the opportunity to assist your attorney in your defense?"

"Yes, I have."

"Did he explain the sentences that may be imposed in return for guilty pleas?"

"Yes, your honor, he did."

"Do you understand that I, alone, will be determining the sentence on each count of aggravated murder, each count of aggravated burglary, and each count of obstruction of justice?"

"Yes, I do."

"Let the record show, the Court finds the plea agreement will stand given the understanding of its ramifications on the part of the defendant.

"Let the record show, I have reviewed the victims' families and friends' statements taken from the transcripts of the Song Lee sentencing hearings.

"In addition, I have heard the testimonies of Angel Morgan's brother, Greg; sister, Amanda; Dr. Rosie Klein; and the defendant, Angel Morgan, herself.

"The Court, hereby, sentences this defendant to 30 years to Life in prison on each of four counts of aggravated murder; 20 years each on four counts of aggravated burglary; and 10 years each on six counts of obstruction of justice. In consideration for the trauma experienced by this defendant throughout her childhood and adolescence, these sentences are to be served concurrently to begin immediately. Court is adjourned."

The gavel banged down with a loud reverberation throughout the room.

Justice had supposedly been served.

Angel's siblings surrounded her and hugged her through their tears. She glanced back at me and mouthed the words, "Thank you." I placed my hand over my heart and nodded. Verna Mitchell led her out the side door to the County jail where she would board a State van and be transported to Marysville. Her belongings were already loaded onto the van as there was no question that she would be going to prison. The question had been for how long?

The current sentence was a minimum of 30 years for which she thanked Dr. Klein whose testimony and work in gathering the other witnesses assisted the court to allow concurrent rather than consecutive years to be served.

Attorney Singer followed Rosie out of the courtroom.

"Very nice testimony on your part, Rosie, and hers. Thank you for preparing her for the proceedings and demonstrating genuine caring toward her."

"You're welcome. I know you did what you did to safeguard her life. But, I must say with the testimony of the defendant and mine, presented to a jury, I truly believe the jury may have come back with much reduced charges. The siblings validated her horrible childhood. With those mitigating circumstances, they might have found her guilty of second-degree murder, or conspiracy to commit murder instead of aggravated murder. The death penalty would not have been on the table, Dan, and she wouldn't have been scared into taking such a plea deal."

"You may be right, Rosie, but we'll never know. Judge Brown showed compassion by having her serve the sentences concurrently instead of consecutively. That means she does have a chance for parole."

"Yeah, Dan, in another 30 years,"the upset showed in her voice.

"I'm sorry, Rosie, but she made her own decisions. I have to get home now; have a nice evening," Dan Singer said.

Rosie walked down the Courthouse steps and watched the mob of reporters waiting to encircle Singer for quotes. She couldn't wait to get home, kick off her shoes, and pet Jocko.

I realize, given the circumstances, that Judge Brown did actually show Angel compassion and mercy because of her background circumstances and family's statements, she thought. *She could have run the sentences consecutively.*

Later, Rosie talking with Bucky, she said:

"But even though that will lessen the time she spends in prison by many years, she will still need all the prayers she can get. She's chosen a hard way to learn her lessons. Living incarcerated isn't really a life, and it's certainly no place to call 'home'."

This story was inspired by a true case which the author has never forgotten. Although some facts have been fictionalized to protect the innocent, the real "Angel" has already served nearly 25 years in prison at the time of this writing in 2019. She will be appealing for clemency soon.

EPILOGUE
TWENTY-FIVE YEARS LATER
2019

From Dr. Klein's Viewpoint:

"The days of my life have flown by since I met and married Bucky Walker. We're returning soon to St. Maarten, where our marriage began, to celebrate twenty-five years of being together. I feel ever so blessed.

"Our blended family now includes twelve grandchildren, six step-grandchildren, and eight great-grandchildren. We have experienced great joy, yet have embraced hardship and sorrow from losses of beloved family members and dear friends along the way. Through it all, we have felt the warm hand of God upon us, and the guidance of the Holy Spirit.

"As I write this, we are in Ohio and have just attended my high school class reunion. Most of us are turning 75 years this calendar year, but no one admits anyone looks it. Such a delight to gather with old friends who shared childhood memories with Bucky. My friends all knew my mother and father, and spent many afternoons and evenings at our home. Their recollections gave Bucky a more complete picture of who I was then, and where I've come from.

"Five years ago, Bucky retired from the University of Toledo's Athletic Department. I sold my private practice to my partners, Steve and Debi. It was so gracious on their part because our practice, unlike medical practices, did not have expensive diagnostic equipment. It was only my name and position in the community that was of value to them.

"Now free of work restraints, Bucky and I bought a large, used RV and spend half the year driving in the West, serving Apache children at an Apache boarding school in

Arizona. We spend three months visiting our children in California, Michigan, Ohio, and Florida. Lastly, we serve in the woods of Vienna, Austria, as short-term workers for an American Christian College. Students, there, are from Eastern European countries and are quietly pursuing masters' degrees from the United States. They come to the Vienna campus for a week while we do whatever necessary to help them focus on their courses. By cooking, cleaning, and tending the gardens, we feel truly blessed by our service to them.

"Today, we are stopping in Marysville, Ohio, to visit Angel Morgan at the Ohio Reformatory for Women where she has spent the past twenty-five years. Perhaps, for her, it has seemed an eternity."

From Angel's Viewpoint:

"I am waiting for a visit from dear Dr. Rosie. She was clearly the most important person in my life during its bleakest season. I don't know how I would have survived the trials, the testimonies, and the sentencing hearing without her.

"The support and encouragement Dr. Rosie gave me was the first time I felt unconditional love from anyone. Maybe she's an angel. Why on earth did my mother name *me* that? She certainly never treated me that way.

"But, I'm told that everything happens for a reason, and the fact that Dr. Rosie came into my life may really have saved me. I felt such guilt, shame, and unworthiness then.

"I, also, remember one guard at the Lucas County Jail by the name of Verna. She instilled in me a love of college football. I remember her on Thanksgiving when the annual rivalry between the University of Michigan and Ohio State is on TV. Seeing that game makes Thanksgiving very special, even though the food here leaves a lot to be desired. Don't get me wrong. I cheer for the team but recognize that's a day to count my blessings, too.

"Yes, Verna seemed to care about me, but, but after all, it was her job, and I never heard from her again once I was transported here to Marysville.

"But, Dr. Rosie stayed with me throughout all these years. The first birthday I spent here, she sent me a women's year-long devotional. Now the pages are tear-stained with many sentences underlined in red. Some words I circled in purple. On my first Christmas in prison, she sent me a Bible with my name inscribed on it. I know she wants me to remember that God knows my name.

"Every Christmas since then, I receive an inspirational book or pretty journal to record my thoughts, which I have done faithfully. Now I'm waiting for her next visit. I hope she will be proud of how I've used my time productively. I really think I'm in line with God's purpose for my life at last.

"I have also tried to impact the lives of other women here in positive ways. My daily work assignment involves sewing flags. I love sitting with the other women and giving them encouragement. They seem to appreciate my interest in them and want to know how a woman like me ended up with a life sentence. They don't realize that who I am now is not remotely like the young woman I was when I made such awful decisions.

"The first five years of being in prison, I spent most of the time feeling angry. My mouth got me in so much trouble that I ended up in "the hole" all alone and scared. The hole is the term we use for solitary confinement. I eventually stopped blaming others and accepted responsibility for all my poor choices.

"Now, I am proud to say that I facilitate a weekly program called Celebrate Recovery where the women who suffer from all kinds of addictions can learn to become free in their minds and hearts. By sharing my circumstances, I hope my story might keep them from going back out there in society and making stupid mistakes and poor decisions like I once did. I pray somehow, someday, I will have a second chance with a pardon from a United States President.

"My health is declining. I struggle with severe back pain, most likely caused from sleeping on a thin mattress with very little support all these years. Only with a release will I be able to get the medical treatment I need to avoid eventually becoming crippled.

"Until that day, I will be grateful for what I have, and not dwell on what I have lost."

Postscript:

Angel continues to write occasional letters to Dr. Rosie Klein.

DISCUSSION QUESTIONS

1. How do you think Angel's childhood would have changed if the store managers had called the police when she first shoplifted food for herself and her hungry little brothers? For better or worse?

2. Discuss the decisions of other adults in her life who decided not to contact authorities even though they recognized severe neglect and possible abuse in Angel's home.

3. How did the Juvenile Detention Facility administration fail to protect residents during their stay in the facility? For example: Protection from sexual predators.

4. What procedures were lacking when Angel was released from the Juvenile Detention Center that might have altered her decisions to join the gang?5. If Marcus' athletic ability had been discovered as a freshman rather than as a junior in high school, what might his future have been?

5. How important is it for children and adolescents to have a father or caring male role model? Did any of Angel's family members or gang members have positive father figures in their lives? How would it have made a difference?

6. If a jury had heard this case, how would they have thought about this young woman's role in the heinous crimes for which she was charged? Put yourself in the position of a jurist.

Discussion Questions continued...

7.   Discuss how the victims' family members felt following the senseless murders of their loved ones. Could they forgive Angel and Song? What about George Emmanuel, the tavern owner? What could he be thinking?

8.   Has Angel made the best of her situation in prison? Discuss her journey in terms of her use of her time, attitude, emotions, and beliefs since her sentencing.

9.   Angel believes God has a purpose for her life. What do you think other women in prison can learn from her story?

10.   How can Dr. Rosie assist Angel in her journey in prison? What should happen following the epilogue?

About the Author

Phyllis Kuehnl-Walters Ph. D.

A retired clinical psychologist from Ohio, Phyllis lives in The Villages, Florida, and writes inspirational self-help books meant to encourage people to joyfully finish their race set forth by God.

Author of "Creating Balance & Purpose in Your Life" and "Worry, Fret and Fear...No More!". She has also written a companion workbook to the second title which helps people through this six week journey.

She is also an inspirational speaker on the topics covered in her books.

In addition to Phyllis' career in private practice, she taught classes at The University of Dayton and Dayton area colleges. Most recently, she has held classes at The Enrichment Academy in The Villages, Florida.

Currently, she is the Academic Dean and instructor at Casa Hope, Christian transitional living house for young men who have struggled with addictions and/ or served time for drug related offenses.

A member of the Florida Writers Association and the Writers League of The Villages, Phyllis also maintains membership in Ohio Women In Psychology, Ohio Psychological Association (Emeritus), and the American Psychological Association (Emeritus).

She can be reached at PhyllisWaltersAuthor@gmail.com